The Suitcase Swap

The Suitcase Swap

LISH MCBRIDE

HODDER &
STOUGHTON

First published in Great Britain in 2025 by Hodder & Stoughton Limited
An Hachette UK company

This paperback edition published in 2025

The authorised representative in the EEA is Hachette Ireland, 8 Castlecourt
Centre, Dublin 15, D15 XTP3, Ireland (email: info@hbgi.ie)

1

A CIP catalogue record for this title is available from the British Library

Paperback ISBN 978 1 399 74326 6
ebook ISBN 978 1 399 74327 3

Typeset in Plantin Light by Manipal Technologies Limited

Printed and bound in Great Britain by Clays Ltd, Elcograf S.p.A.

Hodder & Stoughton policy is to use papers that are natural, renewable
and recyclable products and made from wood grown in sustainable forests.
The logging and manufacturing processes are expected to conform to the
environmental regulations of the country of origin.

Hodder & Stoughton Limited
Carmelite House
50 Victoria Embankment
London EC4Y 0DZ

www.hodder.co.uk

To Joan Wilder, who will never read this because she's fictional: I saw Romancing the Stone *in the theatre as a kid and said, "That. I want to do that for a living."*

My entire career is kind of your fault. (Thank you.)

Chapter One

Sophie Swann didn't think that the people who designed airports were trying to make her life miserable *specifically*, but was amazed at how well they were accomplishing the feat nonetheless. She'd read several articles before she'd bought her ticket – everything from safety statistics to meditation techniques – but the problem was that, once in an airport, one couldn't ignore the very apparent reality of the giant, and often very visible, planes.

Even in the atrium parts of Heathrow Airport where she couldn't look out of any windows, there were actual signs everywhere reminding her that she was in an airport and would soon hurtle through the sky in a metal tube at mind-numbing speeds. Which meant that none of her data, careful planning or deep breathing were doing her any good.

She put her earbud in and opened the app to video-call her son. Tom's face appeared on the screen only moments later, like maybe he'd been waiting for her call. Which he probably had been. She was startled, as she always was, by how much he took after his father, with his dark hair and brown eyes, and somehow was nothing like him at the same time. Tom, after all, was kind and funny, and her husband – ex, *ex*-husband – Andrew was decidedly . . . not.

Tom grinned at her, a crooked smile all his own, and she started talking before he'd even said hello. 'I'm thinking of getting into drugs. Nothing extreme. The heroin lifestyle looks exhausting. Just something that would take down an

elephant for eight hours and could be conveniently pur-
chased in the airport.'

Tom's grin widened. 'You might struggle to find heroin in
the airport, Mum, but I have faith. If anyone could manage
it, it would be you.'

Now that she'd had a chance to study him and look past her
own panic, she could see how tired he looked. The crooked
smile didn't quite reach his eyes and faint purple bruises
underscored the fact that he wasn't getting proper sleep. She
could imagine that good sleep would be hard to come by for
both him and his fiancée, Marisa. Their miscarriage was too
new, the heartbreak too fresh. Grief either handed out too
much sleep or too little. It was just the way of things.

Sometimes Sophie really hated the way of things.

She clucked sympathetically at him. 'How are you holding
up? How is Marisa?'

He glanced away, swallowing hard. It took him several seconds to speak and when he did, it was to mostly dodge the
question. 'I'm very glad you're on your way.'

Well, wasn't that an answer in itself?

'So am I,' she said gently. Out of the corner of her eye,
she saw a toy plane swoop along through the air. A small
girl, perhaps two, held it tightly in her little fist, gurgles of
delight marking the plane's passage. At least someone here
was happy.

'What is it?' Tom asked. 'You look a bit peaky all of a sudden.'

'Giant metal tubes with *wings* and I'm supposed to get
on it.' She focused on the screen in front of her, ignoring
the perspiration suddenly coating the majority of her body.
Sophie didn't even like to drive, something her husb—,
ex-husband – loved to poke fun at. She very carefully taped
up the edges of that idea and hurled it into her mental trash
bin. Then she lit it on fire, just to be certain. 'Bring back the
days of travelling by sea. I could buy a big, floppy hat and
swan about on the deck of a ship being mysterious.'

The image of her son on the screen shifted, revealing another part of Tom's Brooklyn flat. Marisa sat on a lime-green couch, her compact frame wrapped in a Sherpa blanket, smiling back at her. If Tom's face had hinted at exhaustion, Marisa's screamed it. Her naturally tanned skin pale, her usually shiny black hair dull and piled up on her head in a messy bun. 'Hard to be mysterious on a plane. You going to be okay, Sophie? We can still book you on that cruise.'

Sophie was already shaking her head. The flight was cheaper by far, and more importantly, it was faster. Seven hours versus six days and by all appearances, they needed her now, not in a week. She loved London. It was home. But Tom was her heart and at some point, Marisa had become part of that, too. Her heart was breaking and if that meant getting onto a plane, so be it.

'I shall be very brave,' Sophie said, 'and also possibly abuse the bar cart.'

'Those little liquor bottles on planes are one of life's few joys,' Marisa said, her usually bouncy voice deflated. Sophie wished not for the first time that she could reach through the screen and hug them both. Maybe instead of meditation and illegal narcotics, she would focus on why she was going. Her son and soon-to-be daughter needed her, and they needed her now. She was a *survivor*, damn it all, and she would survive this.

An app on her phone helpfully pinged, letting her know that boarding would start soon. She immediately felt over-whelmingly, horribly, ill. 'Okay, my loves. Must dash. See you soon!' She blew them a kiss, enjoyed their chorused good-byes, and ended the call right before sprinting towards the nearest toilets.

Sophie felt she had a solid grasp of irony. For example, she knew there was a spectacular amount of irony in a travel writer having to vomit in the airport loo at the very idea of setting foot on an aeroplane. The fact was, her writing had started as a hobby. She never in a million years would have thought she'd end up in her current career.

After her son had gone to university, she'd had little in her life beyond work. During the day she'd had her hands full running the logistics side of Andrew's business, the one they'd built together, the one that had been *theirs*. Swann's was the kind of place you went to for home DIY projects, to get interesting new fixtures, or to take a workshop on how to build a bird feeder or even a patio. While she organized payroll, managed inventory, and paid the bills, Andrew gadded about charming new clients and building the business.

She'd never enjoyed the client dinners or the travel aspects, so she'd been happy to hand those parts over to Andrew and his assistant, Lori. More fool her. She wasn't sure what was more aggravating: losing the business she'd helped build, losing her husband, or the overwhelming cliché of it all. Losing your husband to his younger, prettier assistant was something that happened on daytime soap operas. Couldn't he at least have used some imagination for his midlife crisis? He could have learned to juggle fire or joined a monastery. But Sophie knew this was a pointless question – Andrew had all the imagination of beige wall paint.

But before all of that, before the mess of her divorce, there had been a few years where she'd found herself at a loose end on weekends and after work. Andrew was always busy. Tom was gone. Since Andrew was allergic, they had no pets. She'd tried joining a book club, but it turned out she didn't like people telling her what to read, especially since one of the members kept picking depressing literature. Sophie had wanted books that would sweep her away, not books that would make her cry.

What she really liked was reading stories that would take her somewhere *else*. Fantasy lands with interesting creatures.

Romance novels set in foreign cities or on sun-drenched islands. Mysteries that took place in catacombs, or on ships, or really anywhere that wasn't the house she'd shared with the same man for over twenty years. The same walls. The same floors, even though she'd torn out the awful carpets that had been there when they'd bought the house. Sophie had wanted at least a taste of adventure.

Which was why she liked travel shows and shows like *Destination: Eats* that took the viewer to interesting new restaurants around the globe. Sophie was the kind of person who liked trying new things . . . she just couldn't go very far to do them.

It was her best friend, Edie, who'd come up with the idea. If she couldn't go far, why not explore what was nearby? After all, there had to be other people who couldn't travel for all kinds of reasons. Thus *Swanning About* was born. Sophie set up a blog for longer posts and attached social media to it. She found things to do on a budget, like free museum days, or classes that had a cheap introductory try-out session. Local theatres with reasonably priced tickets. Happy hours that actually made you happy. Sometimes she caught the bus or a train to go further afield, but not always.

She was surprised at how happy her new hobby made her. She was *more* surprised at how happy it made others, and she was the *most* surprised when she started to make money from it. What Sophie liked most, however, was the community that had formed around it. Every single time she voiced her own fears, told her readers how difficult something was for her, she was rewarded with support and solidarity.

Her latest post about her fear of flying, which she'd linked to a video about packing tips for a long-term stay, had sparked a chorus of replies.

@LolaLightfoot: you can do it, Swanny!

@MarlaBarla:You're so brave. I know how afraid you are of planes. I wish I could take such a big step!

@Mambo#65:You're brave, too, @MarlaBarla! Like Swanny says, if a big step is too much, a little step will do!

@GoldenGirl:You show those New Yorkers what a London Girl can do!

She let all those voices run through her head as she washed her hands and patted her face with a damp paper towel. She listened to them as she stared at herself in the mirror. Her skin was too pale. A few locks of her brown hair had come loose from her ponytail and were now sticking to her sweaty forehead and cheeks. The lighting certainly wasn't doing the bags under her eyes or her crow's feet any favours. She felt overwhelmed and afraid and wished, just for a second, that she had a hand to reach for. Someone to steady her as she wobbled. It was all simply *too much* sometimes.

If a big step is too much, a little step will do.

Right. She could take her own advice. Sophie blew out a big breath. Placed the cold, damp paper towel against the back of her neck for a second and closed her eyes, ignoring the hubbub of the airport toilets. Then she opened her eyes, got a fresh paper towel and dried her face. She redid her ponytail. She straightened her shoulders and looked herself in the eye.

You can manage one step, Sophie Swann. That's all you have to think about. Putting one foot in front of the other until you're on that plane.You will not let Tom and Marisa down.

Another deep breath in, then out.

'You okay, duck?' The old woman at the sink next to her squinted at her through a pair of rhinestone-framed glasses. 'Because those shoes look new, and it would be a shame to get sick all over them.'

'Thank you,' Sophie said, her voice breathier than she would have liked. 'I think I'm okay.'

The woman seemed dubious but nodded at her anyway.

Sophie gave her a wan smile, dried her hands, and marched out of the toilets with her head held high. She would persevere.

Michael Tremblay, or Mike to anyone he was even slightly friendly with, which admittedly wasn't a large number of people, stowed his overhead suitcase with practised ease. He settled into his aisle seat, mentally preparing himself to be jostled every time a person walked past or the cart went by. Even with his upgrade to a seat that claimed to have more leg room, his long legs felt cramped. Walking past first class had felt like a taunt, those people seeming annoyingly comfortable in their luxury. Despite what people thought, most architects didn't make first-class kind of money.

The young woman behind him chattered away, using the last few minutes to call her boyfriend to let him know she was safely on the plane and when to pick her up. Mike felt an unexpected pang of jealousy, not unlike the one he'd felt in first class – *here's something that's really lovely, but it's not for you.*

Unlike not being able to afford first class, this hadn't always been the case.

Once upon a time, he would have been making the same phone call, but Mike hadn't had someone to notify about his whereabouts for years. His children sometimes had a general idea of where he was, but he often forgot to give them exact information. Both were busy, Amaya with her studies and Rahul with his family.

And his Tara, well, she'd been beyond hearing for ten long years.

Knowing that fact certainly hadn't kept him from trying to reach out.

He still sometimes found himself stretching a hand out for her late at night. Not all the time any more, just every once in a while. It had become an occasional emotional love-tap instead of a constant pummelling. Sometimes he'd read a funny line in a book or see a mangy dog on the street and he'd be reaching for his phone before he remembered she was no longer around to receive his texts. He could still imagine taking a picture of an awkwardly put-together dog, all spiky fur and overbite, and sending it to her with the text: *A face only a mother could love*.

Just like he could imagine her response: *Who wouldn't love that face? That is a dog with* character.

Those imagined interactions didn't catapult him into heavy grief any more, at least. It was more bittersweet now, the sadness overtaken by the simple joy of having known Tara. For being gifted so much of her life.

At times like this, sitting in the plane, listening to the young woman coo at her boyfriend, it brought home the fact that he'd known what it was like to be a necessary part of something, a necessary person to someone else, and now . . . he mostly had his work. He sometimes felt a little extraneous, like an old power cable that you didn't need any more but kept just in case.

It wasn't that he didn't love his children or didn't feel loved by them. He was extremely grateful for Amaya and Rahul. They just didn't need him on a daily – or even weekly – basis any more. He could probably be out of the country for a month before they'd notice.

Mike took out his phone, planning to switch it to airplane mode, when he saw a text had appeared in the family group chat. He grimaced. Amaya had sent him a link to an article about dating apps for people over fifty. The idea of dating didn't appeal to him; the idea of using an app to do so actively repulsed him. He took a second to tap out a reply. *Thank you, love, but I'd rather not.*

Dots appeared instantly as Amaya responded. *Don't be the kind of man who only dates women in their twenties, Dad. Don't be ageist against your own generation.*

Mike very much thought 'to each their own' when it came to dating, but the idea of dating anyone close in age to his own daughter made him shudder. *It was a blanket 'I'd rather not' and not anything about people my own age. I can promise you, if I ever date again, she won't be that young. What would we even talk about?*

It was Rahul who responded. *This is why I love you, Dad. Most single hetero men wouldn't be concerned about conversation. They'd only be thinking about hot sex with nubile women.*

Amaya's response was instant. *Ew. Please never use any of those words together again.*

Mike rubbed at the space between his brows with his thumb. He wasn't going to get into a discussion of his sex life with his children. He'd had sex since he'd lost his wife, but it had been fleeting. Like candy floss on the tongue, here and then vanished, leaving a faint hint of sweetness behind.

What he really missed was that connection he'd shared with his wife. To have someone touch him and have it feel familiar, almost a relief. As if their hand on his skin was like aloe vera on particularly bad sunburn. He missed having his morning tea while sitting across from Tara's scowling face (she hadn't been a morning person). He missed date nights where they talked for hours. He even missed arguing with her.

Mike wanted sex, to be sure, but he wanted the kind of sex that felt as essential to his life as breathing.

Not that he'd say a single one of these things to his children, even if they were grown up. It was none of their business. *I would also like to ban the use of the word 'nubile' from our chats.*

Amaya sent a laughing emoji, followed by, *We just want to see you happy, Dad. If you were genuinely content on your own, we wouldn't push.*

I would push, Rahul texted. He sent a picture of a squalling infant, face red, mouth open in a howl, nestled into the crook of his arm. *Archie needs another grandparent to spoil him rotten.*

Mike smiled automatically at his grandson's angry face. It still stopped him short, sometimes, that he was a grandparent. Inside he felt like he was still the same awkward young man, working up the nerve to buy his first pint. Not a man of *fifty-three*. He wouldn't give up Archie for anything, or his older sister Stella. Reminders of age aside, they helped fill the empty spaces in his heart.

The flight attendant made an announcement telling everyone to buckle their seatbelts. Mike quickly typed out a message while he could. *And where's my Stella?*

Noah took her to the Natural History Museum. She wanted to, and I quote, 'go and see the dead things.'

That's my girl, Amaya wrote.

Takes after her barmy aunt. Rahul added a laughing emoji to that.

You love me! Admit it!

I do, Rahul responded, *but then I'm barmy, too. I'll have Noah send you both pics.*

The overhead announcement told them all to put their phones on airplane mode. Mike typed quickly, *It runs in the family. Tell Noah thank you. Got to dash.*

Amaya sent a heart. *Tell us when you land!*

Will do. He turned off his phone, tucking it into the pouch on the back of the seat in front of him. He might not feel useful, but he did feel loved, which was a wonderful thing, and something he didn't take for granted. He got out his tablet, hoping to get a little work done during the flight. When he was finished with that, he would read for a while. If there was one thing Michael was good at, it was filling his time.

Chapter Two

Sophie wasn't sure she'd seen anything grander, anything more wonderful than JFK Airport. She would doubtless feel very differently if she had been there to get *on* a plane. Since the airport was the first available piece of terra firma after disembarking, it had taken on elements of holy ground. For a split second she considered actually kissing the carpet.

That was the exact moment she realized she'd made a tactical error. Drinking on the plane had helped take the edge off her anxiety. But the thing was, beyond the odd glass of wine, she rarely drank these days. She'd also been concerned she would be sick again, so she hadn't eaten. Those factors, plus the fact that she hadn't been prepared for drinking at altitude meant she had somehow managed to step into JFK Airport both still slightly drunk and partially hungover at the same time.

She felt *wretched*. Her stomach rolled, her head was absolutely splitting and the relentless noise wasn't helping, either. The lights were too bright. It was all basically too much – including the taste in her mouth, which was horrid.

People flowed around her in a constant torrent as they hustled to get to their luggage and head to customs. She was repeatedly jostled, the smell of various perfumes, colognes and body odour hitting her in waves. She did not want to be sick in two different airports within the same twenty-four hours. All she had to do was make it through customs. Tom was meeting her on the other side and escorting her back to the flat. She could endure until then.

Sophie lurched through the crowd, finding an out-of-the-way spot by the bins to catch her breath. Which was good because that was when her legs decided they'd had quite enough, thank you, and gave up. She didn't faint so much as *wilt*. Sophie sat down hard, leaned her head against the wall and closed her eyes. Breathe. She just needed to breathe. In a few moments, she'd get up, head through customs and carry on, but right now she would take a tiny sliver of the day to get her bearings.

'Pardon me, but are you all right?' The unwelcome voice was deep and pleasant and any other time Sophie would have enjoyed it. Right now, she wanted it to go away, which she knew was unfair of her. He was just being kind. 'Only, you look a bit peaky.'

'Flying,' she said without opening her eyes, 'is unnatural.'

Whatever the voice had been expecting, it apparently wasn't that, because it was silent for a few seconds.

'Perhaps for humans,' the voice admitted. 'The act itself isn't unnatural. Birds do it. Bees do it.'

'Even monkeys in the trees do it?' She couldn't help but finish the line, smiling a little despite her current state. Her mother had loved that song. Judging by the ensuing silence, the voice hadn't caught the reference and was now considering whether or not she needed medical attention. 'I'm fine. Just a bit unwell. I tried to steady my nerves by drinking on the plane, and it either worked too well or not at all. Jury's still out.'

'I see.'

The way he said it, she was pretty sure he *did* see, but was also faintly amused. Not in a mean way. Andrew had often got a bit nasty when he felt she was being silly like this, but whoever the voice was, he was amused with her rather than against her.

She found herself apologizing anyway. 'I'm sorry.'

'I take it that you're a bit anxious about flying?'

'Yes,' she said, breathing in deeply. 'Just a bit.' The voice had nice cologne. Subtle and spicy. She laughed a little. 'In fact, I'm fairly certain that I've cornered that particular market.'

He hummed thoughtfully at her. 'Hold on a moment.'

She heard him walk away. Despite his words, she wondered if he was going to come back. She would have understood if he'd decided to leg it to the nearest exit. *Monkeys in the trees. Damn it all.* She breathed slowly, willing her stomach to settle.

To her surprise, she heard footsteps coming over to her a few moments later, then the faint rustle of cloth as he lowered himself down. Something popped, probably his knee.

'Hold out your hand, please.'

Bemused, Sophie did as he asked. Chilled plastic met her palm. A water bottle. Startled, she opened her eyes and suddenly felt sick all over again, but for a very different reason.

Blue-green eyes. Crooked grin, causing charming crow's feet. Deep brown hair that was slightly dishevelled after the long flight, going a little grey at the temples. Dark stubble, solid jaw, and a well-tailored suit with no tie.

Oh no. He was *handsome*.

Sophie was suddenly very aware that she looked like something the cat had refused to drag in because even felines had standards. She sat frozen, holding the bottle of water and staring at him.

Luckily, he'd looked away and was digging through his bag. He plucked out a little disposable pouch, the kind medicines sometimes came in, and showed it to her. 'I've been sick on planes before and it's awful, so I always carry something. This should help with your stomach and any headache, if you have one.' He gestured to the water bottle. 'May I?'

She nodded.

He unscrewed the top with a satisfying snap. Then he tore open the packet and carefully poured the powder into the water. After he was done, he threw away the empty packet and resealed the water bottle, swirling the contents around. 'Sip it. You'll feel much better soon.'

She unscrewed the lid again, taking a small sip. Cool water flooded her tongue, along with a hit of artificial citrus and something medicinal. She took a few more careful sips, waiting to see if the liquid would stay put.

The man smiled at her and she swore she felt it in her bones, which was absolutely absurd. Still, she smiled back, though only faintly. His was the kind of smile you responded to, one honestly meant.

His brow furrowed slightly, the corners of his mouth turning down. 'Are you going to be okay?'

'I think so. Thank you.'

He waved it away as if it were nothing, and Sophie would have felt the same way if they'd swapped places. If she'd been the one handing out water and medicine, it would feel like the bare minimum, but the men she'd known until now had a very different definition of those words. He checked his watch. 'I'm sorry. I'm afraid I have to go. Would you like a hand up?'

Sophie shook her head. 'I'm going to sit another moment and then be off.'

His frown deepened. 'Are you sure? I hate to leave you sitting on the floor.'

Sophie cocked her head at him. He meant it. Extraordinary. She took another sip before recapping her water. 'How about a compromise: you help me up, then I'll lean against this wall until I feel ready to move on.'

He hesitated.

'I promise you won't read headlines like, "Woman keeled over in airport – police looking for heartless man who left her splayed on the floor".'

His lips twitched as he checked his watch again. He sighed and held out his hand. 'I will have your word, madam, that there will be no such headline.'

'Did you just "madam" me?'

He winced. 'It sounded better in my head.'

'I bet it did.' She took his hand, his warm palm sliding against hers. She shivered.

He frowned at her some more. He was good at that, too. A sexy frowner. She bet he gave good glower, as well. Perfect. She was cracking up at JFK Airport.

'Maybe I should walk with you.'

She waved him off as she leaned against the wall. 'No, no. You have somewhere to be. I promise I'm okay.' She waved a hand at her legs. 'See? Nary a wobble. I'm wobble-less.'

He glanced down towards the baggage claim sign, frowning, before checking his watch again. When he returned his attention to her, his face relaxed as he shook his head. 'I can't do it, I'm afraid. You're stuck with me until customs at the very least.' He splayed a hand over his heart. 'Think of my reputation. If those headlines get out, I'll be ruined.'

Sophie took another long sip of her water. Deciding she felt slightly less wobbly, she straightened up. 'Suit yourself.'

They moved together down the corridor, the man keeping pace with her, watching to see if she was okay. She was reminded of the time she'd taught her son how to ride his bicycle. The first time he'd pedalled on his own, when she'd let go and run beside him, hovering in case he needed help. A sweet sort of vigilance. When she paused to sip her water, he paused with her, making sure she wasn't jostled by the flow of passengers. She had the oddest sensation of them being in their own bubble, a sense of connection that had snapped into place despite the fact that they were strangers.

He'd also not glanced at his watch even once.

'You really don't have to stay with me,' Sophie said. 'I'm feeling much better.'

The corner of his mouth hitched up. 'Nice try. Every time you take a sip, I can see that your hand is still shaking.'

She hadn't even noticed. 'I don't want to keep you from whatever you're rushing off to do. Unless it's something dreadful like a meeting.'

'It's something dreadful like a meeting,' he confirmed, guiding her around a family that had stopped in the middle of the walkway to comfort their child.

'Will you get into trouble?'

He shook his head. 'Travel delays happen. I don't need to be specific about it.'

They got to the luggage carousel, immediately plunging into the chaos. There was so much bustle in an airport, so much noise and confusion. People trying to rush off to the next step of their travels dodging around people who looked as dazed and exhausted as she felt.

The man grimaced as he leaned this way and that, trying to catch sight of the luggage as it slowly rotated around the belt. 'I'm convinced that any modernization of Dante's *Inferno* would take place in an airport.'

Sophie blinked up at him. 'I don't follow.'

He waved a hand at the crowd. 'Tell me you wouldn't picture this as limbo?'

'Only limbo?' Sophie asked. "Not something worse?"

'It's only baggage claim,' he said. 'Wait until you hit customs. That's pure seventh circle.'

Sophie tried to remember what the seventh circle was, but her tired brain refused to cooperate. 'Which one's the seventh?'

'Violence,' he said grimly, though she could see a glimmer of laughter in his eyes. 'Which is generally how I feel while I'm waiting in line for the customs agent.' Hold on, I think

I see mine.' He darted forward, weaving through the crowd before she could respond.

Sophie finished off her water, wandering over to the side to look for a bin, when she spied her own luggage twirling by. She dodged around several people, muttering apologies despite the fact that they were the ones making it difficult, and grabbed her suitcase handle. The black case looked much like several others around it, but she'd spotted her luggage tag printed with the swoops and swirls of Van Gogh's *Starry Night*. She righted her bag, draping her carry-on and cardigan over the top.

She turned and almost bumped right into the helpful man, and realized she hadn't even asked his name yet. She opened her mouth to say something, only to be jostled suddenly by a man chasing after his toddler. He shouted an apology but didn't look back as Sophie wobbled.

The helpful man's hand shot out, catching her elbow and righting her quickly. 'Got your luggage? Excellent. Let's get out of here before we're trampled.'

He carved a path for her as they weaved their way out of the crush. Sophie, who had been plodding along, focusing on his suit jacket and paying very little attention to anything else, was brought up short when she realized they'd moved on to customs and immigration.

The man turned back to her, a questioning expression on his face. 'Are you okay?'

'My son warned me, I just—' She let out a breath. 'They're *armed*.'

The man followed her gaze towards the police standing off to the side. He didn't look pleased, but he also didn't seem surprised. 'First time in New York?'

She nodded.

For a second Sophie thought he might reach out and squeeze her hand or hug her, but instead he cleared his

Lish McBride

throat and when he spoke, his voice was gentle. 'There are many ways that New York will remind you of London. This . . . isn't one of them.'

'It's okay,' she said, though the wobble in her voice belied her words. 'Just a shock.'

He assessed her for a moment, then obviously decided to let it drop. She started to follow him again, only to realize that he was heading for a sign that said 'Global Entry'. Which Sophie didn't have.

She looked forlornly over at the regular queue. Seeing her stop again, the man turned and, without speaking, seemed to understand the situation.

'You didn't sign up for anything?' he asked.

Sophie shook her head. 'Not exactly a frequent flyer.'

He pursed his lips as he examined the queue she was supposed to join. Sophie laughed, holding up her hands. 'Oh, no. You're not going with me. I've delayed you enough.'

He hesitated, frowning. 'You're absolutely sure?'

'I am.' She held out her hand, palm down. 'See? Steady as a rock.'

'Okay,' he said, though he seemed like he wanted to argue. 'Promise me I won't see headlines?'

'Promise.' She turned her hand, ready to shake on it.

He shook her hand automatically, then seemed momentarily startled by the contact, like he hadn't expected her to touch him at all. Then he smiled, and she was once again walloped by how handsome he was. 'It was a pleasure. Except for the part where you didn't feel well.'

She continued to shake his hand, slightly dazed. 'Same.' They smiled at each other for a second more before he reluctantly stepped back, adjusted his suit jacket and his bag, then turned to walk away. Sophie watched him go. He had nice shoulders and long legs and she *really* didn't want to get into the queue for immigration.

Ah, well. It was neither the time nor the place. She was tempted to shout after him – not that she had anything to say, she just wanted to see that smile again. But what would she shout? Welcome to New York? Nice arse? Surely she could do better than that. She was a writer. She considered words to be her friends, but as she watched him get smaller and smaller, she felt betrayed. Sophie felt like an artist in front of a blank canvas without any paints.

It wasn't until he was totally out of sight that she realized she could have said, 'Thank you.' Or even just asked his *name*. She covered her face with her hand.

Sometimes, Sophie, you are a complete and utter pillock.

At least she was starting to feel better. She grabbed her luggage handle and made her way to the back of the queue.

By the time she'd made it through the gauntlet that was the JFK customs and immigration system, she was dead on her feet. The only thing that made her feel better was seeing her son Tom waiting for her. When he caught sight of her, he brightened, smiling wide. 'There you are! I was about to send the hounds after you.' He enveloped her in a warm hug. 'Wow, Mum, you smell like gin.' His grin was highly amused. 'Have a good flight, then?'

She groaned. 'For the rest of the day I don't want to hear anything about planes or gin. I want a shower, a nap and something to eat, not in that order.' Now that the medicine had worked its magic, she was feeling *much* better.

He gave her a squeeze before taking her bags from her. 'Come on, then. Marisa is waiting for us and the shower is calling your name.'

'You're an angel. Have I ever told you that?'

'No,' he said with a laugh. 'It was usually the other way around.' He threw his free arm around her and gave her another long squeeze. 'I'm really glad you came, Mum.'

'Me too, darling. Me too.'

'What do you mean you didn't get her name?' Rahul's incredulous voice drifted from the phone. Mike had texted his children as instructed as soon as he got to the furnished Manhattan flat his office had found close to the work site. He was exhausted down to his marrow and wanted nothing more than to collapse onto the bed. Instead, he'd accept Rahul's video call.

He'd mistakenly thought his son might distract him from the fact that he couldn't stop thinking about the woman from the airport. Her good humour. The way her hand had felt almost familiar in his own. Or the fact that he had, somehow, forgotten to get even her name. Instead, talking to his son was only making it worse.

'I'm not normally the type of person who chats up ill women,' he said dryly as he set the phone on the dresser, propping it against a decorative vase so that Rahul could still see him as he unpacked. His son was in the middle of making breakfast, the knife flashing as he sliced fruit on the chopping board. Mike wished for a second that he wasn't in New York at all, but back in London, sitting in the same room as his son instead of watching him through a screen.

'I'm not saying you had to go full, "Hey, what's your star sign?" but exchanging names – hell, exchanging numbers – wouldn't have been weird. Especially since you were worried about her.'

Mike snorted and hoisted his suitcase up onto the bed. The luggage tag smacked against the hard plastic shell as it landed. '"Hey, what's your star sign?" When did you turn into your grandfather?'

'Hey, Granddad had game, and you're dodging the discussion.'

Mike sighed, running a hand through his hair. 'I honestly didn't think of it. I'm going to be busy with work while I'm here anyway, so it's not like anything could come of it.' It was just . . . her sitting there, unhappy and rumpled and speaking nonsense. She'd been oddly . . . cute. He'd liked talking to her, even it hadn't been for long, and he'd been reluctant to go. He should have stayed with her through customs. He could have said to hell with his schedule and made sure she was actually well, at the very least.

'You don't have to marry the woman, Dad, but I know you. You're going to work the entire time you're in New York. You'll either skip meals or keep working through them. You deserve more than that. If you'd got her number, you could have met up with her and had lunch or something. One fun thing, Dad. I'd like you to do one fun thing while you're there.'

'You're a bully, you know that? I have no idea where you get it from.'

Rahul's voice quietened. 'From Mum, that's who. If she was here, she'd be chewing your ear off, Dad. She wouldn't like you working yourself to death.'

He couldn't argue with his son – Rahul was right. 'One fun thing?'

'Just one. That's all I ask,' Rahul said soothingly as he slid the sliced fruit into a bowl.

'Okay,' he said, unzipping his suitcase. 'I can do that. I promise.' He flipped open the case and stopped. That wasn't his jumper, and he was certain he didn't own a make-up bag. There was something decidedly lacy to the side. Without thinking, he picked it up, letting the silky cloth unfurl.

'Good,' Rahul said. 'That's all I—' Abruptly, he stopped speaking.

Mike looked at the screen.

Rahul was frozen, knife still in hand. 'Dad, whose pants are those?'

'I have absolutely no idea,' Mike said honestly.

Rahul snorted a laugh. 'Well, I can admit when I'm wrong. You clearly live a more exciting life than I thought.'

'I really don't,' Mike said, staring at the silky green underwear.

'I don't judge, Dad. As long as you're happy, you wear whatever kind of pants you want.'

'Oh, shut it.'

'What else is in there?'

Mike scowled at him. 'I'm not going to go digging through someone's private things.'

Rahul shrugged. 'How else are you going to find out who it belongs to?'

'It's an invasion of privacy,' Mike grumbled, but he was looking at what was on top, to see if there were other clues. It wasn't as bad, was it, if he wasn't digging through everything? There were a few plastic objects, one an odd shape and he couldn't help but pick it up and examine it.

'That's to hold your phone,' Rahul said, fruit and knife forgotten as he peered at the screen. 'You know, for hands-free stuff, like what you could use instead of propping your phone against things.'

'My way works,' Mike said, as he peered into another plastic container next to it. It was round, like a compact. Medicine, perhaps? It might have a name on it. He popped it open and froze.

Rahul perked up. 'You found something. What is it?'

'Nothing,' Mike said, snapping the case shut and putting it back. 'None of your business.'

Rahul leaned closer. 'It's a vibrator, isn't it?'

'No, absolutely not.'

'That means yes.' Rahul grinned. 'I'm beginning to like this person. Fancy knickers, hands-free phone-holder, vibrator – maybe you should have asked for *their* number.' He tilted his head. 'Does it look like a professional set-up? Maybe they've got an OnlyFans.'

'Maybe you should stop talking.' Mike put a palm over his face. 'We're terrible people.'

Rahul snickered, setting down his knife and wiping his hand on the tea towel thrown over his shoulder. 'How did you mix up bags? I thought you marked yours.'

'I did. I have a luggage tag – the one we got from the Van Gogh exhibition. I saw it, grabbed the bag and left. I was in a bit of a hurry to make up lost time,' he said absently.

'Well, I'd take the time to flip that tag now,' Rahul offered mock helpfully.

Why hadn't he thought of the tag before? He was a reasonably intelligent individual. *Because you saw green, silky knickers and lost your mind, old man.* Mike huffed. 'I don't like how much you're enjoying this.'

'I'm a stay-at-home dad at the moment. I take my laughs where I can.'

Mike flipped over the luggage tag. Where he had expected to find his name, he instead found the name *Sophie Swann* in a slanting script. 'It's the exact same brand as my luggage. Exact same tag. What are the odds?'

He'd meant them as rhetorical questions, but his son answered him anyway. 'You have good taste in luggage, and half of London probably went to that exhibition. I'd say the odds were fairly good.'

Mike put his head in his hands and groaned. 'I'm going to have to phone this poor woman and tell her I saw her pants.'

'I'd leave out that last bit if I were you.' Rahul resumed his food prep. 'Women get a little weird for some reason when a stranger starts talking about their unmentionables.'

Chapter Three

Sophie hadn't been able to believe her luck when she'd found an apartment to sublet in her son's building, and now that she was seeing it, she felt doubly lucky. It was a floor above them, with a small living space and the tiniest kitchenette, which pleased her greatly. Sophie could make tea and had an excuse to never cook again. Andrew had liked a good roast, and during their marriage Sophie had spent a large portion of her time at home cooking for her family. Which at one point, she'd loved. She still liked to cook for friends on occasion. When she *chose*. It was the expectation that she had to that had weighed her down. Not just to cook, but to cook what Andrew liked. She didn't even particularly care for a roast.

This, however, was perfect for her needs. It felt like a good omen, like New York was welcoming her. The apartment owner obviously loved a bright palette – the walls were aqua blue, with hanging plants and vibrant art hung here and there. The loveseat was orange, the ottoman pink and the ceiling a bright yellow. A small red table with two chairs sat next to the kitchenette. It felt a bit like being inside a parrot.

The bedroom wasn't large, containing only the bed, a bedside table, and a small chest of drawers wedged into the cupboard. The owner was clearly also big on textures, because there was a faux fur throw across the mattress.

Marisa sidled up next to her, nudging her with her elbow. 'What do you think?'

'I think it's one mirrored coffee table and a line of cocaine away from the 1970s,' Sophie said honestly. 'And I love it.'

Marisa didn't quite laugh, but she *did* smile a little, which was something. 'Good to hear it.'

Tom wheeled the suitcase in behind her, along with a bag of groceries they'd picked up on their way in from the corner store, which Marisa had referred to as a 'bodega'. 'Only one suitcase, Mum. I'm impressed.'

Sophie plucked the bag of groceries from him and set them on the counter. 'Oh, I don't need much. I have my laptop, so I can work. My e-reader. I can wash my clothes, so I didn't need to bring my entire wardrobe or anything.'

'Here,' Marisa said, stepping forward, 'let me put away the groceries. You settle in.'

Sophie followed Tom into the bedroom, letting him heft her single piece of luggage onto the bed. She didn't want to open it in front of him – there were a few things in there she didn't particularly want her son to see, even if he was an adult himself. But he didn't linger, instead stepping in and checking out the cupboard-sized bathroom.

She took the opportunity to pop open her bag, hoping to sneak her toy into her make-up bag, only . . .

Only to find an array of clothing, mostly in dark colours, that was definitely not hers. She didn't own blue trainers. Despite her shock, she took a moment to admire the organization at work. Everything was neat, tidy, folded. The boxers were in perfect rolls, lined up like a pack of sausages.

Tom peered over her shoulder. 'What's this?'

She splayed her hands out helplessly. 'Not mine?'

Tom nudged her out of the way and started rifling through the clothes, being careful to keep things folded at least.

'What are you doing? Those aren't yours!' The last word, she was sure, came out in the decibel range only some really precocious dogs could hear. 'Stop it!'

'Why?' Tim moved on to the other half of the bag. 'We need to find out whose bag this is, don't we?'

'That's what the luggage tag is for!' She pointed at the small plastic rendition of *Starry Night* resting at the top. 'How would you feel if this were your luggage?'

Tom only shrugged. 'Life is short, find joy where you can.' He straightened, putting his hands on his hips. 'Absolutely nothing interesting. Congratulations, Mum. You got the luggage of the most boring man in England. No condoms, no pills, not even a smuggled marmoset.'

She frowned at him. 'I'm a little jet lagged, so forgive me if I'm being obtuse, but why would anyone be smuggling marmosets out of England?'

'Why do people do anything?' He tucked the clothes back into place and zipped up the case, finally turning the tag over. 'I guess you can ask Michael Tremblay when you phone him.'

Sophie gave him a bewildered look. 'You want me to ask him why he doesn't smuggle tiny monkeys in his bags?'

'No, ask him why he's so boring.' Tom crossed his arms with a huff. 'Next time I travel, I'm going to put something inexplicable in my luggage, just in case this happens. Like a roll of duct tape and a single can of sardines. Anything to avoid the possibility that someone would open my luggage and go, "Bit boring, innit?"'

'That's a little judgemental,' she said. 'Besides, you have no idea if this luggage is indicative of him as a person. The luggage might be a clever ruse. Maybe he's just good at his job and whatever he's smuggling is on his person, or in a hidden compartment.' She clutched her son's arm. 'Do *not* go looking for a hidden compartment.'

He smiled at her, amused. 'You never let me have any fun.'

Marisa poked her head into the room. 'What's going on?'

'Mum got the luggage of the most boring man in England,' Tom said.

'Oh,' Marisa said. 'That's too bad. It would have been a lot more fun if he'd had something cool in there. Like fetish gear or a puppet.'

'I suggested duct tape and a can of sardines, which now feels like amateur hour compared to your idea.' Tom eyed his fiancée speculatively. 'I'm not sure if I should be impressed by how quickly you came up with them or disturbed by your pairing.'

She sniffed, tilting her nose in the air. 'Impressed.'

Tom put his arms around her and kissed her forehead. 'I'm always impressed by you.'

Instead of enjoying the sweet scene before her, Sophie was nailed in place by a sharp jab of panic as she remembered what was in her bag. 'Oh no. No, no, no, no, no.'

A slow grin unfurled on Tom's face. 'Now I'm wondering what's in *your* bag.'

'Smuggled marmosets, mostly,' Sophie replied absently, her mind circling with worry. Maybe she would get lucky. Maybe Michael Tremblay wouldn't open it at all. Surely he would just read the tag and *know*. Except . . . she hadn't, had she? She could say it to herself all she wanted, but she didn't believe it. She simply didn't have that kind of luck.

She'd been so looking forward to a shower, too. Oh, she could take one, but the idea of putting on the same clothes didn't sit well.

'Since he's the most boring man in England, he's probably going to turn you in for smuggling, but I'm sure it's just a fine,' Tom said. 'No jail time needed. Which is good. I don't think you'd do well in prison.'

Marisa shook her head. 'That's where you're wrong. Your mom's got steel in her spine. I bet she'll start her own gang and have an underground trading ring of highly sought-after prison wine. And think of the ratings for your blog when you get out.' Marisa patted her shoulder. 'You'll be like Martha Stewart.'

Sophie considered this. 'I wouldn't mind being friends with Snoop Dogg.'

'He makes wine,' Marisa offered. 'Like, actual wine that you can buy and not the kind made in a prison toilet.'

Tom tilted his head. 'I can't tell if I want you to go to prison now or not. I don't want to see you behind bars, but I would love to see photos of you and Snoop Dogg spread all over your socials.' His expression went flat, his tone turning dry. 'I'd absolutely love to forward those along.'

He didn't say to whom, but they all knew, nonetheless. Andrew's name hung in the air like a particularly aggressive spectre. It took a long minute for Sophie to banish him from her mind, but she eventually managed. She refused to let him ruin her post-marriage life by spending her days angry. Not that she wouldn't feel that way sometimes, but she'd already devoted so much of her time to that man, and she refused to give him a minute more of it.

She clicked open her phone and typed in Michael Tremblay's number.

'You're not going to call him, are you?' Marisa asked, the tone of horror in her voice not unlike the one people reserved for things like stabbings or not ordering enough food for a dinner party. 'Haven't you ever seen *Dateline*?'

Sophie frowned at her. 'No. What's *Dateline*?'

'It's a true crime show,' Tom said. 'Full of murders.'

'Sounds very American,' Sophie said, not unkindly.

Marisa sighed. 'I'd love to argue with you, but you're right.'

Tom's brow furrowed. 'I'm not sure calling a strange man is a good idea. He could be a serial killer.' He waved at the plain luggage. 'The more I think about it, the more his neatly folded clothing has sinister undertones. What if he's in a cult? A murder cult?'

'You've been here too long,' Sophie said. 'Not everyone is in a murder cult.'

'Oh, like we don't have those at home,' Tom said. 'It's just not safe, giving a stranger your phone number.' He put his hands on his hips and blew out a breath. 'You could use my phone.'

'What if I'm not his type and he needs young men for his murder cult?' Sophie asked with a grin. He scowled at her instead of laughing as she'd expected. Perplexed, Sophie turned to Marisa with a wordless question.

Marisa put her hands out flat in a sort of shrug. 'He's been a bit in overdrive lately because . . .' She made a face, waving at her own stomach. 'Protective with occasional slides into bossiness.'

'I see,' Sophie said neutrally. She placed a hand on her son's arm. 'My darling boy, light of my life. I'm going to text a man about his luggage, not sign up for a blood sacrifice.'

'No one knows they're signing up for that, Mum,' Tom said ominously. 'People work up to that sort of thing.'

Marisa grabbed him by the shoulders, herding him out of the room. 'I'll manage this one and remind him that you're a grown-up who can make their own choices. You text the most boring serial killer in London.'

'Thank you, love,' Sophie said. 'You're an angel.' She tapped out a message to Michael Tremblay. *Hello, Mr Tremblay. I'm afraid there was a mix-up and I seem to have your luggage. Hoping we can exchange soon?*

Mike had only just picked up his phone from its awkward position against the vase – Rahul having signed off to deal with a fussy Archie – when the text came through.

Hello, Mr Tremblay. I'm afraid there was a mix-up and I seem to have your luggage. Hoping we can exchange soon?

He stared at her open suitcase guiltily for only a moment before replying. *This must be Mrs Swann. I was just about to message you. I'm afraid my schedule is full for the next few hours. Possible to meet up after?*

Mike had already been annoyed at his schedule – no one should have a meeting directly after arriving – but that was hardly anyone's fault as his original flight had been for the night before. His plan of meeting, dinner, nap, however, had been thoroughly derailed. Now he was going to have to venture off to some far-flung corner of the city instead.

He closed his eyes and took a deep breath. Nothing he could do about it. It had probably been his fault in the first place. He'd been tired after the long flight, and somewhat overloaded by the sensory overwhelm that was JFK Airport. His mind hadn't exactly been on the task, or really anything it should have been on. It had been on the woman he'd found resting against the wall.

He rubbed a hand over his face. *Get a grip, old man. She wasn't even that pretty.*

But even he was calling himself a liar when his phone buzzed again.

My dreams of a shower and a fresh change of clothes go up in smoke. Alas, I shall soldier on.

Mike smiled. Even over text, Sophie Swann was funny. His mind helpfully reminded him of the silky green between his fingers from earlier and before he thought better of it, he typed a response. *A pain I understand deeply.*

Would be happy to come to you and apologize for the incon-venience with dinner?

As soon as he'd sent it, he regretted it. What if she was awful? What if she thought his offer was awful? Was it strange, asking her to dinner? It was just a meal. It wasn't like he was asking her on a date . . .

He tapped his phone against his head. This was why he didn't date. He hardly knew what to do any more. To be fair, he hadn't known what to do in the first place, really. His wife had been a patient woman who had somehow, miraculously, seen past his shortcomings. What were the odds that anyone else would?

His phone buzzed again. *How do you feel about paella?*

Mike only had a vague memory of what paella was – his love of food had seemed to die with his wife. He knew there had been a time in his life when he'd enjoyed going out to eat. Food these days was mostly fuel, eaten as he read or worked, only hazily aware of what he was putting in his mouth. But he wasn't going to say that to a stranger, no matter what delightful things he'd found in her luggage.

He thought for a moment before typing out his response. *There are few things I love more than paella. It's right up there with children's laughter and puppy videos.*

Once again, he regretted it after he sent it. Professional, polite: that's what the rest of the world got. Usually he kept this kind of messaging for his children. Jet lag. That was his only excuse. At this rate, she was probably going to throw his luggage at him and leg it.

That is high praise indeed. I'm now concerned that the meal won't live up to your standards. Shall we say eight o'clock?

Mike let out his breath in a whoosh. *Eight is perfect.*

She sent him a link to the restaurant where they would meet. Mike clicked on it as he freshened up quickly to get ready for his meeting. He sent Sophie another text as he walked to the nearest subway station. *How will I know which one is you?*

He didn't see her response until he was smashed up against a cross section of the New York populace, various colognes and sweat clashing in his nose.

That's easy. I'll be the one with the suitcase.

Mike found himself smiling as he responded. *I suppose I should have thought of that. I'm blaming jet lag.*

It does cover a lot of sins.

He barked a laugh at her response, earning him a couple of quick glances before he was ignored. New York's subway was much like the tube back home – he would have to behave a lot more weirdly if he expected anyone to really notice.

The meeting ran over. Mike wasn't entirely sure how, since he was certain the meeting itself could have been an email. A *short* email. By the time he'd collected his luggage and made it to the restaurant in Brooklyn, he was twenty minutes late, tired and not a little sweaty. The air in New York had a weight to it that it didn't have in London. His temper, usually a long, slow boil, had burned so hot during the meeting that all liquid had evaporated, leaving him feeling hollowed out and waspish.

And he was starving.

As such, he was not in the best of moods as he dragged the luggage into the narrow restaurant. The place teemed with people – he didn't see any empty seats as he peered around for Sophie. The restaurant itself was charming – exposed brick walls, sconces that looked like old-fashioned gas lamps surrounded by copper fixtures that reflected the light. Lots of greenery and colourful splashes here and there in the tiled walls and artwork. It was a warm, happy kind of place, smelling of spices and sizzling meats. His stomach didn't so much growl as roar.

He awkwardly wheeled the suitcase as he sought his quarry. Finally, a man waved at him from a table tucked into the back corner. His expression wasn't unfriendly, but it was assessing, and it suddenly occurred to Mike that he might have accidentally asked someone else's partner to dinner. Maybe the man was with Sophie and didn't appreciate some stranger taking his girlfriend out. Shit. Was he going to need to apologize? Surely Sophie would have said something. He hadn't meant anything by it. Maybe he could offer to cover the man's meal as well.

There was a woman seated next to him who was also waving, an amused expression on her face. There was no one else at the table, so this would have to be Sophie. He hadn't realized until that moment that he'd been hoping for something – some*one* who he connected with as much as he had with the woman in the airport. Disappointment weighed him down, making it hard to smile in greeting, but he managed.

The waving woman was beautiful, but too young and obviously taken. That was okay. It had been a silly idea anyway, and it wasn't like he had time or really the inclination to date while he was in New York. Work ate up the hours. He'd just been trying to fulfil his son's request, really, which he could still do by having a nice dinner with these two strangers.

It was a relief, actually. So why did he feel let down?

He pulled the case to the end of the restaurant, coming to a stop at the table. Then he stuck out his hand to the woman. 'Sophie, I assume. Thank you for being so patient about my schedule.'

A slow smile bloomed on the woman's face as she took his hand. 'Oh, I'm not—'

There was a clatter to their left, all of them turning to look at once.

A woman – *the* woman – had frozen in the middle of the narrow aisle, her eyes wide, her lips slightly parted. Behind her, a busboy was bending down to pick up the silverware he'd dropped. He was apologizing but kept sending her dirty looks that implied it had been her fault, probably for stopping in the middle of the aisle.

Mike noticed this absently, the details filtering into his brain as he stared into familiar hazel eyes.

'It's you,' she said.

Mike nodded as if this was something he needed to agree to; that he was, in fact, himself. She looked a lot better now than she had – there was colour in her cheeks, and her skin no longer had that clammy sheen to it that people sometimes got when they didn't feel well. His deeply unhelpful brain decided to gleefully announce that this, *this* must be Sophie of the green, silken knickers, and chose this second as the best time to conjure up images of her wearing them.

His mouth went dry. If he licked a stamp right now, nothing would happen. When was the last time he'd licked a stamp, anyway? Also, why was his brain such a traitorous bastard? He'd never thought they were friends, but he'd at least thought they were uneasy allies.

And why, why was he so fixated on her knickers? Lingerie had never really been a thing for him before. Was it just that it had been ages since he'd held anything like that in his hands? Maybe his kids were right. He did need to get out more if this was all it took for him to act like his brain had melted. He hadn't even greeted her yet. His mouth had stopped working, which might be a good thing, considering the mess his thoughts had become.

He was just . . . staring at her. To be fair, she was staring back, but it had to be unnerving. How long had they been like this? When had timed stopped moving properly? What was wrong with New York anyway, that it just let time do whatever it wanted? He felt a fine mist of sweat break out on his brow. Without thinking, he grabbed one of the glasses of water off the table and drank it.

'Pretty sure that was mine,' the man said, a hint of amusement in his tone.

'Sorry,' Mike replied, but didn't relinquish the now empty glass. He cleared his throat. 'No headlines, then?'

'You're safe from mobs crying for retribution.' She smiled and held out her hand. 'Sophie Swann.'

He reached out to take her hand, realized he was still holding the empty glass, and set it down hastily. 'Michael Tremblay.' Her warm palm slid against his and he felt it all the way to the backs of his knees, which made no sense. His brain continued to mutiny and chose that moment to point out that Sophie-of-the-green-knickers didn't have a wedding ring. She also didn't have anyone there with her currently. Which didn't mean anything, damn it, it was just dinner, only dinner.

Mike swore he could hear his own brain laughing at him and wondered if he should maybe see a doctor.

Someone cleared their throat. 'And I'm Enrico. Any chance I can get through? Table nine has been waiting for a fork for, like, ten minutes.'

Mike blinked at the busboy. 'The ones that were on the floor?'

Enrico shot him a scathing look. 'I took those to the kitchen already. These are new.'

'I'm so sorry,' Sophie said, stepping out of the way. She pulled Mike with her, which made him realize he was still holding her hand. He dropped it, regretfully, dragging the suitcase out of the way.

The other man at their table stood up and took the handle. 'I'll put it back here with your suitcase. It's out of the way.'

'Thank you,' Mike said. He looked to Sophie. 'I can't believe it's you.'

'I can't believe it's me, either,' Sophie said, moving around him, taking the seat by the wall. 'Sit down, sit down. Marisa, Tom, this is the man who helped me earlier at the airport.'

Tom brightened at this. 'That was you? We owe you a bit of thanks, then.'

'That was me.' Mike sat, a little like someone had cut his strings. He couldn't fathom it. He'd never acted this way in his entire life – at least not sober. What was wrong with him? He ran a hand over his face.

The younger woman across from him looked at him sympathetically. 'Long day?'

'Today has been the second longest day of my life,' Mike responded honestly. His brain still had that melted feeling, his usual social filter gone in the aftermath.

The woman cocked her head to the side. 'What was the first?'

'The day my wife died.' Mike could have bit his own tongue. He hadn't meant to say it. Over the years, it had got easier to tell people; it was no longer a sharp blade in his organs every time he mentioned her. He'd boiled it down to simple words – I had a wife. She died. Most people left it at that. Gave a tut and patted his arm sympathetically. No one really wanted to talk about grief. Not really.

But while it was easier to say now, he didn't usually offer it up like that. People had to ask first. He certainly didn't blurt it out to people he'd just met for dinner. Not even *over* dinner. They hadn't ordered yet. Was this how he was going to be now? *Hi, my name is Mike and my wife is dead?*

'Jesus,' the young man said, picking up the glass of water that had been in front of the woman and taking a sip. 'Forget getting you a water. Sounds more like you need the cocktail list.'

'On it.' Marisa plucked a small menu from her side of the table, her accent telling Mike that if she wasn't from here, she'd lived here quite a long time. She leaned across the table, placing the cocktail menu in front of him, her expression sympathetic. 'You need a drink?'

Mike, who had been doing a spectacular re-enactment of the facepalm emoji, lowered his hands to the table. 'I could murder a pint right now.'

The young man, apparently named Tom, choked on his water.

Chapter Four

Marisa pounded Tom's back with the flat of her hand as he choked on his water.

'That usually only makes it worse,' Sophie pointed out, surprised that her voice sounded normal. Sitting next to Michael was . . . well. She didn't know how to describe what it was. Their legs weren't touching, but she swore she could feel the heat coming off him nonetheless. The subtle spice of his cologne teased her nostrils. She wanted to lean in, like he was a flower in full bloom, and take a sniff.

'I know,' Marisa said cheerfully, continuing to smack Tom's back.

'You're hilarious,' Tom wheezed. 'Now please stop.'

She laughed, her pounding now replaced by soothing circles. Tom turned to her, kissing her cheek.

Mike leaned close to Sophie, dropping his voice. 'Is this okay? If I'm intruding, we can swap the suitcases now and I'll get out of your way.'

He started to stand, but Sophie stopped him by placing a hand on his arm. 'What were you going to do for dinner?'

He opened his mouth, made a face, then closed it. 'I would sort something out.'

Sophie shook her head. 'We're already here, in this nice restaurant. The food smells amazing. Why not eat with us?' She dropped her hand. 'Unless you've changed your mind?'

He gave a sharp shake of his head. 'No, no, of course not. If you're sure.'

Sophie smiled at him. 'I think today has been very long, and sometimes very bad, but also very good, and I think a nice dinner would put it more squarely into the good column. I don't know about you, but I could use some more of those kinds of days.'

Michael seemed to accept this, taking the napkin off the table and placing it across his lap.

The waiter stopped by the table, dropping off two delicious-smelling dishes as he took Michael's drink order.

'We ordered a few appetizers for the table,' Sophie said, picking up her spoon and a small plate. 'I hope that's okay.'

Michael picked up his own plate, relief on his face. 'Thank you. I haven't eaten anything except a handful of mixed nuts since I left the airport.'

'We got burrata and the *dátiles*, which are dates stuffed with cheese and wrapped in bacon,' Marisa said. 'Are you a Michael or a Mike?'

'Mike, usually.' He filled his small plate before nudging it towards Sophie. 'This all smells delicious, thank you. Have you been here before?'

As Tom and Marisa launched into a discussion of their favourite dining spots in the area, Sophie put a few things on her plate, trying very hard to pretend that she wasn't watching Marisa. Tom was doing the same thing, both of them waiting to see if Marisa was eating. Tom had said she hadn't been very hungry, more just nibbling at things than eating proper meals. He didn't want to make a big thing out of it, as she was stressed enough already, but he'd also been concerned because she'd started to lose weight.

Marisa continued to chat with Mike as she put one of the dates on her plate. Tom's shoulders relaxed, and he turned his face to his own plate to hide his relief. In the short time that Sophie had been with them, she'd noticed several

instances like this – Tom wanting desperately to take care of
Marisa, but stopping himself out of apparent fear of becoming smothering.

'I'm very sorry,' Marisa said suddenly, snapping Sophie
back to the conversation. 'About your wife.'

'Thank you,' Mike said, his voice rough. 'It's been a long
time, but . . .'

Marisa dropped her eyes, picking at the date with the tines
of her fork. 'It stays with you, doesn't it? Losing someone.'

'It does,' Mike said softly. Then he handed Marisa
his napkin.

Sophie had been so focused on those fork tines, the ones
slowly and systematically tearing apart the bacon, that she'd
missed the quiet tears sliding down Marisa's cheeks.

Marisa took Mike's napkin, holding it to her face. 'I'm so
sorry. I didn't— I'm sorry.'

Tom put his arm around her, pressing his lips to her
hair. 'It's okay, Risa. It's okay.' He closed his eyes briefly,
and Sophie was certain she could see his heart breaking
for the hundredth time with not only his own pain, but
Marisa's too. She wished she could wrap them both up in
soft blankets and hold them tight until they'd weathered
the worst of it.

'Why don't you take her home?' Sophie said gently, knowing that Marisa wouldn't be comfortable with her grief and
pain out there for all of the strangers around them to see. 'I
can bring dinner for you.'

Marisa sniffed into her napkin. 'I hate this. Hate it. I just
. . . I wanted a nice dinner out. That's all, and I—' She cut
herself off with a slow shake of her head. She tipped her face
up, eyes red. 'Not much of a welcome for you, is it?'

Sophie reached out and clasped her hand. 'It's been a *wonderful* welcome. My plane didn't crash into the sea. I got to
hug my two favourite people. There wasn't any cocaine in

my flat, and no one smuggled a marmoset. I literally cannot think of a better reception.'

'I think,' Mike said, 'that either I missed something significant, or I'm having a stroke.'

Marisa gave a wet laugh as she wiped at her face with the napkin. 'I like you. Sorry I ruined dinner.'

Mike reached out, touching her hand with the tips of his fingers. 'You did no such thing. I mean it.' A moment of understanding seemed to flow between the two, causing Marisa to smile slightly.

'You do not need to be happy all the time,' Sophie said, her words no less firm for how gently they were delivered, 'not for me. But you do need to care for yourself just as much as you'd care for us. Tonight that means letting Tom take you home and having me drop off delicious paella at your door.'

Tom looked at her gratefully. 'Thanks, Mum.' His expression turned amused as he glanced at Mike. 'If you're sure?'

She waved him off. 'I'll be fine. He didn't help me in the airport just to murder me in the middle of a restaurant.'

Mike turned his head and looked at her, confused. 'Am I the murderer in this scenario?'

'Yes,' Sophie said. 'My son was just a little concerned about me meeting up with a stranger earlier.'

Tom nodded, pushing back his seat and stood. 'He could be playing the long con and the airport was only the first step in his dastardly plan. Maybe this is what he does: lures people places to retrieve their luggage, only to murder them in cold blood.'

Marisa sniffed. 'That would be silly. Too many cameras in the airport. They'd catch him too easily.' She set her napkin on the table as she stood. 'I think he's smarter than that.'

'Thank you,' Mike said. 'I'd like to think I'd be at least halfway competent, even when it comes to committing murder.'

Tom slid his empty chair back against the table. 'I feel like I should point out that the only things we know about him is that he doesn't recognize his own luggage and he drank my water. That's not exactly a ringing endorsement.'

'People usually follow up that kind of statement with "no offence",' Mike said evenly.

Tom just looked at him, then laughed, unable to keep a straight face.

Sophie sighed. 'I don't think either of you should watch this *Dateline* show any more. It can't be good for you.'

'If I was in your son's place, I'd honestly have the same concerns.' Mike dug out his wallet, fishing around in it for a moment, before placing something on the table. 'There's my driving licence. Take a picture of it. That way if anything happens, you'll have it.'

Tom took out his phone and snapped a photo. 'Thank you.' He put out his hand. 'Thank you for understanding.'

Mike shook it. 'I have two kids. Anytime either of them went on a date, I was worried until they checked in. Still am.'

Tom let his hand go with a nod.

Marisa took his hand next. 'We promise not to steal your identity.'

Tom squeezed her to him. 'I'm not promising anything.'

Sophie looked at her son, feeling the duelling emotions of overwhelming love and frustrated irritation in her chest. 'I can take care of myself, you know. I do it at home. All the time. Have for years.'

Tom moved around the table to kiss her on the cheek. 'Yes, I know, but just because you can, doesn't mean you should have to all the time.' He straightened, putting his arm around Marisa. 'Goodnight, Mum.' He nodded at Mike. 'Nice to meet you.'

'Likewise,' Mike said. He nodded at Marisa, their earlier understanding still vibrant between them.

Then they were gone and Sophie realized that both her and Mike were seated on the same side of the table, and that felt incredibly awkward on several different levels. The memory surfaced of the only time she'd walked in on Andrew and his assistant, Lori, on a date while the divorce was being finalized. They'd been sitting cosily on the same side of a booth in the pub, feeding each other. Sophie was the type of person who would ordinarily have found that romantic, but the fact that these two people were the ones doing it had made it nausea-inducing. She'd turned on her heel and walked out, messaging her friend as soon as she was outside that they'd have to meet elsewhere.

She stood, moving to the other side of the table until she was seated across from Mike. 'I've never been one of those people who sit next to their dates. Not that this is a date.'

Mike gave her a small smile. 'Me either. My wife—' He stopped, dropping his gaze.

The waiter appeared then, dropping off Mike's drink and taking their meal order. Sophie ordered a few things for takeaway, all the while considering whether or not she should let Mike's half-statement drop. Most people she knew would drop it, letting him keep his feelings to himself. She'd only just met this man, after all, and yet she instinctively thought that was the wrong move. It would be leaving an old wound to fester.

'Your wife?' she prodded gently.

Mike sipped his pint, his thumb tracing the line of the glass. The silence grew to the point that Sophie wasn't sure he was going to respond to her prompt at all.

'My wife was a romantic.' His smile was so faint, it was like his mouth had a shadow.

'She would have sat on the same side of the table with you?'

Mike shook his head slowly. 'No, she would have sat across. Tara said you needed space to build tension. The back and forth of it.' He grimaced. 'I'm not explaining it well. It's the body language of it: when you sit across, there's the table between you and all this empty space. It takes effort to cross it. Will the other person put themselves out there? How vulnerable are they willing to make themselves? Do they think you're worth it?'

Sophie absorbed this, breaking the idea down in her head while absent-mindedly noting that Mike sat fully on his side of the table, arms tucked in close, the body language of a closed-up shop.

He was staring hard at his beer now. 'It was all about anticipation. Hard to build that when you're plastered to their side.' He sliced the date in half, taking a quick bite of it. 'Of course, not everyone wants that. Some people want the same side of the booth.'

'I'm with her on this, I think,' Sophie said.

Mike nodded, his gaze flicking up from his beer, his fingers idly tracing through the condensation. 'Not that it's any of my business, but is Marisa going to be okay?'

Sophie hesitated for only a moment, deciding what Marisa would want shared with an absolute stranger and then adjusting that to what Marisa would want shared with *this* stranger. Mike, who had sat down and shared his own grief so matter-of-factly. 'They were pregnant. Now they're not.'

'Oh,' Mike said softly. 'I'm so sorry.' He grimaced. 'That doesn't seem like enough, sorry.'

'I think there are times when something is so crushing that there aren't really enough words to truly convey it, so it's best to keep things short.' Sophie sipped her drink, deciding to move the conversation onto safer ground. She wanted to keep Mike talking, because he was not only interesting, but she liked the sound of his voice. 'What brings you to New York?'

'Work,' he said. 'I'm an architect.'

'I'll admit, I have no real idea what an architect actually does.'

That earned her a genuine smile. 'Most people don't, which is why I say "architect" and not "design architect", which just confuses them further.'

Sophie refilled her plate. 'What does a design architect do?'

'I work with the client to help them realize their design and reconcile their wants with the budget and other things like that. Then I hand those designs over to the architect of record. They're the main architect on the job.'

He finished his pint and Sophie was temporarily distracted by the tip of his tongue as it slid out to collect a bit of the foam left behind on his lip. He had amazing lips, curved and lush, inviting your gaze to linger on them. Except this wasn't a date, and she needed to stop staring at this man. 'I didn't realize architects did more than the design part.'

Mike nodded. 'The Architect of Record will also manage things like zoning and codes. Sometimes projects have a single architect who wears both hats, but that wouldn't make sense in this case because these things are very different in New York than they are in London.

The waiter returned, taking their orders for fresh drinks and whisking away the plates they no longer needed.

'So why are they bringing you over here, then?' She grimaced. 'Is that a rude question to ask?'

'Not at all,' Mike said. 'The owner's concept is an event space that's sort of a fusion of classic British teahouse meets cocktail bar aesthetic. My work fits what they're looking for. How about you?'

'I'm a travel blogger.' Sophie smiled up at the waiter, accepting her fresh sparkling water. After the flight, a cocktail hadn't sounded good at all.

Mike blinked at her. 'But you're terrified of planes.'

'Yes,' Sophie said dryly. 'I'm aware.' She braced herself for the sudden mockery, the derisive stare. Andrew's barbs about her hobby-turned-profession had been so consistent that she half expected all men to respond in the same way. Or to think it was 'cute'.

Mike's brow furrowed, his expression one of open curiosity. 'Surely that makes your job difficult?'

She smiled. 'I usually keep it local.'

Before she knew it, she was telling him all about her blog – the early triumphs as well as the initial missteps – as they ate their meal. 'So there's my friend Edie, holding my phone so we could get a short video and not wanting to interrupt, but trying desperately to signal to me that Fergus had started chewing on the hem of my blouse.'

'Fergus being the 800-kilogram Highland steer?' Mike scraped up the last of his paella with his fork.

'The very one,' Sophie said, shaking her head. 'He ate the entire back of my blouse. Edie had to throw her jacket over me.'

Mike was laughing now, the sound contained as he hunched over his plate, the fork in his hand shaking. 'I would dearly love to see that video.' He wheezed and Sophie wondered at how contained he was, even now, in a moment of joy. 'Do you have plans for when you're here, then? The Empire State Building? The Statue of Liberty?'

Sophie scrunched up her nose. 'The blog is more neighbourhood gems. I feel like everyone knows about the tourist highlights.'

Mike watched her carefully as he leaned back in his chair. 'Surely every day won't be work? You've never been to New York, right? Don't *you* want to go and see those things?'

'If I have time,' she said, shrugging it off, even though yes, she would love to see those things. Especially the Empire State Building – there was just so much romance attached to it. 'I'm mostly here to spend time with Tom and Marisa. I'm sure Tom is over the tourist thing and I'll need to spend my free time going to places for the blog.'

Mike tapped his fingers along the table, that careful gaze fastened on her. 'It's okay to do things just for you, you know.'

'I know,' she said defensively, suddenly wanting to get the conversation off her, feeling like he was seeing too much. 'I assume you've done the tourist thing?'

Mike smiled, flushing a little – not out of embarrassment, she didn't think, but something else. 'Oh, yes. I took Tara to New York with me a few years after we got married. She absolutely *had* to go to the Empire State Building. It was non-negotiable.' He laughed. 'She was a movie buff. Loved rom-coms. After she saw *Sleepless in Seattle*, we had to watch *An Affair to Remember*. Come to New York and not see that iconic building? Absolutely not.'

His expression turned faraway and hazy, like he was happily drunk on the memory. Sophie tried to picture Andrew thinking of her with that expression on his face and she failed. 'Did it live up to your expectations?'

Mike straightened, shaking the mood off. 'It was magical, but then, anywhere with her was. You should go, just for you. Get yourself some of that magic.'

'If I went, I'd probably get stuck in the lift, or get my shirt caught on something, tear it, and accidentally flash a nun.'

He grinned and she thought how much fun it might be, making this man laugh, *really* laugh, head thrown back with complete abandon. To get him to, if for only a moment, let go. How would it feel to be the person who made that happen?

She decided not to think about it too much, as she was convinced that she would never be the one to know.

He'd stayed firmly on his side of the table the entire meal, showing no indication of wanting to close that gap.

Which she was *fine* with. After Andrew, she hardly wanted to go after anything serious, and she was pretty sure that Mike was a serious kind of guy. So really, it made no sense to want anything between them.

And yet, she felt a pang of disappointment when Mike leaned back in his chair and signalled for the bill.

The restaurant was only a few blocks from Tom and Marisa's building, but Mike insisted on walking Sophie back. He could say it was because it was dark, she was alone, and he'd promised her son, but if he was honest with himself – which he tried, but often failed, to be – it wasn't really for any of those reasons. No, his real reasons were both simpler and more concerning. He liked talking to her. He liked looking at her. He liked that he never really knew what was going to come out of her mouth, so every conversation was like an adventure. So while he could say it was for her safety, selfishly he simply wanted a few more stolen moments with Sophie in his life.

The heat of the day had faded only a little as night came along, the air staying muggy and close. They pulled along their matching luggage, the wheels making identical whirring sounds he could barely hear over the bustle of the city around them. New York truly never slept, unlike London, who would ask you to turn the lights out at ten, thank you very much.

While simply being with her was lovely, he was aware of the seconds relentlessly slipping away and he desperately wanted to hear more from her; conversations he could use to brighten up the long, lonely nights. Mike cleared his throat. 'Why marmosets?'

Sophie grinned at this. 'I'm surprised you didn't ask about the cocaine.'

He manoeuvred around a slow walker, coming back to her side. 'I thought I'd ease into the cocaine.'

'Just a joke my son made about my luggage,' Sophie said, flushing in the dim light. 'I told him I was smuggling them in my bags and he was going to have to spring me from jail if I was caught.'

Mike racked his brain, trying to think of anything interesting to add to keep her talking. What would Sophie find interesting? A detail surfaced and he spat it out before he could second-guess himself. 'There are monkeys that live in a temple in Bali that have trained themselves to steal from tourists. They've learned which items are high reward – phones, glasses, wallets – and will barter them for bigger, more exciting treats.'

Sophie almost stopped in the street but caught herself and kept moving. 'Is it wrong that I want to go there just to have monkeys steal my phone?'

'The heart wants what the heart wants,' Mike said. 'And what your heart wants is to be burgled by monkeys.'

'It's true,' Sophie said. 'Sadly, it's not on the cards. I barely made it onto the plane to get here.'

'It must have been very important to you,' he said softly. 'To manage such a feat.'

Her laughter held a note of bitterness. 'Hardly a feat. People fly every day.'

He didn't care for that note. No one should disparage Sophie Swann – even herself. 'You don't fly every day,' he said evenly. 'There are people who jump out of planes all the time. For fun. Put me up there with a parachute and I'd be clinging to the seats, terrified out of my wits.'

'I guess you're right,' she said, her voice taking on a strange tone he couldn't identify.

'So for you, major feat. Most people, they wouldn't face one of their major fears like that.'

She peered over at him. 'Even you?'

He nodded. 'Especially me. I wouldn't consider myself claustrophobic, but there is nothing that could make me go caving.'

She paused, staring at him, her lips parted.

He wondered, idly, what she might taste like.

He very carefully tucked that thought away. 'What is it?'

She shook her head and started walking again. 'It's nothing. I was just trying to imagine Andrew admitting any of his fears, and realizing I couldn't.'

'Andrew is your ex?' Mike had never met the man, but his name felt odd in his mouth. Prickly and slightly poisonous, and he had the oddest desire to spit.

'Yes.' She spoke the word like she wanted to spit, too.

He shouldn't ask. It was none of his business and she obviously didn't want to talk about it. 'That bad, huh?'

'Left me for his assistant and took the company I helped him build.' Her words were delivered evenly, casually, but they sounded to Mike a lot like the way he explained to people that his wife was gone. A carefully curated account that lessened the sting.

'I'm sorry.' What else could he say to such a thing?

She huffed out a breath. 'Me too.' Then she stopped, waving a hand towards a brick building off to her side. 'This is me.' Her smile was just the barest curving of lips. 'Thanks for dinner. And for earlier, at the airport.'

Mike wondered why suddenly, for no real reason, he felt like crying. He cleared his throat and stuck out his hand. 'It's been a pleasure, Sophie Swann.'

She stared at his hand for a moment, before setting her takeaway containers onto her suitcase. Then she stepped forward, putting her arms around him in a hug. She pressed her lips, warm and silken, against his cheek and he closed his eyes, his arms going around her automatically. She felt soft and good and Mike wondered when the last time had been that someone had hugged him like this, and he came up blank.

For a moment, he wanted nothing more than to pull her tighter against him, to bury his face in her neck and breathe her in. She was wearing something – he wasn't sure if it was perfume or what – that reminded him of peaches and honey. He didn't give in to the impulse, though, keeping it a hug and not an embrace.

'Take care of yourself, Michael Tremblay,' she said, then started to let him go.

He regretted it, even before she stepped away. 'I will,' he said, his voice strangely thick.

'You ever want to get dinner again, you've got my number.' Then she smiled, turned and walked to the doors.

She hadn't offered anything else – only dinner. Which was good, because that was the limit of what Mike could really accept. It was the most he could offer. He knew he was shit at dating, that after losing his wife he couldn't make himself that vulnerable again. He just couldn't.

And if one simple dinner with Sophie had already twisted him up like this, it was probably a bad idea to see her for a second one.

Which was fine – better than fine, really. They'd had one good night. One good dinner.

It was enough. It was for the best. He *knew* it.

And if a tiny, long-ignored voice in the back of his mind called him a liar, well, he could just ignore it.

Chapter Five

Mike peered at his daughter's face on the screen, most of which was covered by greenery. 'You got me a plant? I'm here for the next three weeks *minimum* and you got me a plant? Why?'

She lowered the plant, setting it on his countertop. 'Because you're lonely and you need a friend. You won't make a real one, so you get Barney. He's your plant friend.'

Mike rubbed his tired eyes, which already felt gritty and red from staring at a screen. His day had consisted of a short meeting with clients, a truly epic number of emails for not only this job but other projects he was still a part of, and then sketching on his tablet. His eyeballs felt like old grapes rolled in sand.

It didn't help, either, that Amaya was right – Mike had no real friends. Not any more. When he'd lost his wife, some of his friends had avoided him, like his condition might be catching. A few friends had tried, but he'd let those relation-ships wither and die with time. They hadn't done anything wrong; he just couldn't see the point any more. He had work. He had his kids. He would make a life of that and be happy. He sighed. 'I'm going to murder Barney. You know that, right?'

Amaya frowned at him, her mouth curving down into a natural pout that reminded him so much of Tara that he felt his chest squeeze tight. His wife had never had purple streaks in her dark hair, mind you. But they would have suited her.

It was so unfair that he got to see Amaya fully grown and Tara never would.

Amaya bracketed the plant with her hands like she was covering its ears. 'Why would you say that in front of Barney? You'll hurt his feelings.'

He would argue that plants didn't have feelings, but that would only make his daughter send him several articles about plants that he didn't want to read, especially since she was teasing him anyway. 'Greatest apologies to Barney.'

She put her hands on her hips. 'Seriously, Dad, your flat is lifeless and sad. No pets. No people. No plants.'

'Lots of people live that way,' Mike said.

Amaya's mouth was pursed, her brows furrowed, every inch Tara when she'd been stern. 'You are not lots of people. You need a livelier space.' She pointed at the plant. 'So you get Barney.'

He rubbed his eyes again. 'Fine. Thank you.'

Her scowl deepened. 'Why do you keep rubbing your eyes like that?'

'They're a little dried out from looking at the screen.'

Amaya made a muffled screeching sound. 'Dad! Use the eye drops! What is wrong with you?'

'If only Barney were here,' Mike muttered as he grabbed the phone and took it with him to do as she demanded.

Her exasperated expression morphed into one of concern. 'You sound grumpy. You don't usually sound grumpy. Are you okay?'

He set down his phone and dug out his drops, blinking as the liquid hit his eye. 'A little worn out, that's all.'

It was more than that. Mike was the first to admit that he functioned mostly like a machine these days, except for the rare times when he was able to be with his family. The rest of his days were full of work and only work. This didn't usually bother him. He liked work. What else did he need?

And yet, his mind kept swerving back to Sophie. It had been three days since their dinner. He didn't know her. They'd shared a meal, that was all. So why did he keep checking his phone for texts and getting disappointed when there weren't any? He also kept picking up his phone to text her . . . well, anything, really, just to see what she would say.

But he hadn't and he wouldn't, and it was making him crabby, like little Archie when he hadn't had his nap.

Amaya made a thoughtful *hmmm* noise. Her eyes narrowed and grew speculative as she tapped her fingers along her hips. 'Ra says you had dinner with the luggage lady. The one with the OnlyFans.'

'She does *not* have an OnlyFans,' he said sharply. Too sharply. 'Or maybe she does. I don't know.'

Amaya looked like she wanted to reach through the phone and pat his shoulder reassuringly. 'It would be okay if she did, Dad. Nothing wrong with porn.'

Mike sighed and dropped his head back. 'Sometimes I wish my relationship with my children was a little *less* open.'

'No you don't,' Amaya said automatically. 'Okay, so that's a maybe on the OnlyFans. What do you know about her?'

'We had one dinner, Ama. One.' A dinner so warm, so lovely, that it had smoothed out the irritations of the day.

A slow, Cheshire cat smile unfurled on his daughter's face. 'The lady doth protest too much, methinks.'

'I also regret taking you to see Shakespeare.' He gave up, getting his phone and heading to the kitchen. He popped the cap off his beer and took a sip, propping his phone up against a fruit bowl as he rested his elbows on the counter. 'She has a travel blog. A son named Tom and his wife or maybe fiancée, Marisa. They were very nice, though Tom seems worried that I'm up to no good.'

'We only wish you were up to no good.' Amaya opened her laptop and started clicking. 'What's her name?'

'Sophie Swann.' He took another long swallow of his beer. 'She's funny. A little weird.' He picked at the corner of the label on his bottle. 'I liked talking to her.'

Amaya made a thoughtful noise but kept clicking.

'She's divorced.' He bit down on the other words that wanted to spill out of him. *She smells like peaches and honey and it felt good to hold her. Her eyes have more brown than green in them; she laughs with her whole body; and I can't stop thinking about the things I found in her luggage. Was that her only toy, or just her favourite? Does she have more? Did she buy those lacy underthings to please other people, or were they just for her?*

Mike rolled the chilled bottle of beer against his forehead and wondered if he was getting a fever.

Amaya was focused on her laptop. 'Have you read any of her blog? It's funny.'

He'd been very carefully, very deliberately, avoiding it. He had a feeling that if he read it, the last fragile band of his restraint would snap. And then what? 'No.'

'You should read it, Dad.' She clicked again and raised an eyebrow. 'Ah, I *see*. She's kind of fit, isn't she?'

The chilled bottle wasn't working. He definitely had a fever, or a virus, or maybe something worse, like malaria. 'I didn't notice.'

That Cheshire grin was back. 'You do like funny women, Dad. Why not ask her out? Go . . .' She trailed off. 'Do whatever old people do on a date.'

Mike thunked his bottle against the counter. 'Oh, fuck off.'

She laughed. 'You're blushing. I can *see it*. Ooooh, wait until I tell Ra. He's going to shit.'

Mike took a long pull of his beer. 'I tried to raise you with manners, I swear. I don't know what happened.'

'We didn't listen, thankfully.' Amaya huffed a breath, causing her fringe to float up. 'Okay, I'll back off, just . . . message her, okay? Talk to her. Don't think about dating. Just have a good time.'

He didn't want to lie to her but he also really thought it would be a terrible idea. 'I'll consider it.'

Amaya checked her phone. 'I've got to go, but Dad?'

'Yes?'

Her expression was concerned, her tone serious. 'When you do go out with her, make sure you have condoms. You have no idea how many STI outbreaks they've had at retirement homes. Just chlamydia all the time around there.'

'Bit of an ageist stereotype, don't you think?'

She threw up her hands. 'I have data! It's not an unfair stereotype if it's real!'

He grabbed another beer. 'I'm also not in a retirement home! I'm fifty-three, for fuck's sake!'

'At least if you were in a home, you'd be getting some action. If you don't use it, Dad, it falls off. Ra told me that.'

'That's not remotely true, you're both weirdly fixated on this, and I'm hanging up now.'

'We just want you to be safe and happy!' She cackled as he reached over and turned off the phone.

Mike had meant to stick with his plan, avoiding all temptation where Sophie was concerned, he really had. But as he was drinking his second beer, he sat down in front of his laptop. Since he was in front of his laptop, he tapped it, bringing it to life. Now that it was awake, he might as well search for Sophie Swann's blog. It was a little bit like that book, *If You Give a Mouse a Cookie*, but with some light internet stalking instead.

He found *Swanning About* easily, a picture of Sophie front and centre, leaning over and laughing, a giant Highland steer chewing on her blouse. There was so much joy in that photo, he had to smile, almost like he was contractually obliged. He clicked on one of the links at random, finding a post from a year earlier when she'd gone to Little Venice in London.

> *I found a cafe where I could sit and sip my tea and watch the lively waterways. It's such a bright, fun corner of London. Walking along the canal felt like I was in a charming story-book, the people kind and friendly. (I did see a drunk fellow relieving himself in one of the side streets, but that's neither here nor there.) One of the boats along the canal had been converted into a little bookshop! The afternoon felt like a dream, and between transport, tea and my book, it still came in under forty quid . . .*

The next link took him to a post where Sophie and her friend Edie had tried a free pottery class. It hadn't gone well for Sophie – she was covered in clay, her bowl entirely misshapen. Edie's didn't look much better, but both of them were smiling like they'd made something worthy of display in the Louvre. What must it be like to live with that much joy inside you all the time?

He started reading through the comments, which was usually a mistake. There were a few nasty ones, but her core followers were nothing but supportive. He could see why they were so enamoured of her. Her style was so casual, her writing so kind, and the things she wrote about easily accessible. Reading her words felt like talking to a friend. Not all posts were long, some just linking to her Instagram. He found one from the day he'd met her in the airport. Her picture was unfiltered – she looked pale, like she might be sick at any moment, but she looked determined, too.

I've made it on the plane. I can do this. Thanks to all of you that reminded me that a small step would do.

As he was staring down at her face, he realized that he missed her. A few conversations and one meal and he *missed her.* This was so dangerous.

His hands shook a little as he clicked on the last link, posted the day after their dinner.

I cannot tell you the relief I've felt, being on land again! The flight itself went smoothly, but after *the flight was full of turbulence. I felt vastly unwell when I got off the plane. (Note to future Sophie, limit your G&Ts on your next flight.) I had to sit down on the floor on the way to customs. Despite my triumph over my fears, I was feeling very down and self-critical as I sat by the bins, hoping I wouldn't embarrass myself. Luckily, a kindly gentleman checked on me and gave me some medicine and water. He even walked me to customs. Kindness, my loves, is out there. Revived, I made it to my son and my temporary new abode!*

My new apartment is very American – it's loud, full of colour and over the top. I'm a bit in love with it. I'm sitting in the kitchenette now, enjoying my tea and simply feeling grateful for the fact that I am here. I get to hug my son and his beloved, and that means more than I can say.

But it wouldn't be Swanning About *without a few bumps and hiccups. I immediately lost my luggage upon arrival. Or more accurately, my suitcase was accidentally mixed up with someone else's! At the time, I wanted nothing more than a shower, a nap and a meal, not in that order, and so I was quite irritated that this plan had been thwarted.*

But as I often tell you, my Swannies, sometimes ruined plans lead to better stories. Do you know who had my luggage? The kindly gentleman, that's who! My first dinner in New York involved my son, my daughter in all but legalities, and the kind of man who made a travel-sick woman feel one thousand times better. I couldn't have imagined this welcome dinner, and I'm so glad things went awry. As I always say, you'll have a lot more

*fun if you stay flexible. (And yes, I know that's a bit of a double
entendre, and I won't apologize for it one bit.)*

Suddenly the ache in Mike's chest was too much to bear. It
seemed so silly, not talking to her. He was a grown man. He
was perfectly capable of keeping it friendly. He could talk to
her, surely, without risk of it becoming *more*.

He took out his phone and stared at it. It had been three
days. He couldn't simply send her a, 'dinner was lovely' kind
of text. Sending her a text for no reason felt . . . risky. Like it
was saying too much. He tapped his fingers along the table-
top. A reason. That's what he needed. A good excuse for
texting her after three days of radio silence.

His gaze drifted back to her blog. What if he texted her
something related to that? Maybe an interesting building to
visit? She probably already had a list of prospective places –
this was her job, after all, and she was very good at it. What
did he know about travel blogging? Nothing. He did know all
about architecture, however, and New York had some very
interesting spots. What to send? Something joyful. Full of
whimsy. It had to be something to catch her attention, but
also be a good fit for her blog.

He took a deep breath and started typing. *Have you ever
visited Jane's Carousel? It's in Brooklyn Bridge Park. At night
the lights show off the beautiful artistry of the restored carousel
and make the glass enclosure glow like a beacon.*

He hit send, then realized that out of context, it might
be a little . . . weird? Like he was just sending her random
trivia. Or maybe she'd think it was a lead-in to a, 'we should
go there on a date' conversation, giving her the wrong idea.

Mike quickly sent her a follow-up message. *Thought you
might find it interesting.*

Well, that didn't help *at all*. He might have actually made
it worse. His body, unhelpfully, erupted into a panic sweat.

A casual observer might think he was doing something dangerous, like disarming a bomb, not trying to have a normal, human conversation with a woman he fancied.

He wiped his forehead with a free hand, drying it on his jeans, then sent another text. *For your blog.*

There. Perfect. He'd fixed it. Assuming she'd saved his number into her phone and not thought some rando was texting her. Mike groaned. This. This was why he didn't date. This was why he didn't even *friend.*

He was just going to have to send another text. *This is Mike Tremblay, by the way.*

He tapped his phone against his forehead as he blew out a long breath. *Mike Tremblay, you absolute muppet. At this rate, it's just going to be you and Barney the houseplant for the rest of your life, and you're probably going to kill the houseplant.*

He sighed and went to get himself a glass of water.

Chapter Six

Sophie had spent her first full day in New York on her son's couch fighting jet lag and watching *Dateline* with Marisa. The jet lag was gone, but now she was a little worried about going outside because that seemed like a good way to get murdered. Or be forced to join a cult. Or be forced to join a murder cult. The second day was spent cleaning her son's flat and convincing Marisa to watch anything *but Dateline*.

Now she was on her third day and typing up a post about jet lag, which she was considering subtitling, 'Nature's way of confirming that planes are unnatural and no one should fly to a different time zone'. She wasn't getting very far on the post. Her mind was unhelpfully pinging between worry about her son and Marisa, and the very real probability that she might try and order some of the cologne Mike had worn just so she could smell it. If she'd known what it was called, she would have already done it.

She felt like she'd just finished thinking about Andrew, and she didn't want to think about another man – any man. She'd been happy and focused on her new, unfettered life stretching out before her. Why would the universe decide to set this distraction before her *now*? She supposed it could be worse. She could be on Andrew's social media, obsessing over posts about him and Lori.

Thankfully, that was no longer a temptation. To her, Andrew was now about as attractive as holy water was to vampires. The very sight of him made her recoil and hiss. Lori was welcome to him.

Mike, however . . . zero recoiling. No hissing. Pure temptation.

She bet he had really nice forearms. She was a sucker for a man's forearms.

Sophie's head thunked against the table. She didn't *need* a man, she really didn't. She made her own money, had her own friends, and owned several different vibrators. Her sex life, sadly, had more joy and variety now than it ever had when she was married.

If she had to think about a man, she'd prefer to think of one so unattainable that he was basically fictional. Keanu Reeves. Idris Elba. Those clips of rugby players in the rain, roaming the pitch like errant gods, thighs straining against the wet material of their shorts. Men she could dream about who would never betray her or let her down.

Only now, inevitably, those players ended up with blue-green eyes and a crooked smile. It was *irritating*. He was ruining her ability to fantasize properly.

She straightened in her chair. 'Right, Sophie Swann. Get a hold of yourself. Focus. Get to work. Stop thinking of Mike Tremblay.'

Her phone buzzed. She looked at it and groaned as *Mike Tremblay* showed up on the screen. The universe had a sense of humour and it was *mean*. She could ignore it. It felt rude, but there was no law against not responding to a text.

It buzzed again. And again.

She gave up, snatching the phone off the counter. She read his messages with a smile on her face. Then she read them again. Was he inviting her to go? She didn't *think* so. Still, he had at least been thinking about her enough to text.

She clicked on her browser, pulling up Jane's Carousel. It did look like the kind of thing she liked to do. She jotted it down on her list of possibly posts so she wouldn't forget to look into it further after she'd finished today's post.

There was a knock on the door, making her frown. She hadn't ordered anything and as far as she knew, Tom and Marisa were out at an appointment.

Another knock sounded, followed by a scratchy voice. 'Come on, Gabi. You're not answering your phone, and I know you're in there.'

The voice didn't sound angry, or even irritated, but *tired*. Sophie stood, making her way to the door so she could see who it might be. Through the curving lens of the peephole, she could make out a small, brown-haired man, holding a dog. She didn't recognize him, but pulled open the door, leaving the chain on. 'May I help you?'

He blinked at her rapidly, like a goldfish. 'You're not Gabi.'

'I'm not, no,' Sophie answered, even though he hadn't really asked a question. She was somewhat transfixed by the blue flecks of glitter in his eyebrows.

He groaned, putting a hand over his face. 'Gabi's on sabbatical. You're her renter. I forgot.' He dropped his hand, and she could see a fine sheen of sweat on his forehead. In fact, she wondered if he might be unwell. His tanned skin had a sickly greenish undertone to it.

'Are you feeling well?'

He sighed, setting the small dog down on the hallway floor. 'I feel like hot garbage, to be honest, but I live alone and dogs don't care if you're sick. Gabi sometimes walks Stanley Poochie for me when I'm in a pinch.'

Sophie peered down at Stanley Poochie. She wasn't sure what kind of dog he was. He looked like the kind of creature that might result if a French bulldog and a Pomeranian somehow managed to have sex with a gargoyle. He peered up at Sophie, his small pink tongue lolling out. He was hideous and she adored him. 'I can walk him for you.'

The man's eyebrows squished together, his voice uncertain. 'Really?'

Sophie brightened. 'Of course.'

He examined her suspiciously. 'You're not going to steal my dog, are you?'

She stared down at Stanley, who was currently licking the wall. 'I promise you I will not.'

He sighed, his shoulders drooping. 'Normally, I wouldn't hand Stanley off to a stranger, but I'm desperate.' He gave her the leash, fishing a poop bag out of his pocket. 'There's a little park on the next block.'

She took the leash and bag. 'I'll be right back. Go and rest.'

He nodded, jerking his thumb towards the door next to hers. 'I'm right here. Just knock.'

Stanley Poochie didn't seem to be in a hurry, so Sophie didn't rush him, using the time to compose a future post in her head.

Dear Readers, you should know that Brooklyn has stolen a place in my heart. I might need some of you to remind me why I love London so dearly. There's an astonishing variety to Brooklyn. The air is spiced with different languages, some of the voices flowing in and out of English with a dexterous grace that I envy. Every time I turn onto a different block, I feel like I'm in a new country. My travel-loving heart could gorge itself here.

She smiled at Stanley, taking a quick picture of him with her phone as he panted up at her. *I'm making handsome new friends, my Swannies. I could be very happy here, I think.*

She tugged gently on Stanley's leash, leading him back to his home. His owner – she hadn't managed to get his name – might be worried if she was gone too long, and she didn't want to add to his misery. Nothing was worse than being sick and having to take care of yourself.

As they grew close to the corner store, Sophie scooped Stanley up, making an impulsive decision to go in. Why not grab a few things for her sick neighbour? If her neighbour – she was really going to have to ask his name – relied on Gabi when he needed help, that likely meant he didn't have anyone else close by. Sophie had survived the last year with the help and support of friends and neighbours and knew full well how sometimes the smallest of efforts could have a long-lasting impact for those in need of a little extra care.

Shopping done, she let Stanley lead her back to his apartment. He plopped down in front of it, panting happily at Sophie while she knocked.

The neighbour opened the door, somehow looking even more wretched than before. 'I was beginning to worry about you.'

'I was gone a bit longer than planned. Sorry if we worried you.' Sophie handed him the leash. 'Stanley was a perfect gentleman. I would be happy to walk him later for you if you're still feeling poorly. Knock on my door, or I can give you my number to text me.'

He took the leash. 'That's very kind of you.'

'It's miserable being sick, isn't it? I'm sorry, I didn't get your name before.'

'Manny,' he said. 'Gabi told me your name, but it went right out of my head.'

'Sophie. I'm here for a few months, visiting my son and his fiancée. They're down in 3C.' She handed him the bag of groceries. 'I picked up a little care package for you. Juice, tissues, that sort of thing. I hope that's okay.'

Manny gazed into the bag, pulling out a plastic takeaway container. 'You got me soup?'

'From the nice woman at the Thai pop-up in the corner store. It's a bit hot out for soup, but I mentioned my neighbour was sick and she made me this. It's chicken noodle.

I was surprised how quickly she threw it together, but she already had some broth in the fridge. She told me it was "street food" style. I'm not sure how that's different to regular Thai chicken noodle soup, but it smelled delicious.'

Manny clutched the soup to his chest. 'I'm now convinced that I've hallucinated you, that this isn't really happening, and I'm going to wake up on my couch and cry because there won't be any soup. Thank you. I don't know how to repay you.'

Sophie dropped down and petted Stanley goodbye. 'Oh, I don't mind – and now I know the park is there.' She levered herself off the floor. It wasn't *quite* as easy to get up as it used to be. 'I like to explore my neighbourhood. It's kind of my job.' When Manny looked at her questioningly, she continued a little self-consciously, 'I write a little travel blog back home in London. I keep it local, trying to find the hidden gems, encouraging people to take full advantage of what's around them.'

Manny nodded. 'Well, this neighbourhood is full of those. When I feel better, I can tell you about a few – if you'd like?'

'I'd love that,' Sophie said. 'If you don't mind. In fact, I snapped a few photos of Stanley while we were out and about. Is that okay? I won't use them if you don't want, or I can delete them altogether.'

'Are you kidding me? Stanley is made for the limelight. I can give you his handles. Stanley is all over social media. Besides' – he held up the soup container – 'you've saved my life. It's the least I can do. In fact – hold on.' He disappeared into his apartment for a moment, coming back seconds later without the groceries or Stanley's leash, a neon blue slip of paper in his fingers. 'I have a friend that gives dance lessons. Do you know how to salsa?'

Sophie shook her head.

'My friend puts on these socials twice a month. Live DJ, salsa dancing. It's only about twenty-five bucks. The next one's tomorrow night. If you go an hour before, he does a quick tutorial for beginners who want to try it out. It usually costs a little more, but he owes me a favour. It's a lot of fun.'

Sophie stared at the paper with mingled excitement and trepidation. 'I haven't been dancing in ages.'

Manny leaned against the wall. 'No time like the present.'

She gave him a determined nod. 'I think you're right, Manny. I would love to learn how to salsa.'

He took out his phone. 'Give me your number. I'll text you more details after I talk to him.'

She rattled off her number, thanking him again for the tip, and left him to get some rest.

A few minutes later, she got a message from an unknown number. *It's Manny. You're all set. Javi says you can come alone, but it's best if you can bring a partner with you.*

Sophie bit her lip. A partner. If she were at home, she'd already be calling up Edie, but she wasn't home, and Tom and Marisa had plans with friends tomorrow.

She knew exactly one other person in the entire state of New York . . . and he *had* just texted her. Before she over-thought it, she messaged him. *Carousel sounds delightful. I'll check it out. What are you doing tomorrow? I have an in on a dance class, but I need a partner. Any chance I can talk you into it? I'm not above bribery. Drinks on me?*

She set down the phone, refusing to stare at it until he responded, deciding to work instead. The phone vibrated a few seconds later, surprising her. *Well, that was fast.*

I'm a very mediocre dancer but would be happy to join you. My children have been threatening me to get out more, and I'm worried about my continued health if I don't heed their warnings. So really, you're doing me a favour.

Sophie pressed her fingers against her lips as if she could stamp the small smile on them more deeply upon her soul. It was unsettling, how happy a little text could make her. Her phone vibrated again.

Should I meet you there? What time?

Sophie's sharp, surprised laugh echoed in her flat. *He was a bit keen, wasn't he?* She thought about it for a second before texting him back, *You're staying in Manhattan, yes?*

Yes.

She chewed on her lip as she tapped out her reply. *Probably makes more sense to meet there. Dance lesson at six. Does that work? Five thirty if we want to get a drink first.*

Dots appeared, vanished and reappeared. *I'll have to move things around a bit, but I don't dare go into that dance lesson without a cocktail. Five thirty it is.*

Sophie sent him the address for tomorrow, delight making her feel like she was full of champagne bubbles. Which suddenly, abruptly stopped when she realized that she had nothing she could wear salsa dancing. Marisa probably had something, but they weren't the same size at all. She sent Marisa an SOS text. *Help. Salsa dancing tomorrow. Need dress!*

Marisa texted her back instantly. *What? Yessssssss. Fun! I'll come over as soon as we get home.*

Mike got up early and worked through lunch in order to meet Sophie at the bar before the lesson. He had just enough time to take a quick shower, shave and ditch his laptop before catching a taxi to the address she'd sent him. It wasn't a date. He needed to remember that. But the nerves were the same.

The bar reminded him of a dapper older gentleman past his prime – elegant, classy lines gone charmingly to seed, managing the delicate balance between sophistication and a hole in the wall. The bar top was scarred wood, lovingly polished, with stools and only a few scattered tables. Mike perched on a stool and ordered a cup of coffee from the bartender, wanting a punch of caffeine to compensate for the early wake-up before he started drinking.

The bartender, a wiry man more stylish than Mike had ever been in his entire life, grabbed the pot, his mouth set in a line. 'You sure you want coffee?'

'Yes?' Mike wasn't sure why his answer sounded like a question, except that he hadn't been expecting the pushback on coffee.

'It looks like you're about ready to vibrate out of here as is,' the bartender pointed out, grabbing a mug and filling it. 'You're jiggling your leg so hard I'm surprised the bar isn't shaking.'

Mike paused, realizing he was correct. 'How did you know?'

Bartender pointed at the ornate wall mirrors lining the wall behind Mike's back.

'Ah,' Mike said. 'So you're not psychic.'

He shook his head. 'Just a good bartender.'

Mike took the cup from him. 'I'm fine, just nervous. I'm meeting someone.'

'Ah,' the bartender said knowingly. 'Hot date. Got it.'

Mike sipped the coffee. He usually put cream in it, but he thought taking it black might be more bracing and he desperately needed some bracing. 'It's not a date. It's a . . . I don't know what it is.'

The bartender's pierced eyebrow went up. 'I see.'

Mike rubbed a hand over the back of his head and let out a breath. 'Maybe I should just make excuses. This is a terrible idea.'

The bartender was already shaking his head. 'Don't do that, dude. You respect this person?'

'Yes,' Mike said, wondering how this bartender kept asking him things that surprised him. 'Of course.'

The bartender planted his hands on the bar, expression set. 'Then respect them enough to be here when they arrive. No one likes to be ditched last minute. I see it a lot. It's brutal.'

Mike stared at the man. 'What's your name?'

'Vince.'

'Have you considered becoming a life coach, Vince?'

Vince rolled his shoulders. 'Nah. Lots of pressure. This gig pays well, and I can help people, but also throw out the assholes I don't like.'

Mike nodded, drinking more of his coffee. 'I want it to be a date, Vince, but I also don't want it to be a date.'

Vince thought this over as he popped open the small dishwasher behind the bar, releasing a draught of steam. 'Lots of red flags?'

Mike shook his head.

Vince nodded. 'You're scared.'

Mike opened his mouth to argue, then grimaced. 'Yeah, I guess.'

Vince started taking glasses out of the dishwasher, quickly putting them away. 'I get it, but to my mind, we get this one life. I'd rather have a long line of failures than one of regrets. You miss all the shots you don't take, you know?'

Mike finished his coffee and shoved the mug across the counter. 'Vince, you might be the wisest person I've met in a long time.'

Vince scoffed. 'I think that says more about the people you've been around than anything about me.' He reached below the bar, then tossed something small onto the bar top. 'Here.'

Mike looked at it, realizing it was a mint. 'Is this a subtle hint?'

Vince went back to unloading the dishwasher. 'Coffee breath is a thing and you've got a not-a-date to impress, yeah?'

Thinking Vince might have a point, Mike accepted the mint, unwrapping it and popping it into his mouth. 'You are a god among men, Vince.'

The bartender simply nodded, as if this was expected, pointing at the tip jar, which had a few dollars in it, but also a QR code for those that didn't have cash. 'Just remember that when it's time.'

Mike was about to say something, when the door opened, and he turned. Sophie had pushed it open with her hip as she tucked something into her bag. She was wearing an off-the-shoulder burgundy dress that hugged her body, the skirt the kind that would twirl if he spun her. Heels. Her hair up, a few strands falling around her face. Mike felt like he might swallow his tongue.

'Ah,' Vince said. He slid another mint across the bar. 'Just in case.'

'Thanks,' Mike said, sounding winded, absently shoving the mint into his pocket.

Sophie straightened, her expression nervous until she saw Mike. Then she smiled.

Her smile was a donkey kick directly to his gut. 'Fuck.' He'd said it softly, but Vince managed to hear him.

The bartender set a glass of mints on the bar. 'You better tell that woman she looks phenomenal.'

'She does look phenomenal,' Mike muttered.

'I'm just saying, she might need to hear it.' Vince pulled out two glasses, filling them with water, sliding one to Mike and one to the spot next to him, then he went to the other side of the bar to fill an order for one of the waitresses.

Sophie stopped in front of him. 'Hi.'

Mike wanted to touch her. He wanted to lean over and kiss her cheek. He wanted . . .

He wanted.

'You look amazing,' he said, not bothering to hide the reverence in his voice. What was it about her that turned him inside out?

Her smile brightened. 'Thank you.' She smoothed a hand over the dress self-consciously. 'Marisa helped me pick it out. I wanted something that would look good for the blog, but . . . you don't think it's too much?'

'If it's too much,' Mike said, 'then too much is a good look on you. You look beautiful.'

She blushed, taking the seat next to him. 'Thanks.' She looked up at the menu, which was chalked onto the wall behind the bar. 'You nervous about dancing?'

'Oh god, yes,' Mike said. 'It's been a while.' He watched her out of the corner of his eye. He'd been nervous, and that was still there, that startled moth feeling in his gut of anticipation, but there was something else, too. Being with Sophie eased something inside him in a way he couldn't quite wrap his mind around. He just somehow knew that with her here, he would have a good time.

'I've danced with friends,' Sophie said. 'But I haven't danced with a partner in years.' She grimaced. 'Which now strikes me as a bit sad. Not that I need someone to feel complete,' she added quickly. 'More that I supposedly had someone, but we'd stopped dancing together.' Her mouth twisted in another grimace. 'Which is probably more than you wanted to know.'

'I think,' Mike said slowly, 'that there might not be a limit to what I want to know about you. And that while you're with me, while we're both here, we shouldn't worry about being too much. We should just have fun.'

Sophie watched him for a long moment, as if trying to make sense of his words. 'All right. I'll probably get someone to take pictures of us if I can. Do you mind being in them? I can put something over your face if you'd prefer to stay anonymous.'

'I don't mind being in the photos,' Mike said. 'If anything, it would give my kids proof that I took a night off. Might get me some respite from their constant hounding.'

She grinned. 'They sound like they love you.'

'They're good kids,' he admitted. 'I'm so proud of both of them. I just wish . . .' He let out a breath. Probably wasn't good form to talk about Tara when he was on a sort-of date, was it? Sophie hadn't minded before, but he didn't want to cross some sort of line . . .

Sophie put a hand over his. 'Life isn't very fair, is it?' She turned back to the menu, her voice suddenly casual in a way that told Mike she felt anything *but* easy about her topic. 'Tom hasn't talked to his father since the divorce.' She seemed to realize she still had her hand on his and took it back. 'I didn't ask for that. I don't want to get in between them, but with the way Andrew's acting, it's like he divorced both of us. He hasn't tried to bridge that gap at all. It makes me so angry. Tom deserves better. I should have *chosen* better.'

Mike reached out, putting his hand over hers on the bar. 'I'm sure you did the best you could at the time.'

Sophie nodded, swallowing hard. 'It doesn't feel that way sometimes, but thank you.' She turned those big hazel eyes on him, and the effect was disorienting, like he might fall into them. Which was ludicrous. 'From the little you've said about Tara, you did choose well. She would have been proud of her kids, Mike. Maybe it's silly to say that because I didn't know her, but I feel like I know you, at least a little, and . . . I can't imagine you would love her so much if she wasn't the kind of person who would love her kids one hundred per cent. Does that make sense?'

Mike blew out a breath, feeling like he'd been kicked again, but in a way that felt kind of good. 'Yeah, it does. And she was. Thank you.'

Her smile was faint this time, but looked fully meant. 'Anytime,' she said. 'Now how about we get a drink, put everything aside for the night, and try not to be the worst salsa dancers in the world?'

Chapter Seven

Javi was a man of medium build with tanned skin, black curly hair shaved at the top, and the body of a man who danced for a living. Sophie was also convinced that he was possibly some sort of wizard because the way the man moved was magic. Which she felt only highlighted how not-magically she was moving.

'Okay, cross body lead, one two three, here comes the turn,' Javi said, clapping his hands. 'Remember, small steps, no bouncing. At the end of the lead, changing hands, five, six, seven, good!'

Mike placed his hand on her hip, grumbling as he led her in the steps. 'I swear that man is actually a cat.'

'It's uncanny, isn't it?' she whispered.

'He's freakishly talented – I know this is his profession, so of course he should be, but damn, what have I been doing wrong my entire life?' His arm slid around her waist as they moved into the next part of the dance, and Sophie missed her step.

She didn't mind that she was fumbling her way through the dance moves – it was fun, even if she wasn't a natural at it. It was only that she might have been better at it if she wasn't distracted every time Mike touched her hip, or held her for a step. The touches were fleeting, but it also felt like they were layering up, each one building to something inevitable, like flowers blooming in the spring. Or like the *Titanic* crashing into an iceberg.

Mike, even buttoned up in a suit for his professional look, was handsome. It turned out that this side of him, his jacket abandoned, top two shirt buttons undone, sleeves rolled up revealing his forearms, took him a step beyond. Sweat glistened on his forehead, his hair was tousled from him running his hands through it, he was breathing as hard as she was from the exertion, and it was quite possibly the single sexiest thing she'd seen in her entire life.

His eyes glittered with laughter as he flubbed another step, barely missing her feet.

Javi came over to them, his hands still keeping the beat. 'Small steps, move those hips. Show everyone you've still got it.'

'You're a very good teacher,' Mike told him. 'Don't take our butchering it personally.'

Javi clucked his tongue. 'You're having fun and trying. Dance is about joy, and the sensual pleasure of letting your body move. Who cares if you're not perfect? This isn't a competition.'

'Well said,' Sophie said with a laugh as she wobbled on her heel, Mike catching her easily, his arms wrapping around her and *oh*.

'My assistant got some footage and stills of you,' Javi said. 'You should definitely get some shots from the social, though.'

'Thank you,' Sophie said. 'For what it's worth, I'll credit both of you and give you a glowing review. It's been so much fun, even if I've stepped on Mike's toes a million times.'

'I don't mind,' Mike said gruffly, moving them both back into a starting position. 'My toes are at your disposal.'

'That's the spirit,' Javi said. 'Okay, let's go from the top, people. And, one, two, three!'

The social took place in an open room, with a scattering of high-top tables along the edges. A live band was on the stage, already playing the first song. Mike had gone to grab them both a cocktail from the bar while they took a breather before joining the other dancers. There were people of all levels dancing, some from their beginners' class from earlier, some experienced, all of them there to have a good time. The lighting was dim, most of the light coming from colourful hanging lanterns.

Mike joined her at the table, depositing her drink in front of her. 'Your "These Hips Don't Lie", which I am convinced is almost entirely tequila, so I'm recommending caution.' He pulled a bottle of water out of his pocket, placing it next to her. 'For hydration purposes.' He fished out his own bottle of water and set his cocktail down, something with a lime wedge on the rim.

'What did you get?'

'"La Noche",' Mike said, taking a sip. 'Don't ask me what's in it. I've already forgotten.' He took a bigger sip. 'But it's delicious.' He offered it to her, eyebrow up.

She handed him hers, trading for sips.

Mike tasted hers, eyeing the drink suspiciously. 'I'm *certain* that's pure tequila. I watched him make it. He barely waved a lime wedge over it. Why is it so good? Last time I drank straight tequila, I coughed so hard I almost sicked it back up.'

'Really? When was that?' she asked, sipping more of her drink.

'Uni,' Mike said promptly. 'So admittedly, we were drinking the cheapest tequila we could find.'

'Not exactly the best representation of its kind, then.' Sophie laughed. 'Well, this is good tequila. It makes a difference.'

'One point for getting older,' Mike said. 'You can afford the good alcohol.' He snapped open his water bottle, taking a healthy swig.

They fell silent for a few minutes after that, sipping their drinks while they both rested their feet. Sophie enjoyed watching the dancers, taking a few short videos while they waited. Even sitting at their table, she was having a good time. Mike was a relaxing companion, and she didn't feel the need to entertain him.

She liked watching the other dancers, some of them making the same missteps she'd made earlier. Once they'd finished their drinks, Sophie found one of the couples from their class and asked them if they'd mind taking some videos of her and Mike dancing for a few minutes. She offered to pay for their drinks, but they waved her away.

Mike escorted her out onto the floor, getting them into position and putting a hand on her hip. 'Do you ever worry about anyone stealing your phone?'

'Not really,' Sophie said. 'I mean, it's possible, but what else am I going to do? I can't always get someone to go with me. People have lives and I can't afford to hire an assistant.'

Mike peered down at her, his hand moving to the small of her back. They were so close she could smell his cologne, his sweat, his breath that held a hint of lime. Heat unfurled in her belly, spreading fire rapidly through her body. How was it that the smallest touch from this man could do this to her? She thought back to the early days with Andrew and couldn't remember feeling anything like this.

'If you need someone to hold your camera while you're here, call me,' Mike said gruffly. 'Please.'

She blinked up at him. Sophie knew comparing Mike to her ex wasn't a great idea, not if she wanted to banish Andrew from her mind permanently, but she couldn't help it sometimes. Her husband – ex, *ex*-husband – had never helped her with the blog. Not once. He'd never shown even an iota of interest in it. So Mike's offer felt a lot like . . . a gift. 'Really?'

The song started, Mike leading her in the opening steps. 'Of course. There'll be times when I have to work, but I'd be happy to help.' He spun her into a turn, pulling her back against him like they'd been dancing like this their whole lives. 'I'm having a great time.'

'Even though I've been stepping on your toes and sweating through this dress?'

'Turns out I'm very into those things,' Mike said. 'We've discovered my secret fetish.' He leaned in, pulling her tighter against him as they moved, trying to be heard over the music. 'Besides, I love this dress.'

She wrapped her arms around his neck, her body feeling warm and fluid as they moved, either from her relaxing into the dance, or the tequila. He stared down at her, their eyes locked as they moved, no longer paying attention to words, not thinking about their feet or the steps, simply feeling. It felt like magic, a warming glow of a moment crystallized in slow-moving sap, hardening into a memory that would last the ages.

Then the song ended. The world snapped back into focus, slapping her with reality. They stood for a second, frozen in each other's arms. She saw the muscle in Mike's cheek twitch, like he was clenching his jaw, and she felt his thumbs trace down the back of her dress. Then he stepped away from her, eyes lowering. 'I'll go and get your phone for you.'

She let him go, all her unsaid words bunched in her throat.

Two more cocktails and an untold number of dances later, they left the social. Sophie's sides hurt from laughing, the magic of the night weaving its spell far beyond the dance floor. It was getting late, and she knew Mike had to work in the morning, and yet . . .

'I don't want to go home yet.' The words fell out of her mouth unplanned, but she didn't regret them.

'I think,' Mike said, tipping his head up at the sky, 'we need food.' He frowned for a minute. 'Hold on. Don't move.'

He disappeared back into the bar, coming out a moment later. 'Okay, I've got a plan. Trust me?'

'If the first step of the plan is food, I'm game.' She blinked up at him. 'No roast dinner.'

Mike smiled down at her, bemused. 'I'm not entirely sure that's an option here, anyway. No villainous meat and potatoes. No dastardly Yorkshire pudding, or scheming veg. You're safe from the evils of a Sunday roast.' He glanced at her shoes. 'Are you okay to walk a few blocks?'

'I'll regret it tomorrow, but for now, we're good.'

'Let me know if that changes.' As they started walking, he took her hand. Sophie wasn't even sure he realized he'd done it.

Her feet were killing her by the time they got to the food truck, and she almost didn't say anything. He'd made plans and she didn't want to bring the evening down and . . . no, she wasn't doing that! She wasn't biting her tongue, making herself smaller, ignoring her needs ever again. She refused to act like she was still stuck in her marriage.

'My feet are going on strike.'

Mike looked around. 'There's nowhere for you to sit. Can you last until we get our food? I promise a terrifying taxi ride after that where you'll at least be off your feet.'

She considered the very real possibility that her feet might break into a thousand pieces. 'Yes, but only if the food is fast and the taxi soon.'

'On it.' He draped his jacket around her shoulders. 'Anything you can't have or don't want besides roast beef?'

She hadn't even checked what kind of cuisine the truck offered and didn't care. All food was created equal at this point. 'Surprise me.'

He stepped away, getting into the queue. Sophie waited, lifting one foot at a time to find some relief. She loved these shoes, but she also might throw them into the bin when she got back to her flat. His jacket smelled like him, which wasn't a surprise, and with his back turned, she took the opportunity to snuggle into it, turning her nose to capture his scent. It should be illegal for a man to smell that good.

The queue moved at a good clip, Mike returning shortly with a bag full of boxes and two water bottles. 'Okay, taxi time.'

She sighed longingly. 'Never have I heard sweeter words.'

'That's me,' Mike said. 'Mr Romance.' He waved down a taxi with an ease that was, frankly, irritating. She hadn't been in New York long but had already realized that this was a skill she didn't seem to have.

Once inside the taxi, she groaned in relief, it felt that good to get off her feet. Mike rattled off an address while she closed her eyes, leaning against his shoulder, taking a moment to rest. The world was spinning in a lovely way that she didn't want to stop. She wasn't drunk, just . . . happy.

When the taxi stopped, she opened her eyes. 'Where are we?'

'It's a surprise,' Mike said, taking out his credit card.

'You don't need to cover the taxi—'

He shook his head. 'My idea, my money. I don't make the rules.'

She snorted. 'I think that's you literally making the rules.'

'Take me to court,' Mike said, ushering her out of the taxi. 'I have an excellent lawyer.'

'Do you really?'

'No, but it sounded good, didn't it?'

She laughed, adjusting his jacket on her shoulders as they walked, taking in the lights glittering on the water in front of them, the bridges, and the silhouetted shapes of carousel horses around them. This place – he'd mentioned it to her, but she couldn't remember what it was called. 'Where are we?'

'Jane's Carousel,' he said. 'The pavilion was designed by the Ateliers Jean Nouvel, an internationally renowned designer and architect.' He switched the bag to his left hand, so he could point with his right. 'That's Lower Manhattan, the East River, as well as the Brooklyn and Manhattan Bridges.'

Sophie paused, dragging him to a stop. 'Wait a moment.' She brought out her phone, hitting the record button. 'Okay, go.'

He stared at her, perplexed. 'With what?'

She lowered her phone for a second. 'Your thing. If I'm lucky, I'll remember half of this tomorrow at best. Hence the phone. So tell me about the carousel.'

He hesitated a moment. 'This will help you?'

'Yes.'

He sighed. 'Okay.' He went through it again, the bridges, rattling off a few details about each, though it was the carousel he knew the most about. When he was done, he lifted the bag. 'And now we're going to enjoy dinner.'

They found a bench and Sophie almost groaned in relief, getting off her feet again. Mike handed her a bottle of water, then dug out a takeaway container and passed it to her.

'Wait . . .' She brought her phone up.

He laughed. 'You want to record it.'

She felt deflated for a moment, pulling her phone back close to her chest. 'Is that – are you okay with that?'

Mike gave a little shrug as he got his own food out. 'It's your job. Do what you must.'

She brought her phone back up, centring the screen on him. 'Okay, what did we get?'

'We got food from a halal food truck,' Mike said. 'I got us both the chicken and lamb over rice combo.' He set his meal down and held out his hand.

'What?'

'Give me your phone. It's your blog. They don't want to see some sweaty pillock babbling about architecture, they want to see you.'

She looked at him. Considering the fact that a good number of her loyal fans were women, she didn't think they'd complain too much about Mike taking up some screen time. But he was right, it was *her* blog. She handed him the phone.

'Okay,' he said, holding it up. 'Take a bite. Tell me what you think.'

She opened the box, dug her fork in and shovelled a bite into her mouth. Flavour exploded across her tongue and her eyes rolled back a little. 'Oh my god, this might be the best thing I've ever eaten.'

He grinned at her from behind the phone. 'I'm sure the fact that you're starving helps a little.'

'No,' she said. 'This is ambrosia, food of the gods.'

He laughed, bringing the phone down. He gave it back to her, taking out his own phone. Then he squeezed in close, snapping a photo of them both.

She wrinkled her nose. 'What was that for?'

'For me,' Mike said, tucking his phone away.

'Oh, right,' she said, finally understanding. 'Proof to your kids that you're not working twenty-four seven.'

'No,' Mike said, tucking into his own food. 'Just for me.'

'Oh.' She scooped up another bite with her fork, not knowing what to say. He wanted it just for him. That meant something, right? Except she wasn't sure what, exactly. A picture of his new friend, or . . . Sophie shook her head. It didn't matter. That wasn't why she was here. She put those thoughts away and concentrated on her food.

The conversation shifted after that, flowing from topic to topic as they ate. Sophie felt a lot better once the food was gone, her water bottle empty.

As Mike went to find a bin for their empty cartons, Sophie wrapped herself in his jacket, watching the carousel. It really was magical, the horses sliding by, the river behind them.

'Ready to go?' Mike asked.

'Not quite,' Sophie said. 'This place is enchanting.' She eyed him. 'You're good at this.'

'At what?'

'Finding interesting places.' She turned until she was facing him. 'What do you think of collaborating?'

He frowned at her. 'Pardon?'

She waved a hand at the carousel. 'Helping me when you have free time – you know, beyond being a human phone-holder. I'm not sure I would have found this gem without your help. You can also speak much more about the buildings and history than I can.'

'But it's your blog,' Mike said. 'It should be about you.'

Sophie waved this away. 'That won't change. Edie helps me at home. You'll just be my New York Edie.'

Mike gave her a rueful smile. 'Have you consulted Edie on this? I'm not sure she'd be okay with me poaching her role.'

'Edie would love it,' Sophie said. Not only would Edie approve of Sophie getting the help she needed, but she'd also love the fact that Sophie's new sidekick was a handsome, charming man. Edie would probably hope Andrew would see the posts and writhe in jealousy. Sophie didn't care about that. She could be honest enough to admit that she wanted Andrew to share the level of pain she'd felt about their break-up, but she didn't want to waste whatever time or energy it might take to make that happen. She'd wasted enough of her past on Andrew already. Tom and now Marisa were her gifts from that, and she was grateful for them. But she wanted to move on.

'If you're sure,' Mike said, reaching into his pocket. He pulled out a mint and handed it to her. 'Courtesy of Vince, the best bartender in the world. How are your feet?'

She took the mint, unwrapping it and putting it in her mouth. 'Feeling better, while also demanding a soak.'

Mike chewed his mint, looking out over the water. 'We should get them home, then. They've earned some respite.'

Sophie hummed her agreement as she rolled the mint around in her mouth. 'In a minute. This place – I just want to soak it in for a little bit longer.'

He looked around, taking in their surroundings again. 'Thank you.'

She laughed. 'For what? You brought us here.'

He leaned back on the bench, placing his hands behind him. 'I never would have come here without you. My kids are right. I would have stayed in my flat working until I went back to London. That's what I do.'

Sophie kicked off her heels, bringing her feet up onto the bench and stretching out her toes along the chill of the wood. 'That doesn't seem healthy.'

'No,' Mike said. 'It's not, but it's all I've got.'

Sophie shook her head. 'I don't believe that. You have family who love you. Friends, too, I assume. Why make your life all work?'

He stared at the carousel, his hands absently taking her feet, stretching her legs out over his lap. He dug into the arch of her foot with his thumb and Sophie had to bite her lip to stop from groaning, it felt so good. 'I don't think I'm capable of much more than what I have.'

'I don't think that's true,' Sophie said, her voice hitching as he started massaging her other foot. 'But it's your life. You choose how you want it to go.'

He looked at her then, his eyes jewel-bright even in the low light. 'Is that what you did?'

She frowned. 'I didn't choose my husband running off with his assistant, no, but I chose how I dealt with it. I chose how I went on.'

He kept watching her, his gaze dropping to her mouth. 'I'm not sure I'm as strong as you.'

'Then make yourself stronger,' she said. Was he closer now? He seemed closer, but she wasn't sure when that had happened. He still had one hand on her foot, the other on her calf. She couldn't remember the last time she'd had a man's hand on her calves.

Mike let out a shuddering breath, his gaze still locked on her. 'I don't think I want to. If I was stronger, I wouldn't do this.' Then he lowered his mouth onto hers, a soft press of lips. Then more, their breath mingling, his tongue gliding along her lip, a shallow taste of her.

Sophie slid her hand into his hair, pulling him closer, taking the kiss deeper. He tasted of mint, spice and something indefinable, something good that she wanted more of.

He groaned, one hand on her neck, his thumb tracing her jaw as his other hand slid up her calf, the back of her knee, her thigh.

She tugged on his hair, asking for more, her blood bubbling pleasantly from the contact. The taste of him, the feel of him, was headier than full-bodied wine. She could get drunk on this man.

He pulled away, lips tracing her jaw, her neck, her shoulder. 'This bloody dress.' His words were mumbled, garbled, like maybe he was drunk on her as well. He stayed there, breathing deeply, his hands clutching her.

She wanted to cry, ask him why he'd stopped, but she didn't, knowing that if she pushed him now, he'd run. Sophie stroked his hair, coaxingly, as if she were trying to convince a feral creature that it was safe.

'We should go,' he said, his words hot on her neck. Then, close on the heels of his first statement, a second one delivered with an edge acknowledging that out of the two of them, only one of them was regretting the way the night had gone. 'I need to go.'

Sophie's chest felt thick, full, as if an entire flock of emotions had tried to land in the same nest. Frustration flapped its wings. Hurt fussed its feathers, making room for Sorrow. But it was Pity, ultimately, who commandeered the nest. Pity bugling out a sad noise for a man so shut down and fractured that he couldn't enjoy a single stolen moment of pleasure.

Or maybe she was wrong and there was some other reason he was putting a stop to things. She guessed it didn't really matter, because her response was the same. 'Okay.'

He let go of her, helped her put her shoes back on, and stood. Then he summoned a rideshare as they walked back to the car park, neither of them saying a word.

Chapter Eight

Mike was a mess. His body strained for one thing, his mind for another, and his heart sat in the middle, abstaining from this particular vote. He didn't really know what he wanted. Or maybe it was more that he did know what he wanted, but felt bad about wanting it? Either way, he didn't feel good about dragging Sophie into it, but he also wasn't comfortable with putting Sophie in a stranger's car and sending her on her way. They'd both had several drinks. What if he got her a rideshare, tucked her into it, and she never made it back to her flat? He couldn't handle that.

Which meant they were now sharing a very silent, very awkward ride together, the air so thick with tension he could practically scoop it like ice cream. She wouldn't look at him. Was she angry? Hurt? He clasped the back of his neck with one hand. *Tremblay, once again, you're an absolute bell end.*

The driver was chatty. Mike responded, not really paying attention to what he was saying, his mind whirring and cycling through various levels of despair. Kissing Sophie had felt . . . amazing. There was no other word for it. If they hadn't been in a public park – and he hadn't panicked – he was pretty sure they'd both be half naked by now.

Chemistry. Pure, unfiltered, high-octane chemistry. They had it. He couldn't argue otherwise. Sex, if they decided to go that far, would be the kind of sex people wrote songs about. And while his body was thrumming, demanding he do exactly that, the rest of him was a tangled confusion of fear, panic and guilt.

He'd had sex since he lost his wife. It had been nice, generally. Fun, but more like taking care of a chore than anything really passionate. He'd never thought he'd find anything like he and Tara had managed when they were together, but while kissing Sophie was very different, it was on the same level.

And it was fucking with his head.

The driver came to a stop, Sophie's building looming above them. Mike paid the driver, climbing out behind her without thinking. He just knew he wouldn't feel right until he delivered her to her door.

She watched him, her expression unreadable. 'What are you doing?'

'Seeing you home.'

She shook her head. 'You really don't have to do that.'

'Yes,' Mike said quietly, 'I do.' Her expression stayed carefully blank, which he understood, but her eyes were sad, which he hated. 'Please, let me at least see you to your door, Sophie.'

'Fine,' she said. 'Suit yourself, but you're being ridiculous.'

'No argument there,' Mike said. Because he was being ridiculous, but he wouldn't feel better until she was safely home.

They took the lift up, Sophie silent, her mouth down-turned. Mike felt like shit, which was a weirdly comfortable feeling. He was *used* to feeling like shit.

The lift dinged, letting them out on her floor. Mike followed her, hovering behind her as she wobbled on her heels. He waited as she got out her keys and opened her door.

The door clicked and she stepped out of her shoes before crossing the threshold. She tossed them inside, looking up at him, not saying anything.

He wasn't entirely sure what he wanted to do, but he didn't want to leave it like this, either. 'Sophie—'

She shook her head. 'Not sure I want to hear whatever you're going to say in that tone.'

He shoved his hands into his pockets. 'Fair enough. Despite—' He stopped, reorganizing his thoughts. 'I had a good time tonight.'

She scrunched up her nose and for fuck's sake, why was that so cute? 'Really?'

'Yes,' he said. 'I really did, but I shouldn't have . . .' He ran a hand through his hair, flustered. Why were words so bloody difficult? He had a lot of them running through his head, but the only ones that came out were, 'I shouldn't have kissed you. I'm so sorry.'

Sophie paled.

As usual, he was making it worse. 'That wasn't . . .' He had no idea how he was going to finish that sentence.

Sophie shook her head. 'Wow, okay, please stop. I would pay fifty pounds to not have this conversation right now. Let's just leave it, please.'

'Of course,' he said. 'I'm so sorry.'

She handed him back his jacket. 'Here.'

He took it, lips pressed tight, swimming in misery. This was why he didn't date. This feeling right here.

She sighed, suddenly looking tired. 'Thank you for the dancing.'

He nodded, miserable.

Then she very quietly shut the door and Mike stood there feeling like the worst human on earth.

He heard footsteps behind him, which he ignored until a wiry younger man stopped at the door next to him, his gaze narrowed on Mike. 'Did you make her cry?'

'Probably.' Mike closed his eyes for a moment and grimaced. 'Most definitely.'

The stranger made a disgusted sound. 'No one should make her cry.' He pointed at the closed door. 'That woman right there, she's a gift. You kiss her feet, you don't make her cry.'

'I know.'

'Then why did you do it?'

Mike sighed. 'Because I'm a fucking miserable git.'

'I don't know what that means,' the man admitted. 'But from your tone, it's not a good thing.' His glower deepened. 'Maybe you should go home. Don't come back until you can treat her right.'

Mike nodded, but he wasn't sure the man saw him before that door clicked shut in his face as well.

Mike had been miserable when he got home. He'd taken a shower, hoping to wash away the bitter end to the evening. His heart felt leaden, sinking down into his gut. As soon as he was dry enough, he pulled out his laptop and typed out an email to his work team that he'd be working from home tomorrow because he wasn't feeling well. He was supposed to meet them at nine, but the idea of going about his day in the morning felt about as appealing as splitting open his own chest with his bare hands right now.

Once he'd sent the email, he climbed into bed, naked, his hair still wet from the shower, and immediately passed out.

And apparently left his ringer on, because he was woken up by it the following morning. He couldn't think of who would be calling him at this time. Mike climbed out of bed, blinking at his phone. It was *noon*. He couldn't remember the last time he'd slept that long. He pulled on a pair of pyjama trousers and stumbled to the kitchen. His phone had stopped ringing, which was good, because he wasn't going to speak to a single person before he had a cup of coffee in his hands. As he got the coffee brewing, his phone started up again.

Mike gave up and fetched the infernal device. Rahul's name flashed across the screen, a picture of his son kissing his husband's cheek flashing right below it. Mike let out a breath, set the phone up on the counter and clicked the accept button.

His son appeared on the screen, cigarette in hand, as he leaned against the side of his house. 'Well, thank fuck, there you are.'

'Here I am.' Or as here as he was going to get right now. He felt blurry from sleep, his mouth thick, his movements clumsy.

Rahul took a drag on his cigarette, his gaze razor sharp. 'You look absolutely wretched, Da.'

Mike propped his elbows on the counter. 'You're not supposed to be smoking. Noah's going to lose it.'

Rahul pointed at the screen. 'That's between me and the love of my life. I'm not calling about that.'

Unable to wait any longer, Mike fetched a mug and placed it directly under the coffee spout. 'Then why are you calling?'

'Because your daughter has been blowing up my phone for the last hour, that's why.'

He frowned. 'Amaya? Why? Oh god, has Barney died already?'

'Who the fuck is Barney?' Rahul asked, then flicked his hand. 'Never mind. No, that's not why she was calling. She was calling because you showed up on a certain blog this morning.'

'Oh no,' Mike groaned. 'Was it bad? Does she hate me?'

Rahul's eyes narrowed. 'Why would you ask that? What did you *do*?'

Mike sighed, grabbing his coffee and setting the jug back with his other hand as he sipped. Cream, he definitely needed cream. 'I'm not sure I want to get into this particular topic with my son.'

Rahul made a disgruntled noise. 'Who you going to talk about it to, then? Amaya?'

'No,' Mike said, his voice firm. 'That's even worse.'

'Then I'm it, aren't I?' Rahul asked, looking off screen. 'Shit.' He threw down his cigarette and stomped on it.

'Yes, because I absolutely didn't see you smoking just then.' Noah's dry voice drifted in from off screen. Then his face appeared, blond hair slicked back, grey eyes merry. 'Is that your dad?' He grinned. 'Michael, how are you?'

'He's fucking miserable, that's what,' Rahul said, his tone softening as he continued. 'Sorry. I know I said I'd quit—'

Noah rolled his eyes indulgently. 'Later, love. Why's your dad miserable?'

'That's what I'm trying to find out. All I know is he had a cameo on this woman's travel blog and when I called him, he looked like something you'd find on the floor of the tube.'

Noah made a face. 'Wait, the airport woman? *Swanning About*?'

'Yeah,' Rahul said.

Noah held up a finger. 'Wait please.' He took out his phone, pulling up Sophie's blog.

Mike took this opportunity to stir cream into his coffee and drink it, wishing, not for the first time, that he could just dump it directly into his veins.

Noah stared at his phone, his eyes wide, his hand over his mouth. By the end of it, he had his hand on his chest. 'Michael Tremblay, I didn't know you had it in you.'

Mike groaned, his hand over his eyes. 'I haven't seen it. How bad is it?'

'Honestly?' Noah said, his brows high. 'You're adorable together. The energy between you pops on the screen.' He shook his head. 'There is much buzz in the comments.'

He pinched his eyes shut. 'Sophie's probably livid.'

'Why?' Noah asked. 'I know you haven't seen it yet, but the fans *love* you. They're asking who you are and if you'll show up in more videos. Honestly, the comment section is usually a mire of troll behaviour, but this one is oddly wholesome.'

Rahul peered over his shoulder, looking at the comments. 'Who's Andrew?'

'Her arsehole of an ex-husband,' Mike said into his coffee. 'They're comparing me to that bastard? Is Sophie?' The first wouldn't be great, but the second . . .

'Contrasting, mostly,' Noah said. 'Lots of "you go, girl" energy.'

'That's something, at least,' Mike said with a sigh.

'I think we're going to need it all, Dad,' Rahul said. 'Spill.'

'Boundaries— '

Noah cut him off. 'With all due respect, Mike, boundaries can go hang. You cannot dangle this kind of delicious morsel in front of us after years of *nothing* and expect us to ignore it.'

'He's right, Dad,' Rahul said. 'You've really only brought this on yourself. We want the tea.'

'The tea?' Mike asked.

'The gossip,' Noah clarified. 'And quickly, please – my mum is only here for another thirty minutes, and she's handling the children.'

Mike's instinct, the one that had been keeping him alive since Tara's death, was to stay silent. Close off and deny. It had kept him safe, but it had also been utterly *exhausting*. He was so very tired of keeping everything locked down and inside. Still, he wavered on that tightrope, his instinct screaming at him to protect his kids from this. They'd had enough pain, they'd had enough *grief*, they'd—

'Da,' Rahul said, his voice sharp. 'I've let this slide. Both Amaya and I – leaving you be, waiting for you to heal . . . We know you loved Mum. Putting yourself out there, *trying* – Da, she'd want that. We want that. So please, for the love of fucking everything holy on this spinning orb, tell us what happened.'

And really, what was he going to say to that? Mike gave up and told them an edited version of the previous night, leaving out the more . . . personal bits. The softness of her skin, the taste of her, the feel of her body beneath his hands as they danced, the pulse of his desire like a second heartbeat. Some things you just didn't share.

By the end of this tale, Rahul was banging the back of his head against the side of the house and Noah was frowning.

'Well,' Noah said to his husband with a sigh, 'I'm starting to understand why you were so difficult when we got together.'

Rahul turned his head, his expression irritated. 'What are you on about?'

Noah waved a hand. 'I'm just saying, a lot of stuff is making sense. You are *just* like your father.'

Rahul scowled at him. 'What does *that* mean?'

Mike poured himself another cup of coffee. 'Not loving that I'm being touted as a negative here, but weirdly I also can't argue against it.'

Noah placed a hand on Rahul's chin. 'You've worked hard, my heart, but remember how long it took you to tell me you loved me?' Rahul looked disgruntled by this, but softened after Noah kissed his cheek.

Noah leaned into his husband and let out a sigh. 'And you're even worse, Mike. I love you *dearly*, but you're making yourself miserable. Did you have a good time last night?'

'Yes,' Mike admitted.

'Then what's the problem?' Noah asked gently.

It was the gentleness that undid him, making the words that Mike wanted so desperately to hold close to his chest spill out. 'I can't give her what she needs. I can't – I don't know if I can love anyone again the way I loved Tara.'

Noah's face was sympathetic, while Rahul dropped his gaze, his throat working.

'I loved her so much,' Mike said, his voice breaking. 'She was my *heart*.'

Noah made a soft sound, an understanding hum. 'I never got to meet Tara, but from what I know, Mike, she would hate that you're denying yourself happiness. Be upfront with this woman. Tell her that you might not be able to give her anything permanent. Why can't you enjoy *now*?'

Mike's head snapped up. 'That seems . . . She deserves more, surely?'

Rahul sighed. 'I'm so glad I'm not straight. Straight men are *exhausting*.'

Noah shook his head. 'Mike, has it occurred to you that she might not want more right now either? She just got divorced. In her place, I'm not sure I'd want to be looking for anything but a for-now kind of hook-up.'

It had literally never occurred to Mike that Sophie might want anything other than something long term. He blinked at them, words failing him.

'Bloody hell, Dad, did you even talk to this woman?' Rahul looked at Mike's expression and shook his head. 'For fuck's sake, try and catch up with the times. You'd better phone this Sophie and apologize on your knees.'

'He's right,' Noah said gently. 'You made a pretty big assumption there. At the very least, you need to apologize for how you acted and try to explain, if you want to salvage any kind of friendship with her.'

'And go big, Da. There's no way you can go too lightly on the grovelling here,' Rahul said. 'Learn from my experience.'

'I have been married before,' Mike grumbled. 'And I was just as much of a pillock then. If your mother taught me anything, it was how to make amends after things had gone pear-shaped.'

Noah made a sympathetic face. 'You might have to get creative.'

Mike sighed and finished his coffee.

Chapter Nine

Sophie sat on Tom's couch, eating pizza and watching *The Great British Bake Off*, which for some reason was called *The Great British Baking Show* here.

Tom was at work, but Marisa was watching with her, though she also had Sophie's phone, and her attention was mostly on the video from the previous night. She puffed out her cheeks. 'Holy shit. Watching you two.' She fanned her face with her piece of pizza, which didn't so much fan as flop.

Sophie made a noncommittal noise.

'Interesting,' Marisa said, dragging the word out. 'You disagree? Because I'm sensing a story here.'

Sophie had also watched the video, obviously, in order to edit and post it. The process had been difficult for her as she'd tried to decide what any of it meant. Mike had held her close, his hands possessive, but that was also a requirement of the dance. He'd looked at her – how had he looked at her? Hungrily? Or was that just what she'd wanted to see?

After the divorce . . . well. She didn't trust herself to assess such situations any more. After all, she'd been surprised by Andrew's cheating. Then she'd had to face that she'd been ignoring the very real fact that it had been a sad, miserable kind of marriage at the end. It was so obvious now. If she'd been able to miss all *that*, then who was she to judge any of Mike's actions properly?

He'd been interested enough to kiss her, and while the kiss had been scorching, maybe he was just a good kisser?

Chemistry didn't necessarily mean compatibility. Ultimately, he'd been the one to stop. Which was his prerogative. She certainly didn't want him to do anything he didn't want to do.

That being said, she wasn't sure if she could have put on the brakes herself. It had been intoxicating, and she was mortified by the idea that he hadn't felt the same. The evening had left her with a strange mixture of desire and shame that she didn't care for, and underneath that a little bit of hurt as well. It was an off-putting emotional cocktail and she was cutting herself off. No more of that, thank you very much.

'That's a whole lot of thinking going on there.' Marisa took another bite of her pizza, her eyes narrowing. 'You know I've got all day, right? I can wear you down slowly over time.' She made a face. 'Normally I wouldn't press you. None of my business, right?' She slumped heavily into her seat, an annoyed cast to her features. 'It's just – have you ever been so sick of your own bullshit? I know I need to process everything. I know I need to deal with the trauma, and that takes time, but I'm so exhausted by everything being about me.' She reached for another slice of pizza, her hand hovering in indecision. 'So for the love of god, Sophie, let me wallow in your drama for a minute. Forget that I'm engaged to your son. We're just two women sharing hot goss. Spill the tea. I've seen how much of it you drink. You should be full of the stuff, so *share*.'

Sophie really didn't feel like talking about it – her insides felt *raw*. But she couldn't pass up the opportunity to take care of Marisa a little. She was also starting to understand what Marisa meant by being *so sick of her own bullshit*. 'Fine. I'll talk about it if you eat another slice of pizza.'

'Blackmail, Sophie? Really?' Marisa selected another piece. 'You're ruthless.'

Sophie grabbed her own slice. 'I'd apologize, but I'm not really sorry.'

'Don't get me wrong, I respect it,' Marisa said, taking a big bite. 'I'm a big fan of women speaking up for what they want.' Her eyes narrowed. 'And now that I've held up my end of the deal . . .'

Sophie sighed, setting her pizza back onto her plate. 'We kissed.' Kiss was such an oddly simple word for a complicated thing, glossing easily over what was sometimes such an impactful action.

Marisa's eyes widened. 'Ohhhh. This is even better than I'd hoped.' She tipped her head to the side, examining Sophie. 'Kissing usually doesn't lead to that face, though. That's an unhappy face. Was it bad? Dead fish bad, or plumber going after a blocked drain bad? Terrible breath?' She scrunched her nose. 'I'd always hoped older men would be better at this sort of thing. Surely they must learn as they go. You've extinguished a great hope that I held dear, Sophie. He's so hot, too. I had higher hopes for Michael.'

Sophie looked at her, exasperated. 'Do you want to actually hear about it, or spin a ton of conjecture first?'

'Conjecture,' Marisa said instantly. 'That's the fun bit. *Then* I want reality. But I'm done now, so carry on.'

'The kiss was . . .' Sophie struggled for a word to describe it. How to convey the chemistry of it, how good it had felt, and how thinking of it now made her want to cry? In fact, she'd wanted to cry the second he'd stopped. She made a helpless noise, her hands fluttering at her sides.

'Oh,' Marisa said, her tone knowing. 'It was really *good*, wasn't it? One of those knee-weakening, fairy tale kinds of kisses that make you feel like they should be illegal. Panty-melting.'

Sophie made a noise like the saddest balloon with a slow leak.

'Those are good kisses,' Marisa said. 'And since we're pretending we're two friends, I will admit that those kinds of kisses are why I'm engaged.'

'Really don't want to think about that,' Sophie said. 'But also happy for you.'

'Okay, so if Michael laid one on you that unleashed a sexy kraken—'

'I do not understand that statement at all.'

Marisa batted this away with one hand. 'There's an 80s movie, my mom loved it. Greek mythology. We'll watch it next, because I think you'll love it. Let's focus. If it was that kind of kiss, why the sad face?' Her lip curled. 'Please do not tell me it made you nostalgic for your ex. I'd like to put Andrew into some kind of wicker man.'

Sophie tapped her fingers on her plate. 'Seems . . . extreme.'

Marisa shrugged. 'Lots of weird leftover hormones right now, plus I do not like what that man did to you and Tom. If we were on the *Titanic* right now and it was sinking, I'd rather drop an empty lifeboat into the ocean than let him get into it.'

'Wow,' Sophie said. 'I'm honestly a little impressed with your level of spite right now.'

'I don't like it when someone hurts the people I love,' Marisa said simply. 'And that includes myself. You and Tom should try it. Be *less* forgiving to those that hurt your loved ones, and that list should start with yourself.'

Sophie digested this quietly for a moment. 'I think you might have something there.'

'I'm wise beyond my years,' Marisa said dryly. 'Now focus.'

'Right. Well, the good news is that it didn't make me miss the Wicker Man,' Sophie said. 'Bad news is Mike shut it down pretty quickly. Done, over, got me into a Lyft, dropped me at my door.'

Marisa groaned, throwing back her head. 'Noooooo. Mike, you're killing me, buddy. Please tell me he didn't apologize for kissing you.'

'He did. Very "so sorry, that shouldn't have happened" kind of nonsense.'

'Uggggghhhhh.' Marisa shoved the last of her pizza into her mouth, chewing angrily. 'Why are men? *Why?*'

'I don't know.'

'Well, I'm sorry,' Marisa said. 'That's shitty. And . . .' She eyed Sophie, like she wasn't sure how the next bit would be taken. 'Probably felt extra terrible, after what the Wicker Man did to you?'

'*Yes,*' Sophie said, with more force than she'd intended. 'Thank you – you get it!'

'Rejection squared,' Marisa said. 'It becomes exponential when they're back to back like that.'

'It wouldn't be so bad,' Sophie admitted, 'if we hadn't been having so much fun. Honestly, yesterday . . . I don't know when I last laughed like that, except when I'm with Edie.'

'Edie's a good friend,' Marisa said with a nod. 'The kind you could have fun with even if you're stuck somewhere really terrible.'

'Yes,' Sophie said, 'she is. But last night . . . I had such a good time dancing, then dinner at the park, with the river and the lights and the carousel. It was honestly magical.'

Marisa nodded solemnly. 'And then Mike had to shit all over it.'

'There has to be a nicer way to say that,' Sophie said. 'But yes.'

'Nicer, perhaps, but you can't argue with the accuracy. So what are you going to do now?' Marisa asked. 'Are you going to see him again?'

Sophie shook her head. 'I don't know. He said the offer was open if I needed any help with my blog, but I'm not sure I want to court that kind of trouble.'

Marisa nibbled a fresh slice of pizza. 'I completely understand why you'd be hesitant.'

'I think for now I'm just going to concentrate on why I'm here – to be with you and Tom. To help. And my job. The things that make me happy. I really don't need a romantic relationship adding a layer of complexity right now.'

Marisa sighed. 'I was really hoping you'd at least get some good, sweaty sex out of it. I can't imagine the Wicker Man being anything but a selfish ass in bed.'

'Thank you,' Sophie said. 'I think. I'm choosing to take that statement as one of being hopeful about my future happiness.'

'That's how it was meant,' Marisa said, picking up the remote. 'Now, how do you feel about mechanical owls?'

They were just at the scene where the temple was falling apart when there was a knock at the door. Sophie had given up working, cuddling down into some blankets on the couch with Marisa. Neither of them were expecting anyone.

Marisa paused the film, getting up to check the peephole. 'Well, that's interesting.'

'Who is it?' Sophie asked.

Marisa looked back at her. 'Mike is at the door. He does seem to be bearing gifts. What would you like me to do?'

She was very tempted to tell him to go away. She *really* did not need more drama in her life from a man. 'I'm not sure. Andrew—'

'In this apartment he is now and forever the Wicker Man,' Marisa said firmly.

'Fine, the Wicker Man has given me plenty of drama this past year or so. I'm not sure if I want any more. Still, Mike isn't Andrew and it doesn't seem entirely fair to be equating them.'

One of Marisa's brows went up. 'Who said we need to be fair? We get to decide who we keep in our lives. There's no guaranteed second chances. It's not like you signed a contract. If he's adding too much, he's adding too much, full stop.'

Sophie got up from the couch and hugged Marisa fiercely. 'Have I told you recently how much I adore you?'

'Four times yesterday and twice this morning,' Marisa said. 'But I'm always accepting accolades.'

Sophie sighed. 'How does he look? Sad? Uncomfortable?'

'He looks like he's about to tell someone he accidentally killed their goldfish.'

'Oddly specific, but you do paint a picture.' Sophie straightened. 'Okay, you can answer it.'

Marisa waved her back before she cracked open the door. 'Mr Tremblay. What are you doing here?' She paused. 'Also, I find it suspicious that you knew which apartment was ours.'

'I stopped by Sophie's apartment to give her something – she wasn't there, so I texted Tom. I hope that's okay. Is she here?'

'She might be,' Marisa said. 'But then again, she might not be. I find that it entirely depends on your intentions.'

Sophie could almost feel Michael's wince through the door; even though she couldn't actually see him, she still had a sense that he felt bad. Andrew had never liked getting his nose rubbed in it when he'd messed up, often getting nastier and lashing out in consequence. He'd eventually apologize by bringing her a bouquet of roses – which she didn't actually care for – and never quite saying he was sorry.

Normally she didn't like people feeling upset or uncomfortable and would often leap forward to close the gap and smooth over the problem. But today . . . today she felt like seeing how this played out. If Mike stomped and pouted, their conversation would be short and final. Same if he was rude to Marisa, because her almost-daughter was right. She was under no obligation to put up with any of it.

The other side of the door was quiet for a long moment. 'My intentions are to check on Sophie and to issue an apology for some of my behaviour.'

'Okay,' Marisa said. 'Hold on.' She shut the door. 'What do we think?'

Sophie considered for a moment. 'How sincere do you think he was being?'

Marisa tilted her head, thinking. 'He seemed honestly contrite and miserable, but maybe he's a good actor?'

Sophie shook her head. 'He can be a closed book, but I've never had the feeling he would pretend like that.'

'Trust your gut, then,' Marisa said. 'What do you want to do?'

Sophie sighed. 'My gut has been notoriously untrustworthy, but I guess I'll talk to him.'

Marisa didn't question her, she simply opened the door and ushered Mike in. He was dressed casually today, in a T-shirt and shorts, but he didn't look well. Oh, he was as handsome as ever, but Sophie got the distinct sense that he'd slept poorly and wasn't feeling great, which – and she felt bad about this – had the odd effect of making *her* feel better.

'Hello,' Sophie said. 'What are you doing here?'

Mike stared at her for a second before dropping his eyes and swallowing hard, his hands fussing with the wrapped package he was holding. 'I wanted to talk about last night.' His gaze flicked to Marisa. 'I recognize that this is your home and a bit awkward, but could we have a moment?'

Marisa's eyes narrowed. She spun around slowly towards Sophie. 'Do *you* want a moment?'

Sophie couldn't help but smile. 'Yes, please, if you don't mind.'

'Fine,' Marisa said. She pointed at her eyes, then V'd those fingers back at Mike. 'But I'm in the next room. I hear raised voices? I will chase your ass out with a broom.'

'Understandable,' Mike said.

Marisa glared at him for another moment, then swept out of the room.

After a long moment of silence, Mike cleared his throat. 'She's terrifying.'

'I like her,' Sophie said stiffly.

Mike smiled a little at her defensive tone. 'Me too. She reminds me of my daughter, who is also terrifying.'

Unsure what else to do, Sophie stared at him, her arms crossed.

He sighed, rubbing a hand over his face. 'Can we sit?'

For a second, she considered arguing, but then she softened and waved a hand to the couch. After they'd both settled, he watched her for a moment. 'I had a speech,' he finally said. 'A long one. Very grovelly.'

'Can't wait to hear it.'

'I think it would test your patience,' Mike admitted. 'I've been told, repeatedly, that I was an arsehole. Mostly by myself, but also by outside interested parties.'

She wasn't going to argue with him about that, but she also wasn't sure what to say. She hadn't realized how ingrained she'd become to Andrew's way of arguing, his methods of fighting, until just now. Mike wasn't red-faced, his words weren't biting. In fact, he didn't seem angry at all.

'I find I agree with their assessments.' He fidgeted with the package in his hands. 'Last night – I had a great time.'

'Me too,' Sophie said quietly. 'Until the end.'

Mike winced. 'That's on me, you understand? You didn't do anything wrong. You were wonderful. I was a mess.' He frowned thoughtfully down at the package. 'I *am* a mess. I'm very sorry my behaviour hurt you. Can you forgive me?'

Sophie pursed her lips, watching him. He did seem honestly contrite. Still . . . 'When you say, "your behaviour", are you still referring to the kiss, or after?'

'After,' Mike said firmly. 'Only after.'

Sophie nodded, her throat tight. 'While I would never, ever ask you to do anything you weren't comfortable with,

I neither want, nor need, another man causing havoc in my life.'

Mike swallowed. 'Fair enough. What about a friend?' His voice quietened. 'I really did have a good time yesterday. I'd like – if you're amendable – I'd . . .' He gusted out a breath and shook his head, before turning his gaze on her. 'What would you like? Do you even want to spend time with me after last night?'

Sophie blinked at him. What did she want? She wasn't used to being asked that. Andrew had always barrelled forward, assuming he knew what she wanted or that she would want the same thing as him. If she was honest with herself, she wanted another kiss, but was too raw to consider it. 'I think . . .' she said slowly, 'that having a friend here would be a good thing.'

He nodded sharply. 'Then that's what we'll be.'

Sophie couldn't detect any dismay in him at her choice, but she didn't detect any relief, either. He was frustratingly difficult to read. For herself, she felt an odd mix of both, and couldn't quite tell how she felt about the decision. Still, she forced herself to smile. 'Friends.'

He held out the package, his manner deliberately casual. 'I got you a little something.'

Sophie couldn't hold back her smile. She *adored* presents, and the sad fact was, she rarely got them any more from anyone except her son and Marisa on special occasions, and Edie. Inside the parcel was a very nice journal, the cover bound in the *Starry Night* print, a subtle nod to the way they'd met. There was also a very nice pen.

Mike frowned at the gift. 'It seemed like a good idea at the time, but now I'm feeling like even more of a muppet. I just thought – you said you made lists of your ideas. For work. I use these same journals for my work, and they're very good.' He grimaced. 'Should have got flowers . . .'

The journal prismed in her vision as her eyes welled up. She threw her arms around his neck and hugged him tightly. 'I love it.'

He gave a startled laugh and hugged her back. 'I'm so glad. Thought it had gone pear-shaped again.'

'No,' Sophie said, giving him another squeeze and then letting him go. 'It's perfect.'

And that was the worst of it – it really *was*, the gift beautiful and thoughtful at the same time. Which was fine. Great, actually. That just meant he'd be the perfect friend. Which was exactly what she needed. Nothing else.

Despite how firmly she said this to herself, she wasn't entirely sure she believed it.

Chapter Ten

'You're sweating,' Sophie said. 'Are you okay? We can stop at any time.'

'Absolutely not,' Mike panted. 'We're doing this.' Even if it killed him, they were doing this. And it might. It might actually kill him.

'We don't *have* to do this. Do you want me to stop recording?'

'No. I'm enjoying it,' Mike grunted. 'Promise.'

'You don't *look* like you're enjoying it.' Sophie sounded sceptical. She had every right to be sceptical. *He* was sceptical.

'My pride is at stake here, Sophie. I have staying power. I can prove it.' Mike swiped at his forehead, breathing hard, his voice sounding husky to his own ears. 'I'm seeing this through.' He was somewhat relieved that only half of the tables at Xi'an Famous Foods were full. Fewer people to watch his downfall.

Sophie laughed, digging her chopsticks into her bowl. 'I thought you liked spicy foods.'

'I do,' Mike said plaintively. He grabbed his napkin, dabbing at his forehead. 'My kids are going to mock me relentlessly, and I can't say I blame them.'

Sophie smirked as she dug into the container for a spicy cucumber. 'Why is that?'

'Tara's grandparents were from India. She cooked a lot of curries. I *like* curries.' Mike downed half of his water. 'How are you not dying?'

Sophie shrugged. 'I like spicy food.' She used her chopsticks to expertly shovel another wide noodle into her mouth, then rolled her eyes and groaned in pure bliss. 'These are *delicious*.'

Mike was sweating, his mouth on fire, and the sight of Sophie groaning in almost orgasmic bliss almost shorted out his brain. *Friends*, he reminded himself. They were *friends*. His unhelpful brain chose that moment to pipe up, pointing out that friends didn't usually know how each other tasted. He took another bite of his dumpling in an attempt to get his brain to shut up.

Sophie snickered. 'Why do you keep eating?'

'Because they're delicious,' Mike said. 'And I never learn.'

'It's a different kind of spicy,' Sophie said. 'Or maybe you're out of practice. When's the last time you had spicy food?'

Mike placed his palms flat on the metal table. He was pretty sure that when he removed them, he'd see a steamy outline of each of his fingers on the shiny surface. 'It's been a while,' he admitted. Indian food had been intimately linked with thoughts of Tara and after she'd passed, he'd been unable to face any of his favourite dishes unless his children were present. Even then, he'd still felt sad, he'd just tamped it down, unwilling to ruin their own happy associations with his grief.

'Maybe you need to build your tolerance back up.' Sophie nudged the cucumber salad towards him. 'If you want any more, now is the time. Otherwise, I will eat the entire container.'

Mike gamely scooped up another bite with his chopsticks and put it in his mouth. The cucumbers were crisp, the marinade delicious. He swallowed them, then grabbed another, getting a chilli this time. He ate it anyway because he refused, *refused* to shy away.

Sophie grabbed another dumpling. 'I read somewhere that spicy food is good for your sex drive.'

Mike choked, coughing the chilli pepper he'd just swallowed back up. Which wouldn't have been a problem, but it landed somewhere in the back of his sinuses. And it *burned*. Oh god.

Oh *god*.

It was practically volcanic, the sensitive area lighting up like one of those pinball machines from the 70s.

He started coughing into his napkin.

'Oh dear,' Sophie said. 'I shouldn't have said that. I wasn't thinking. Are you okay?'

Mike shook his head, still coughing.

'You're turning a very concerning red.' Her eyes widened. 'Are you choking?'

He shook his head furiously. He kept coughing, which only lodged the pepper deeper. He was going to die, right here in front of a bunch of strangers, face down in a bowl of dumplings. While Mike was certain there were worse ways to die, he was pretty sure there were also *better* ways. Ways that weren't so mind-numbingly stupid.

He wasn't entirely sure the situation could get worse. His vision was going black around the edges.

'Should I call someone?' Sophie asked, her eyes even wider now. 'Get you water?'

He gagged.

Oh *no*. Turns out it could get worse.

Mike lurched from his seat, bolting for the toilets.

'I can never go back there.' Mike was stretched out on the grass in Prospect Park, his arm over his eyes. The trees above covered them in dappled shade, so it was less about blocking out the sun and more about avoiding his self-reproach. 'I have disgraced my family.'

Sophie sat next to him, her face turned up to the leaves. 'This is a beautiful park. Also, you're being ridiculous.'

'It's designed by the same people who mapped out Central Park in Manhattan. And of course I am, I'm always ridiculous, it's just this time I'm also being honest – I've brought them shame.' He dropped his arm. Errant slivers of light danced along her skin as the slight breeze moved the leaves above. Mike took a moment to admire the effect specifically, and her in general.

'You have not,' she said, sounding exasperated. 'Sit up and try your shake. It will make you feel better.'

Mike levered himself up before digging out his phone. He tapped in the code to unlock his screen and handed it to her. 'See for yourself.'

Sophie set down her milkshake and took his phone to read through the text chain, her free hand pressing against her lips to stop her growing smile. It didn't work and she spluttered a laugh. 'I stand corrected. Who's Noah?'

'My son Rahul's husband. Noah's usually the nice one. Amaya's the more ruthless of the three, normally.' He eyed the shake she'd offered him, which was resting on the grass. 'Is that the small?'

'They only had one size.'

'Sometimes I think Americans eat like they don't want to live,' Mike said, taking a tentative sip. 'What flavour is this?'

'Strawberry donut. It's a special. If you don't like it, we can swap. I got salted caramel.' She sipped her shake. 'Maybe it's more that they eat like they want to enjoy life?'

'Why not both?' Mike sipped at the shake, which was delicious and soothed his ravaged throat. 'That does feel better, thank you.'

'You're welcome.'

Mike blew out a breath. 'I cannot believe I threw up.'

'You got a pepper stuck in your sinuses,' Sophie pointed out. 'I didn't even know you could *do* that.' His phone pinged and she read it, then laughed. 'Amaya says she wants the video. She also says you have to go back. It's a moral imperative, and you made Barney cry.' She glanced at him. 'Who's Barney?'

'The plant she got me for my sad flat.' He took another long sip of his milkshake. 'You might as well send her the video – that way, my humiliation will be complete.'

Sophie juggled both their phones, dropping the video into the chat. 'If you do decide to go back, I'll go with you. I'm going to be dreaming of those noodles and I might marry those dumplings.'

'They were really good,' Mike admitted. 'Before I puked them all up.'

'Where should we go next?' She started pulling up local attractions on her phone, flipping through different websites. 'We could rent pedalos.'

'Absolutely not,' Mike said. 'With the way today's going, we'll end up capsizing. Let's rain-check that idea.'

'Can you capsize a pedalo?'

'Normal people? No.' Mike moved his shake back and forth between them. 'Us? I'm not taking that chance.'

'Fair enough,' she said, finishing off her shake. 'I'm open to ideas.'

'No food,' Mike said firmly. 'At least, not yet.' He sipped at his shake for a minute, thinking. 'Fancy a trip on the subway?'

'Does anyone, ever, actually fancy a trip on the subway?'

'Of course not,' Mike said. 'But we're taking one anyway.'

An hour later and they were standing in front of, to Mike's mind, one of the most impressive buildings he'd seen in a long time.

'What is it?' Sophie peered up at the structure, eyes wide.

'It's called the Shed – a glorious construction of structural steel, insulated glass, polymers and reinforced concrete. It's energy efficient and it *moves*.'

She blinked at him. 'It what?'

'Moves.' He turned her slightly, pointing to the relevant part of the structure. 'See that bit, there? Those are wheels. The building can expand as needed. It's a centre for the arts, which includes performances, so when they need more space, they create it.'

'Ooooh.' The sound was filled with awe as it escaped her rounded lips. 'I'd love to see that.'

Mike felt an overpowering urge to lean down and press a kiss just to the corner of her mouth, right *there*, and— Friends. They were friends. He wasn't going to break his promise on the same day he'd made it. No, wait, he wasn't going to break it at all. That was how promises worked, damn it.

He cleared his throat, shoving his hands into his pockets. 'They don't do it often. But it does have a bar that I've never been into. Can I buy you a drink?'

'Yes,' Sophie said, taking out her phone. 'After I get some pictures and video first.'

Mike held out his hand. 'Here, I can take some with you in it—'

Sophie shook her head. 'First, let's get a few of us.'

Mike dutifully followed her until she picked a good spot, taking several pictures of them from a few different angles. She examined the photos before they moved on, smiling after a second. 'These are good. I can use these.'

'You can?' Mike shook his head. 'But it's your blog. You don't need photos of me in it.'

'Why not?' Sophie asked. 'It's not like it's only pictures of my face. I include Edie in it all the time. Besides, you're the one that brought me here and you're the one who's going to tell me all about the building.' She frowned up at him. 'Unless you don't want to be in it?'

He shook his head. 'It's not that. I just don't want to take over.'

'You won't,' she promised with a grin. 'Now let's go and check it out. I want to poke about a bit before we head into the bar.'

They never made it into the bar. No sooner had they walked through the front gates than they were confronted with an explosion of people and noise.

'What is this?' Sophie asked, wonder in her voice.

Mike felt a sudden stab of envy. It was like Sophie approached the entire world with a sort of joyous curiosity. When had he stopped being like that? Had he ever been like that?

Sophie peered up at a banner. 'It's a market!' She darted off and all he could do was follow.

The market was full of food vendors, with cuisines from all over the globe. Everything from samosas and meats on sticks to drinks in hollowed-out pineapples, ice cream cookie sandwiches, paper baskets full of arancini – if you wanted to eat it, he was pretty sure the market had it. As he watched, someone pulled apart their cheese toastie, revealing a literal rainbow of cheese.

Just standing as he was at the entrance was a sensory experience. Dozens of food smells wafted through the air, along with people chattering and laughing, while music from a nearby exhibit flowed in the background. Between the stalls and the people, there was so much to look at that he wasn't sure where to start. It was like an explosion of flavour he could hear, see and smell as well as taste.

'I have died,' Sophie said solemnly. 'And the afterlife is wonderful.' She grabbed Mike's hand, tugging him forward. 'Come on!'

Startled by the sudden gesture, he made no argument, letting her tug him along in her wake. Without thinking, he laced his fingers through hers. The movement was so easy, so comfortable, that he didn't even realize he'd done it until they'd stopped in front of a juice stand.

'I want to drink out of a pineapple,' Sophie said breath-lessly. 'I didn't know how much I wanted that until just now.' She cast her gaze around the market, her tone turning plain-tive. 'There's so many things I want to try, but I'm not that hungry yet.'

Mike's stomach rumbled. 'Well, I'm starving.'

She gaped at him, incredulous. 'How? We had that big lunch, and then milkshakes.'

'*You* had a big lunch,' Mike reminded her. 'I sort of rented mine and then gave it back.'

'Oh, right.'

Mike took another long look at the offerings as he thought. 'How about you get your pineapple. Then pick out three small things you want to try. I'll order them, then you can sample as much as you want, and I'll eat the rest.' He peered down at her. 'This will be good for your blog, right?'

Sophie nodded. 'It's perfect.'

He tried very hard to not think about how much he liked hearing her say that while she was looking at him. It was only . . . someone should be doing things to make her happy. To keep that joyful glow going. Her ex had done the oppo-site, and her son, rightfully, was focused on himself and his fiancée at the moment. Sophie had friends, but they were far away. He held no illusions that she wouldn't make new ones quickly. She had that way about her.

Still, he was her friend, wasn't he? That had been the plan. It was a good plan. Very sensible. Only it was getting snarled up in his chest with a bunch of other things, sparking like a rat's nest of tangled-up wires.

He was still holding her hand. Which was fine. It was a friendly gesture. Although it didn't feel friendly, more like essential, and he couldn't name a single other friend he held hands with, but he was ignoring all of that. He'd have to let her hand go in order for her to get her pineapple. Until then, he was holding tight.

At that moment, Sophie turned her face up to him and *beamed*. He wasn't sure why she did it, but it made that nest of wires spark so hard he thought he could smell burning plastic. Maybe he was having a stroke.

He wanted to kiss her. *Badly*.

And it wouldn't end well. He knew that. Their last kiss gave him ample evidence that it would go poorly, and he'd only just returned to her good graces. He didn't want to jeopardize that again.

He cleared his throat as he tugged her gently in the direction of the juice stand. There were only a few people in front of them in the queue. The one time he wanted a queue to be longer, the universe couldn't oblige. Why couldn't it give him this? Because as soon as they were at the front, he'd have to let go.

The juice person moved unforgivably fast and it felt like only seconds later that they were at the front. Which was fine. Absolutely fine.

He dropped her hand.

It felt even worse than he'd imagined, so he shoved that hand into his pocket and tried to ignore it. They were friends, damn it, and he wouldn't do anything to jeopardize that.

Chapter Eleven

Highline Park might not be a hidden gem for New Yorkers, but I thought it was a gem, hidden or otherwise. A wonder of nature, art and architecture, it's a place meant for lingering. You can take a guided tour, or simply wander as we did, checking out the views of the city, finding art installations, or merely watching the bees buzz around the flowers. One could fall in love in the span of an afternoon here, I think – if not with another person, then at least with the city itself.

— *Excerpt from* Swanning About

Sophie spent the next few days working, pottering about the apartment, walking Manny's dog and spending time with Tom and Marisa. She tried very hard to not think about Mike, but it wasn't working. First, because she'd been reading comments on the posts from their day at the Shed and his unfortunate spicy pepper incident. She'd assumed he'd want her to leave it out of the post – there was no way Andrew would have let her post anything that didn't cast him in the best light – but he'd only shrugged and said his misery might as well make a few people laugh.

Even if she'd avoided her posts, he was always texting her. He'd had some long days ahead of him at work, so she hadn't expected him to message her at all. From the way he'd talked about it, he was very focused, often forgetting to take breaks or eat on those days unless one of his kids messaged him.

So she was surprised when she started getting texts randomly throughout his day. Sometimes it was him sending her pictures of interesting things he saw at work. Other times, it was simply him asking her how her day was going. Normal things, she supposed, but what surprised her was not only the ease of their conversation, but the breadth of it.

Mike: You really should go to the Empire State Building, you know. All work and no play, etc. etc.

Sophie: Says the guy who's working right now.

Mike: You're dodging the subject. We could go, you know.

Sophie: You've already been – surely you don't feel the need to go again.

Mike: Empire State Building, the views from the Staten Island Ferry – these are iconic for a reason. Classics don't get old. But if I can't tempt you, let me at least tempt you with a visit to the Guggenheim. I can give you a two-minute spiel about the impact of Frank Lloyd Wright's mid-century masterpiece that you could use for your blog, then a longer rant about how museums should organize paintings in order of whether or not the artist was a terrible human being . . . which you probably shouldn't use for your blog at all.

Sophie: What happened to separating the art from the artist?

Mike: Gauguin cut off Van Gogh's ear and had child brides and Picasso referred to women as 'machines for suffering'.

Sophie: Maybe we should avoid the Guggenheim, then?

Mike: No, ignore me, I'm in a bad mood. My laptop just crashed and I lost an hour's worth of work.

On the second day, Mike's mood had clearly improved, because he spent the whole day texting her silly questions.

Mike: Who would win in a fight, Betty White or Bea Arthur from The Golden Girls?

Sophie: Why are you even thinking about that?

Mike: I'm a man, Sophie. I spend at least half of my waking hours thinking about these things.

Sophie: Why were you even watching The Golden Girls?

Mike: I couldn't sleep last night and it was on the telly. Answer the question.

Sophie: Fine, Betty White, because I think she would fight dirty and I respect that about her.

Mike: Would you rather eat a gallon of dill pickle ice cream or get stuck in the tube for two hours?

Sophie: Pickle ice cream. Wait, is it peak hours on the tube?

Mike: Peak.

Sophie: Ice cream. What's worse than getting packed into a sweaty metal tube with annoyed people for two hours?

Mike: Getting packed into a sweaty metal tube with annoyed people for two hours and really having to pee the entire time?

Sophie: That's just mean.

Mike: Do you think Barney misses me?

Sophie: Do I think the plant you've never met misses you?

Mike: Yes.

Sophie: Who wouldn't miss you?

The third day was philosophical.

Mike: What I love most about Manhattan is the light. In the morning it's all shards of golden and white reflecting on the buildings. It gives everything a dreamlike quality. I feel as though at any moment someone could bump into me, and I'd wake up back in London.

Sophie: I've felt like I've been on a movie set since I got here. This city is like sensory overload, but in a good way.

On the fourth day, she got an invite.

Mike: Do you have plans tomorrow?

She didn't. She'd been spending a lot of time with her family, and she was sure Marisa could use some time to herself. There was a fine line between being there and being supportive, and smothering someone with attention. She tapped out a reply: *Not really, no.*

Mike: The project I'm working on, you know how I said it was to be a sort of take on the teahouse? I found a few local places that do tea. Thought it might be good to check out how the locals do it. Would you like to go?

Sophie didn't hesitate. *That sounds wonderful. I brought my own, but I'm homesick for a good cuppa.*

Mike: Me too. I'll send you the details. Looking forward to it.

And so was she . . . and not just because of the tea.

'This is . . . not what I expected,' Mike said. He was eyeing the atmosphere with a politely neutral expression on his face.

Sophie could admit that it wasn't quite what she first thought of when she thought of teatime, but she liked new things. This just seemed like an odd assortment of things. The multicoloured tablecloths had pompoms, but also proper place settings. 'Is it the jungle fronds? The fancy hats? The gold cutlery?'

Mike tilted his head. 'All of it?'

Sophie laughed, causing him to smile faintly at her. He looked handsome today – he looked handsome every day, really. The shirt he was wearing brought out the green in his eyes, and the sleeves were rolled up, revealing his forearms and a silver watch. Not a smart watch, but a regular watch. Sophie wasn't quite sure why that was attractive to her, but it was.

'It's only . . .' Mike hesitated here, once again taking in the unexpectedly tropical atmosphere of the place. 'That I have *misgivings.*'

Sophie could admit that she, too, was feeling the first faint pangs of misgivings. She considered herself to be a fairly adventurous person. She enjoyed trying new things. And yet . . .

'I'm concerned about our order,' she admitted.

'It made sense at the time.' Mike's tone was an odd cock-tail of defensive and bewildered. 'If you want to get a sense of a place, you ask for the most popular option. The items that they're known for.'

'I quite agree,' Sophie said soothingly. 'Normally.'

'But that was before the full impact of the place set in.' Mike's eyes were wide as he took in their surroundings. 'I think I might have been in shock.'

'Was that before or after you saw the terrarium with the live snake?'

'There's a live snake?' Mike's head whipped round, his body following. 'I saw the caged birds. The skinny fellow with the violin. I even saw the woman with the balloon ani-mals on her hat. I missed the live snake.'

Sophie tented her fingers and pressed them to her chin, a subconscious prayer for patience in this strange new land-scape. 'I'm wondering if you saw the menu.'

Mike blinked at her. 'It's tea. It might be a bit posh and a bit strange, but it's *tea*. Scones. Little sandwiches. PG Tips. A variation on the theme, but the theme remains.'

'I will acknowledge,' Sophie said, 'that there's a lot I don't know about America. You've been here more than me, obvi-ously, but they're a bit notorious for, well, slaughtering a good cuppa.'

Mike dropped his face into his hands. 'What have I done?'

'I'm sure it'll be fine.' Even to Sophie's ears, her tone sounded overly bright, like the neon flash of a false statement.

'I once watched an American put a tea bag into a mug, add cold water and *microwave it*.' Mike slowly dragged his fingertips down his face. 'How could I have forgotten that?'

'That was just one person,' Sophie said, her own hands now fluttering about anxiously. 'This is a restaurant. A restaurant known for tea. Obviously they're not going to do that.'

But as the waiter returned, wheeling their order over on a cart, her doubts not only returned but increased exponentially. The man was all limbs, lanky in floral shirt and trousers. His curly red hair stood out like someone had been pulling at it and his eyes were wide as dinner plates. He unloaded their teapot, along with lemon slices, cream, orange slices and, for some reason, a small dish of cherries that were a bright, improbable red. He also set down a tiered serving tray full of small treats and then bowed, sweeping his arms out to the sides.

'Thank you,' Mike said.

The waiter didn't move.

Sophie tried again. 'Thank you?'

After a long, strange pause, the waiter straightened up with a snap. His smile was wide, but oddly fixed, as he nodded at them. Then he darted away, forgetting his cart.

'Well,' Sophie said slowly. 'That was . . .'

'Odd,' Mike finished. 'Decidedly odd.' He peered at the tray, hand hovering in indecision.

A small smile curled the corners of her mouth. 'Can't decide what you want first?'

'Can't decide what anything *is*,' Mike said. 'I think this has caviar? And there's some kind of green . . . mousse in that one.'

She picked up one of the strange sandwiches and sniffed it. She couldn't smell much beyond the bread, so she took a tentative bite. 'I think it's cucumber?'

Mike's response was a horrified whisper. 'What have they done to it?'

She didn't particularly want to keep chewing – the texture was decidedly strange – but she also didn't want to spit it into her napkin. Tea, the answer was tea. What problem couldn't be solved by a good cup of tea?

She quickly poured herself one, surprised when it came out in a stream of blue. She clutched her water glass, washing down the unpleasant bite of sandwich. 'I'm not sure what they've done,' Sophie finally rasped, 'but I'm certain it's illegal.'

Mike stared at her cup. 'Why is the tea blue? Did I take drugs? Am I on drugs? What is happening?'

'It probably has butterfly pea flower in it. Edie bought some tea like that once.' Sophie picked up the tongs, selected a slice of lemon and put it into her cup. 'It changes colour when you add lemon.'

'It's very pretty,' Mike said. 'And I'm sure I should be intrigued by the science behind it, but I want – I *need* – a cup of tea. Not . . . blue.' He shook his head. 'It's my fault. I didn't read the menu.' He turned in his seat, looking for the waiter. 'I'll order another pot.'

Sophie eyed the tiered tray for a long moment before taking what appeared to be a tiny quiche in a filo pastry cup. 'I haven't seen our waiter since he bowed away. You might need to make your peace with drinking blue for now.' She stared at the quiche with trepidation after the cucumber foam, but it looked innocent enough. Steeling herself, she popped it into her mouth and chewed, relieved to discover caramelized onion and some kind of smoky cheese. 'The quiche is safe.'

Mike didn't question her, just reached for one and popped it into his mouth. His shoulders, which had been slowly inching up, relaxed down to their normal position. 'That's quite nice.'

'Maybe if we avoid the cucumber foam, we'll be fine?' Her tone conveyed it as the optimistic question that her statement actually was.

Mike seemed sceptical about this, but gamely placed a few other items neatly on his plate. Then he sighed and poured himself a cup of the blue tea. He added a slice of lemon, smiling a little as the tea changed slightly in tone, becoming more of a purple. 'It really is very pretty.' He sipped it, his mouth twitching down before taking another small, tentative swallow.

'You don't like it?' Sophie asked, feeling the question was a little unnecessary, but asking it anyway.

He sighed. 'It's not that I don't like it.'

'You just want a cup of proper tea,' she said sympathetically, because she, too, wanted a cuppa.

'I do,' he said. 'I really do.' He leaned back in his chair, once again searching fruitlessly for the waiter.

She plucked an innocuous-looking raspberry pink tart up with delicate fingers and bit into it – but instead of the sweetness she had been expecting, the taste was decidedly fishy, the texture disturbingly silky. To her mortification, she spat it immediately back out, only barely getting her napkin up in time.

Mike's lips twitched into a smile. 'That bad?'

Sophie whimpered and gulped her tea.

He scoffed, reaching across to take the offending tart from her plate. 'It can't be worse than the cucumber.' He put the rest of the tart into his mouth.

Chewed once.

Froze.

Colour drained from his face.

Sophie carefully handed him his napkin. Mike held it up to his face, his jaw working.

He set the napkin back down and drained his teacup. 'That was an affront to nature,' he said, his voice tinged with horror and awe. 'What was it? What did they *do* to it?'

Sophie shook her head, pouring herself another cup of tea. She picked up one of the orange slices and bit into it, hoping it would cleanse her palate. 'I wouldn't be surprised if you told me we'd just eaten people. It felt that wrong. Cannibalism-level wrong.'

'Like we'd committed a mortal sin against nature, just by taking a bite,' Mike said, his voice ominous. 'An abomination.'

'I thought it was going to be sweet.' Sophie had the urge to scrape at her own tongue with her fingers. 'Was it fish?'

Mike shuddered. 'Ham, maybe? Is there such a thing as a ham-fish? Because if there is, they made a tart out of it.' He gave a long blink. 'That was the worst thing I've ever put in my mouth.'

She gave him a faint smile. 'Worse than what happened at the noodle place?'

'Yes,' he said fervently. 'At least the noodles tasted good. Even coming back up they tasted better than that.' He eyed the rest of the things on the tray with trepidation. 'I would rather get a handful of peppers stuffed into my sinuses than eat anything off that tray.'

Sophie silently agreed, turning the tray until she found a toast triangle covered in what she fervently hoped were salmon and dill.

'You have to be kidding me,' Mike hissed. 'Don't touch it, Sophie – that tray is obviously cursed. We've angered a witch.' He stared ominously at his napkin. 'Possibly an entire coven.'

Her hand hovered over the tray, her expression etched with misery. 'But I'm hungry.'

'No one is that hungry,' Mike said, his brows furrowed. 'The ham-fish tart might not even be the worst thing on there. You don't know what other culinary atrocities await.'

She blinked at him. 'I'm not sure my mind can conjure something worse than that.'

'Good,' Mike said. 'Leave it that way.'

It was at that moment that the waiter came back. He was still smiling, and Sophie thought that even for an American, he smiled a great deal. His face was also shiny with sweat, like he'd been glazed with something before coming back out.

'How is everything?'

Mike cleared his throat. 'We were wondering if we could get . . .' His voice trailed off, his face pinched with concern as he watched the waiter staring fixedly at their tablecloth. 'Are you all right?'

The waiter laughed, the sound high and strangled.

Mike looked at Sophie.

Sophie widened her eyes in what she was hoping came across as a 'I have no idea what's going on' kind of expression.

Mike tried again. 'Is something amiss?'

The waiter blinked, giggled, then blew out a long breath. 'I'm going to be honest with you, dude.'

For a long, drawn-out moment they waited for the waiter to say something else. When he didn't, Sophie stepped in. 'You're going to be honest with us?'

The waiter gave another long, slow blink. 'I am?'

'Yes,' Mike said. 'You were. About something being amiss?'

The waiter nodded, absently scratching one of his arms. 'My roommate told me to try microdosing.'

'Microdosing what exactly?' Mike asked, his tone neutral, like he was worried that if he spoke too sharply, the waiter would bolt like a startled horse.

'Mushrooms.' The waiter drew his arm over his face, using his shirtsleeve to wipe away the sheen of sweat.

'Oh,' Sophie said. 'I see.' She wasn't entirely sure she did, but it seemed like the right thing to say.

'Only, the scale was off,' the waiter added. He laughed again, high and strained.

'That sounds . . . not good.' Mike's voice maintained that delicately even tone. 'How far off was it?'

The waiter picked up Mike's mostly full teacup and took a long drink. 'A lot.' He blinked. 'Is this tea supposed to be purple?'

Mike opted to not say anything about the tea. 'So you're not so much microdosing as you are regular dosing?'

'I am ripped out of my gourd right now.' The waiter set down Mike's teacup. 'Just high as fucking balls.'

'I think,' Mike said casually, 'that you should tell your boss that you're sick and go home.' He pursed his lips, thinking. 'How are you getting home?'

The waiter thought about this for a long moment before getting distracted by some of the jungle greenery. 'I feel bad for the snake. Do you think we should set him free? He's a living creature. He should be free. In the wild.'

'I'm not sure even a snake would consider New York to be "the wild",' Sophie said. 'Let's leave the snake for now. What's your name?'

'Lee.' The waiter shifted nervously. 'You're sure about the snake?'

'I am,' Sophie said firmly. 'That snake loves his home. He's safe there. It's his favourite place.'

Lee relaxed. 'Oh, good.'

Mike sighed. 'Here's the plan, Lee. You're going to bring us our bill. Then after we pay, you're going to go home sick. Sophie and I are going to help you get home, okay?'

'You are?' Lee smiled at this. 'That's nice.'

'Go and get the bill, Lee,' Sophie reminded him. The waiter darted away, hopefully to return soon with their bill.

Mike slumped in his chair. 'I'm beginning to think that we shouldn't be allowed out together. Things always go wrong.'

Sophie watched as Lee came back out, pausing in front of the terrarium. She pushed her chair out and stood. 'Well, for Lee's sake, I think it's probably very good that we did.'

Mike followed her gaze and cursed. 'He's going to free that bloody snake and lose his job.' He stood up abruptly. 'We'd better hurry.'

Chapter Twelve

After they'd paid their bill, Mike decided that trying to manage Lee on the subway would be nothing short of a nightmare and ordered a rideshare instead. Twenty minutes later they dropped Lee off to his confused but grateful roommate. As they left Lee's building and stepped back onto the pavement, Sophie rested a hand on Mike's arm. 'I have an idea.'

'That we should charge that tea place with crimes against humanity?'

Sophie laughed. 'No. We're going to go back to my flat. On the way there, we're going to stop at the store and pick up a few things. Then we're going to have a proper cup of tea.'

Mike looked at her gratefully. 'That might be the best thing I've heard all day.'

It was only as they stepped over the threshold to her flat that a few salient facts filtered into Mike's mind, the first of which was that he was going to be in Sophie's flat. The second of which was that they would be alone. This was followed by a swift and almost overwhelming feeling of panic. It washed over him like a big wave and his mouth went dry.

As Sophie started unloading their purchases, he dropped a text in the family group chat as he tried to wrestle with himself. *Having tea with Sophie. Panicking.*

He instantly regretted it. He should have kept it to himself. Mike didn't usually bring his kids into his business like this. Except since he'd met Sophie, he'd been doing it more, hadn't he? What was it about her? And text . . . text made it easier to find the words. That didn't necessarily mean he needed to do it, however. He was just pressing the screen with his thumb in the hope of deleting the message, when he realized he was already too late.

Noah: We need more details. Outside? Cosy setting? What?

Mike: At her flat.

Noah: Ooooooh.

Amaya: It's just tea, Dad. She didn't exactly invite you to an orgy. It will be fine.

Rahul: I thought we'd banned that word from the chat?

Amaya: We've banned sex, nubile, moist and soggy bottoms. We haven't yet banned orgy.

Mike: We're banning it now.

Noah: Can I just say your family chats are sooo much more interesting than mine. Unless Nana has been at the sherry again. Three-drink Nana is absolutely wild.

Rahul: Three-drink Nana is my favourite. I love her.

Mike: Can we focus please?

Noah: Sorry. What's causing the panic? Do you not want to be there? Do you need to leave? Is this a very polite hostage situation?

Amaya: She's not going to force you to do anything you don't want to do, Dad. Do you think she has any expectations?

Mike glanced up at Sophie, who was filling the kettle at the sink. Did he think she had any expectations? He grimaced. *After the debacle of the carousel night, no, I don't think so.*

Amaya: Then just enjoy tea with a friend. She's hardly going to demand that you make out.

Rahul: Make out? What are you, American now?

Amaya: I like learning phrases from other countries. Get cultured, you swine.

Noah: I think Mike's primary concern is that he wants to make out.

Rahul: Not you, too. I'm taking away your Netflix. You've been watching too much American telly.

Noah: Get cultured, you swine.

Amaya: Ha! Noah's on my side!

'Everything okay?' Sophie asked.

'Yes,' Mike said. 'Apologies. Catching up with the kids really quickly.'

'It's good you're so close to them.' She fetched the tomatoes from the counter and gave them a good rinse.

'Sometimes I think we're a little too close,' Mike muttered. Another text appeared on his screen.

Amaya: Deep breaths, Dad. Relax and enjoy your tea.

Rahul: And if you feel like kissing her, go for it.

Mike couldn't deny that he did, in fact, want to do just that. Had wanted to since he'd fucked things up so badly the first time. He'd tried to not think about it but kept finding himself going back to the memory. The feel of her. The taste. The soft sound she'd made when he'd— He shook his head sharply, like he was trying to clear it. *I don't think that would be fair to her.*

Noah: Sometimes life isn't fair. People aren't fair. We make mistakes. Isn't it possible you made one when you decided to just be friends?

Mike didn't have an answer to that. He found the idea troubling.

Rahul: My husband is a wise man. You should listen to him.

Unsure what to say to that, Mike tapped a thumbs-up reaction to it and put away his phone. Then he went to wash his hands, throwing Sophie a tight smile. 'I didn't mean to leave you to it. Point me towards the knives and I'll start slicing cheese.'

After a round of cheese and tomato sandwiches and a cup of tea that wasn't even slightly blue, Mike did the washing-up. To be fair, the dishes were minimal, but he felt it was the least he could do after abandoning Sophie to the lion's share of the tea prep.

Sophie watched him, her chin resting on her fist. Mike realized with a shock that he liked her watching him.

He peeked back at her. 'Making sure I don't miss a bit?'

She shook her head, the movement minimal and slow. 'Just taking a moment to appreciate a man doing dishes. Or any housework really. You should be commended.'

Mike scoffed. 'Commended? My kids would refer to it as the lowest of bars.' He shot her a look. 'I take it your ex didn't pitch in around the house?'

'Not unless it involved a power tool.'

Mike hesitated, unsure whether his next question would be an overstep. 'What about your son?'

Sophie barked a laugh. 'Much to Andrew's disappointment, Tom was never really into power tools and all that. He was more my little buddy around the house, growing up. I wanted to make sure he wasn't like the young men I met at uni who couldn't wash their own socks or cook anything more complicated than frozen pizza.'

Mike thought he'd done well enough there – his son could cook better than he could. 'Were you successful?'

She stared thoughtfully at the ceiling for a moment. 'He met Marisa in a cooking class, so I think whatever I didn't manage to teach him, he's picked up on his own.'

Mike rinsed the last dish, slotting it into the rack to dry. 'You gave him enough to continue on, then.'

'How about your kids?'

'Rahul is a chef normally, though he's home with Archie for a little while yet. Even when he goes back, he'll cut back on the longer hours because of the kids. I'd love to claim he got his culinary skills from me, but my cooking ability is mediocre at best and Tara's was better, but she didn't enjoy doing it often, much to her mother's chagrin. Especially if she was busy at work. Rahul probably learned out of self-defence.' He felt a sudden pang of loss, but it was a gentle one, more of a nudge than a dagger. 'He learned a lot from Tara's parents.'

Sophie smiled at this, as if charmed. 'What about your daughter?'

'Oh, Amaya would be perfectly capable in the kitchen if she had any inclination to be. But she relies on takeaways and frequent meals at her brother's house.' He dried his hands, turning around to face Sophie.

She was looking out of the window now, her thoughts clearly a million miles away, and Mike realized that, rather selfishly, he wanted her attention back on him. He really needed to sort himself out. The problem was, he decided, that he was overcomplicating everything. The other problem was that he wanted to stay safe and alone and unhurt, but also couldn't stop noticing the way Sophie moved. The curve of her mouth when something delighted her. The smell of her skin.

'Do you need to go back to work?' Sophie said. 'Now that you've had tea?'

'I should,' Mike said. He really should. He'd built a bit of a reputation on getting things done fast. He wasn't behind on this project yet, but he wasn't ahead either. It wouldn't take too much to lose ground. Yet the idea of going back to work left a decidedly sour taste in his mouth. 'But I don't want to. Taking care of Lee wore me out.'

'That poor man.' Sophie scrunched up her nose which, heaven help him, continued to be the cutest thing he'd seen in years. 'Do you think he's okay?'

'I think he's better at home than he was at work,' Mike said. 'I can't imagine going in to work like that.'

Sophie stood, stretched, and turned towards her living room. He caught a flash of the skin at the small of her back. He wondered how it felt. Soft – he bet it was soft.

Mike shoved himself off the counter, following her into the living area and sitting across from her on the couch. 'What about you? How are you doing on the work front?'

Sophie gave a little shrug. 'I'm fine. A post ahead, actually. The last few got a lot of responses,' she added, with a quirk of her lips. You're a popular addition.'

'Will you post about today?'

She tilted her head to the side. 'Maybe? Not with names, though. I took a few pictures of the food, but I generally don't post negative reviews unless there's a very good reason. Like if something is unsafe.'

'I would classify that meal as unsafe.' He shifted on the couch so that he was turned towards her, one arm resting on the back. 'Whoever created that menu should be forced to eat it.'

'They must have, to create it in the first place?' It was her turn to shift in her seat, readjusting herself to get more comfortable. Was she sitting closer now, or was that just Mike's imagination?

'There's nothing to say they have to eat it just because they made it,' Mike said. 'It's not like it's a legal obligation.'

'I can't believe I spat it back out.' Sophie gave a little laugh and rolled her eyes. 'It's a good thing we weren't on a date. That would have been mortifying. Nothing so sexy as your date coughing back up a bite of mystery meat tart.'

All the other words Sophie said seemed to sink slowly into the conversational ocean, except for the word 'sexy'. That one bobbed up high like it was its own little boat, and Mike responded without thinking. 'I don't think you could do a single thing that I wouldn't find sexy.'

Sophie's mouth, which had opened to say something, snapped back shut. Mike felt his pulse shoot up. It had been a stupid thing to say. Reckless. Possibly disastrous, especially in light of their agreement. But honest, no doubt about that.

'You're joking, surely?' Sophie said quietly.

She was throwing him a metaphorical rope – an easy out. Smile, laugh, shrug it off as a joke. Stay safe. No risks at all.

But no rewards, either.

Fuck. It.

'I've never been more honest in my life.' Mike could almost taste his own pulse now. He could hear the echoing drum in his ears. His skin felt hot, and he wanted . . .

He wanted.

He wasn't sure who sprang forward first. It didn't really matter. What mattered was her body in his arms. His mouth sliding over hers, hovering, his tongue delving deeper. She tasted like tea, like lemon, earthy and tart. He growled low in his throat, tugging her forward until she was in his lap.

Sophie squeaked, surprised, but didn't pull away. He plunged one hand into her hair, angling her head so he could kiss her deeper. With his other hand, he gripped her hip, encouraging her to settle in against him. Her weight felt so good, his palm moving with a will of its own, dipping back to caress the round globes of her arse.

Mike groaned, pulling away from the kiss to trace her jaw, her cheek, with his lips. Brushing his mouth over her brows, then back to her lips. She welcomed him, her hands in his hair. Her cool fingers sliding along the heated skin at the nape of his neck. She whimpered, a soft uncontrolled sound, making Mike feel like a king. A god.

The kiss became a frenzy. A thing of teeth, of tongue, a movement of pure sensation. He dipped down to her throat, licking the skin there, listening to her sharp, panting breaths.

She clutched him to her, rolling her hips.

Now it was Mike's turn to whimper, the movement feeling so unbelievably good. His hand slid up the back of her shirt, his fingers playing along that skin he'd caught sight of earlier. He'd been right – it was soft. Hot and silky. He wanted nothing more in life than to press his teeth to that spot – not enough to leave a mark, just enough to make her arch her back.

She was yanking his shirt out of his waistband, her own fingers searching for skin.

Her touch was a relief. A cooling rain on a hot night. Something both visceral and necessary. It felt *vital*.

He brushed his knuckles over her breasts, wondering the whole time what her nipples might look like. Small? Large? A blushing pink, rich red or deep brown? Somewhere in between? He was hard, so hard, and she was rubbing over him, there but not quite right. He needed it a little harder, needed her a little more centred.

He palmed her breasts, enjoying the weight of them, the feel through the layers of cloth. Then he slid his hands further down, his knuckles tracing her belly, while his fingers dipped below her waistband.

Her head dropped back, a breathy moan escaping her lips. She looked so beautiful like this – her cheeks flushed pink, her lips slightly parted. Her eyes were screwed shut in fierce concentration. Seeing her like this . . . Mike wanted nothing more than to see her release. To see her in that moment of bliss when nothing on the earth or in the heavens mattered beyond the pleasure sizzling through your veins.

'Sophie,' he breathed into her neck, nibbling along the skin. He slid a hand around, stroking a path from her back to her thigh. He wanted to touch her like this so much, so often, that the sensations, the muscle memory, burned into his brain. He wanted the feel of her tattooed along his skin, etched into his bones.

'Oh, god, Sophie.' His mouth was close to her ear now, the puff of his breath making her shiver. 'Let me make you feel good. Please. Let me do this.'

She made a soft sound, rolling her hips again and again.

He undid the button of her trousers and pulled down the zip. 'Is this okay? Tell me if you want me to stop, if you don't want it.'

She tugged on the hair on the nape of his neck, his name a whisper on her lips.

He could feel his pulse beating through his own body, every particle of him focused on her. He leaned back, his chest heaving, watching his own fingers, moving slowly in case she changed her mind. In case she'd decided this was far enough.

He caught a glimpse of purple, silky material and his mouth went dry. His voice, when he could finally get it out, was raspy and deep. His knuckles hovered over the purple cloth. 'I need to hear you say it, Sophie. Can I touch you?'

She hovered there, eyes hazy. Desire limned every curve of her body, every swoop and angle of her face, but she hesitated all the same.

Mike didn't move, didn't want to convince her with his body, which meant he had to find words, and he was historically bad at those. 'Whatever you want, Sophie.'

She caught her lower lip in her teeth, not quite looking at him.

He tipped her chin up with a gentle nudge of his fingers. 'I mean it. Whatever you want.'

Her gaze was steady as she examined him carefully. 'If I say we're done?'

'Then we're done.' He didn't even have to think about his answer. He was a little worried that she thought he might *have* another answer.

Her next question was more hesitant, unsure. Mike marvelled at it – so unlike the side she usually showed the world, brave and self-assured. 'If I only want to be held?'

'Then I'm a lucky man.' Mike couldn't help it then and rubbed a hand down her back, reassuring.

Sophie snorted a laugh, but he didn't think it was at him, more at some other situation or man in the past. 'And what do you want?'

'Oh,' he said with an offhand shrug. 'Indecent things. My mind is an absolute cesspit of sordid imaginings right now, that's just how it is.' He stroked her back again, just because he could.

She brushed back his hair with one hand, her fingers tracing his ear, his neck, causing him to shiver. 'You're a confusing man, Mike Tremblay.'

'I know.' That was the worst of it, really. He *did*.

Her expression was serious, but she was definitely laughing at him now somewhere inside herself, though not in a mean way. 'I'm going to kiss you anyway.'

'Oh, thank god.'

She leaned in but he met her halfway, folding her deeper into his arms, letting her guide the kiss. Things had cooled between them as they'd talked, but it was like a frost instantly melted by the touch of the sun, soon gone. Sophie took one of his hands, placing it back where it had been, and he could feel her smile as they kissed.

He traced her through the fabric, whisper-soft, not knowing what kind of contact she needed. He couldn't wait to find out. Mike had always been a good student, and he wanted nothing more than to learn what made this woman light up. Sophie shuddered, gasping and leaning in to his touch.

Mike swallowed, his throat feeling thick, his chest heavy. Any part of him not touching her felt too far away, the thin layers of cloth between them taking on the dimensions of chainmail.

A breathy moan escaped her lips as her head dropped forward, her hair hiding her face. Mike let her hide for now, concentrating on how she was moving; applying more pressure, moving in a way to match the thrust of her hips. He realized then that he was talking to her, all of his restraint being used up in order to keep himself in check, to stay where she needed him. Words normally kept behind clenched teeth were bubbling up, flowing towards her like it was the most natural thing in the world. An ancient spring, cutting through well-worn rock pathways as it sought the ocean.

Except his spring was apparently *filthy*, but Sophie didn't seem to mind, shivering under his hands as he spoke. 'So beautiful, so, so, oh god, yes – again. Fuck, Sophie, you're perfect. Let me look at you. I love watching you move. I love feeling you get wet. Is that for me, Sophie? All for me?' It was a litany of praise and suggestion and he couldn't stem it if he tried.

Sophie moaned and rocked harder, the material under his fingers soaked through. He sucked gently on the skin of her neck and nipped her ear. She kept her eyes closed, off in her own little world of pleasure.

Maybe he was selfish, but he didn't want that. He wanted her here, with him. For a brief, heady span of time, he wanted her thinking of no one but him. He wanted her to realize, beyond a shadow of a doubt, that she felt good because he made her feel that way.

He took his finger off the sweet spot, tracing around the material. With his other hand, he reached up and touched her chin, tipping it up until she had no choice but to look at him. Her mouth curved into a pout, her cheeks flushed, her pupils wide. Sophie Swann looked wrecked. Pride flared in his chest as he stole another kiss from that pouting mouth. 'You think you can come like this?'

'Not if you're not.' She huffed and he loved how petulant she sounded. Like he owed her something and she was completely put out that he wasn't delivering.

He traced the tips of his fingers feather light over her most responsive spots. She shuddered, a desperate whine trapped in her throat.

'I know, I'm being terrible darling, aren't I? You're right there. I can feel it.' He leaned in and licked her lower lip, sucking it between his teeth. He let it go slowly. 'So mean. You don't deserve such treatment.' Another feather-light caress, dipping away when she chased the movement with her hips. 'Look at me, darling. Look at me, and I'll let you. I want to see you come apart.'

She breathed deeply, her arms tightening around his neck, and looked him square in the eyes. She was so turned on, her pupils so wide, he could barely see the colour of her irises.

'There you are,' he said, moving his thumb slowly around where she needed it, just a few tight circles. Then he drew it back and tapped her clit hard with his thumb.

Then Sophie Swann came apart in his arms, her eyes glazed with pleasure, and his name on her lips.

Chapter Thirteen

After a night of amazingly heavy sleep, Sophie woke up early and video-called her best friend Edie.

It was a Sunday and Edie loved nothing more than moving as slowly as possible on such days, often lounging about in her sleepwear until late in the afternoon. So it wasn't entirely a surprise when she answered the call in a set of teal pyjamas, her small body swimming in a gold patterned robe. Edie's features were delicate, her nose tilted slightly at the end, and with her mass of auburn hair, Sophie always thought her friend looked rather like a woodland sprite, if woodland sprites had sharp tongues and the libido of a cat in heat.

Her hair was currently piled up high on her head in a messy heap, held together by a plastic clip. Thick blonde streaks twisted here and there through the mass.

'You got highlights,' Sophie said. 'Obviously. Sorry, the tea hasn't kicked in yet.' Likely because she was having a difficult time drinking it. Mike had tasted like tea yesterday. She mentally swerved away from that thought, returning to her best friend.

Edie smiled faintly. 'Reggie said he preferred "natural-looking women", whatever that means.'

'Ah,' Sophie said. 'So the streaks were a spite move?'

'No,' Edie said. 'I refuse to let a man have that much control over me. I'd been thinking about getting the streaks anyway. I just pushed the timeline forward. Me not wearing make-up to our last and likely final date will be my spite move.'

'You think you not wearing make-up will be a deal-breaker for him?' Sophie asked.

'No,' Edie said, laughing evilly into her coffee. 'He likes me too much. His comments happen to be a deal-breaker for me, however.'

'He lasted what, six whole weeks?'

'Seven,' Edie corrected. 'I must be getting more patient in my old age. How are you doing?' She squinted at the screen. 'You're looking a little washed out. Rough night's sleep?'

Sophie shook her head. 'No, I slept well.' Like a rock, actually. She didn't usually sleep that long or that heavily. 'I'm still tired this morning, though.'

'Go back to bed,' Edie said promptly.

'I might later.' Sophie settled deeper into her seat, wrapping her fingers around her mug.

Edie frowned at her. 'Okay, what's going on? You've got a' – she waved one hand around her face and shoulders in a rough circle – 'thing about you.'

Sophie took a deep breath, then mumbled a series of words into her tea that she wasn't sure even *she* could make out.

'I'm going to need that again,' Edie said impishly. 'Except slowly and with enunciation. Pretend that you actually want to tell me whatever it is you're struggling with.'

Sophie puffed out a breath. 'Fine.' With as few words as possible, and many, many intimate details left out, she went over the events of the night before.

'Dry-hump,' Edie said thoughtfully, as she stared at her cup, 'is a terrible phrase. It's better in French – *frottage*, I think.'

'The French have a word for everything,' Sophie muttered into her tea.

'Yes, love, that's how language does tend to work, having words for things.' Edie frowned, holding up a hand. 'Wait a moment, this is the same man who flipped out after a single kiss?'

Sophie wasn't entirely sure if she would classify their first kiss as a single *anything*, but nodded anyway.

Edie leaned closer to the screen, her entire focus on Sophie. 'He kissed you, flipped out, told you he was going to start his own monastery and die an untouched monk, apologized complete with friendship pact and blood offering, and then deliciously molested you on your sublet's couch?'

'I feel like at least half of that is nonsense, and molested is a terrible word that implies unwanted attention.' Sophie might not know entirely how she was feeling about yesterday, but unwanted wasn't part of the emotional tangle. No, his actions had been extremely wanted.

Edie rolled her eyes, set down her coffee and picked up her phone. When Sophie opened her mouth to speak, Edie held up a single finger, making her stop. She scrolled for a second, before lighting up with unholy satisfaction. 'Deliciously fondled, then; held you in a torrid embrace as you delightfully canoodled on the couch in your sublet.'

Sophie scowled at her. 'I'm taking away your thesaurus app. You clearly can't be trusted with even a sliver of power.'

'You got it on with a hot man and had what I am hoping was a spine-melting orgasm. He may be Captain Mixed Signals, but at least he delivered, yeah?'

Sophie thought about the way his eyes had blazed into hers as she fell apart on him. 'Yes, he delivered.'

'Did he, you know?' Edie made a vague gesture that Sophie wasn't sure how to interpret.

She gave it a shot anyway. 'Pet a duck? Play cricket? What are you doing?'

'Did it go both ways?' Edie tried one more time for subtle, mostly in deference to Sophie's slightly more delicate sensibilities, before giving up entirely and getting right to the meat of the matter. 'Did he have an orgasm? Did you take him to a state of bliss? Did you fondle his titbits?'

'Did I fondle his what?' Sophie shook her head. 'Hardly titbits.'

Edie raised her mug in salute. 'Good for him and hopefully good for future Sophie.'

Sophie traced the rim of her cup with her thumb. 'You don't think I should put a stop to things? Because of the mixed signals?'

Edie snorted. 'If that man managed to get you off using only his fingers while you were both fully dressed, I have high hopes for what he can do when he has his entire arsenal behind him. You deserve a good time after Asshole Andrew.'

'Marisa has been calling him the Wicker Man.'

Edie barked a laugh. 'I like her.'

'You really think it's okay?'

Edie pursed her lips. 'You don't have to marry the man. You don't even have to date him. He's only in the city for, what, two more weeks?'

'I'm not sure,' Sophie said, frowning. 'It depends on a few different things.'

'But he'll be there less time than you?'

'I think so.'

'Great,' Edie said, dancing in her seat. 'Better than great. Perfect. There's a built-in timeline. Have fun. End it when he leaves. Until then, emulate rabbits.'

'I'm not sure I can do that.' Sophie sighed.

Edie shrugged one shoulder. 'Won't find out until you try.'

Sophie bit her lip. 'I'll think about it.'

'You do that,' Edie said. 'In the meantime, go and take that nap. You're looking decidedly peaky.'

After signing off with Edie, Sophie took herself back to bed, surprised when she didn't wake up again until noon. She still felt exhausted. In fact, she felt worse than when she'd gone to bed. Her body felt heavy, her throat scratchy. Her nose was somehow stuffy and runny at the same time.

She must be getting ill. That might explain a little of her behaviour yesterday. She'd fallen asleep on the poor man. Had he been put out about that? Maybe he'd been expecting reciprocation? She curled deeper into her blankets, replaying yesterday afternoon in her head. She hadn't had any indication that he'd been upset. But maybe she'd missed it? She didn't entirely trust her gut still.

After she'd fallen asleep in his lap, he'd tucked her into bed, despite the early hour. She touched her temple, sure there had been some kind of kiss planted there before he'd left. Should she feel embarrassed by her actions? Did she owe him anything? With Andrew—

No.

No.

She wasn't even going to go there. Mike had offered – practically begged, if memory served. Sophie decided that until she learned otherwise, she would take the offer at face value: a thing freely given.

With that thought firmly in mind, she shuffled to the bathroom, took the last dose of the pain relief she'd brought with her from London, and dragged herself back to bed.

Mike didn't hear from Sophie the next morning, which was fine. Absolutely fine. It was her prerogative whether or not she wanted to talk to him. He could reach out first. It wasn't like he was a teenager any more, trying not to seem too keen by calling someone too soon. She was used to him messaging her by now, anyway, so he would text her at lunch. If she needed a little time to get to grips with what had happened, he could give her space.

He just wished he knew how she felt about everything. Mike knew how *he* felt about it. The mental film had been playing on a constant loop in his head. The blissed-out look on her face. The satisfying feeling of her in his lap, in his arms. The way she'd dozed against him, snoring lightly once or twice. He'd held her until his legs had gone to sleep.

Then he'd held her a little more.

Once he'd tucked her into bed, he'd pressed his lips to her forehead, closed his eyes and breathed her in. She'd smelled a little like him, and he'd liked that, too.

Then he'd let himself out of her flat, caught a cab and gone back to his place. He'd opened his front door with shaking hands, barely keeping it together at that point. As soon as he was inside, the door locked behind him, he went into the bathroom and proceeded to have what might have been the shortest wank in his entire life history. And that included his teenage years, which was saying something.

So no, he wasn't even a bit conflicted about what had happened the afternoon before. Far from it. In fact, he was more than a little obsessed. He wanted to do it again. Hopefully in more ways and with fewer clothes.

And he was really, really hoping she felt the same way and wasn't deleting his contact info from her phone for the way he'd handled, well, everything. So he decided to text her after lunch and take it from there.

Except he got swamped at work. He'd had to play a bit of catch-up from the day before, and it was almost teatime by the time he took a break. No messages from Sophie. Right. Well, it was possible she'd had a busy morning or was waiting for him to make the next move. It took him a few minutes to figure out what to say. Finally, he settled on something simple: *Thinking about you a lot today. Hope you're well.*

He sent it. Waited. No dots appeared. Well, she was hardly tethered to her phone. And while he was tempted to stare at it like some sort of lovesick adolescent, that would only drive him mad, and besides, he had more work to do.

He tucked his phone into his pocket and got back to it.

She didn't text all afternoon. His phone was maddeningly silent for the entire evening. By bedtime, he was feeling frustrated and concerned, his gut sinking as he stared at his blank screen. Maybe he'd overstepped? Maybe she hadn't really liked it. Maybe afterwards she'd been ashamed or embarrassed or unhappy or . . . something. Something that wasn't *happy*.

He blew out a long breath. Or maybe she was completely fine but hadn't been as blown away by it as he had. He ran a hand over his face, tired of his brain chasing itself in circles. He decided the decent thing to do was text her goodnight. Two texts wasn't veering into stalker territory.

Are we okay? Are you okay?

Nothing. Just a blank, mocking screen. He resolutely set it down, showered and brushed his teeth. Climbed into his cold, empty bed and plugged his phone into his charger. No response. Finally, he texted her *goodnight*, put his phone on do not disturb, and went to sleep.

In the morning, his phone was still silent, except for a message from Rahul sharing some photos of Stella and Archie. An hour later, Amaya sent him a photo of his plant, Barney – she'd written his name on the pot. She'd also added a small plastic dinosaur, standing it in the dirt. He was pretty sure it was a brontosaurus.

But no message from Sophie.

He copied the photo of Barney, dropped it into their chat and added *good morning* under the photo. Once it was sent, he went about his morning routine, diving quickly into work. He surfaced around two o'clock for lunch. No texts.

Was he getting ghosted? It wouldn't be the first time in his life that had happened, though he'd been lucky that he'd only had to deal with it once when he was seventeen and Margo Flanagan had ditched him for her ex-boyfriend, deciding there was no reason to tell Mike any of this first.

But that . . . didn't seem like Sophie. Rather than grassing on Lee to his boss, she'd helped get him safely back to his flat. She'd got on a plane, something she was terrified of, just to be there for her kids in their time of need.

She'd forgiven him when he'd been an absolute fucking muppet.

What she *hadn't* done was ignore him. So this . . . this felt off.

Something was wrong. Maybe her phone was broken? Maybe something had happened to her kids? But he just couldn't see her ghosting him.

By the evening, he was decidedly uneasy.

By the following morning, he was checking his phone every two minutes.

And by nightfall, he couldn't shake the frantic, uneasy feeling seeping into his bones. He'd been going back and forth with himself all day – he was probably overreacting. It had only been, what, forty-eight hours? She was a grown woman with things to do and didn't owe him anything. She hadn't promised him anything. It wasn't like they were dating. But all of those perfectly logical, rational statements felt like the thinnest tissue paper, tearing under the relentless feeling that *something was wrong*. That Sophie would *answer her fucking phone, even just to tell him to leave her alone.*

He could text Tom. Mike had his number in his phone, but at this point Mike wouldn't feel better until he saw Sophie with his own eyes. He didn't bother getting out of his suit, just grabbed his jacket and headed to her flat. If he was overreacting, they could have a good laugh over it, or she could tell him to lose her number. He'd deal with it if those were the outcomes, but at least then he'd know she was okay.

It was raining – of course it was raining – and despite catching a Lyft by the time he got to her flat, his hair was flat against his skull and his jacket soaked through. When he got to her door, he knocked quietly at first, then a little more firmly. No one answered. Had she gone? Was she at her son's flat? He could check – he knew which flat they were in, after all. Or he could knock on her neighbour's door, see if he'd heard from Sophie.

Mike gave a third and final knock, and was somewhat surprised when the door opened.

Sophie stood wrapped in a blanket looking like a furry caterpillar. She blinked up at him owlishly, her eyes glazed, her cheeks a florid pink. A sheen of sweat coated her face, but she shivered as she pulled the blanket tighter. 'Mike?' She licked her dry lips. 'What – why?'

'Sophie, are you sick?' Without waiting for a response, he reached out and put a palm on her forehead. His hand was chilled from the rain, but it felt to him like she was burning up. Sophie leaned into his hand like a cat, but didn't answer him.

He shook his head. 'Come on, back inside. Let's get you settled.'

She let him herd her back into the flat. Mike stripped out of his wet jacket and hung it up while toeing off his shoes. He wouldn't help her by dripping all over her.

'Sit on the couch,' he said, heading for the bathroom. Once inside, he grabbed a towel and dried his hair as best he could before going through the drawers and cabinets. No thermometer. He frowned. No medicine, either, except for a few antacids and a bottle of eye drops.

He hung up the towel and headed back into the living room. Sophie was sprawled on the couch, using a paper towel to wipe her nose. An empty box of tissues sat on the table next to a disturbingly large pile of used tissues and a mostly empty glass of water.

Mike sat on the edge of the couch and put his hand back on her forehead to see if she felt different now that his hand wasn't impersonating an ice lolly. Still hot. 'Sophie, do you have any cold medication?'

She mumbled and had to say it twice before he caught it. 'No.'

'When's the last time you took something?'

She squinted at him, thinking hard, a shiver shaking her body. 'Don't know.'

'Have you eaten?' He wasn't feeling good about the answer.

'Not hungry,' Sophie rasped, right before she covered her mouth with her blanket and started coughing.

Mike brushed some of the sweat-damp hair back from her forehead. 'Okay, I'm going to go down to the shop and get supplies. Are you allergic to anything?'

She shook her head, her lips curved down into a miserable pout.

'Good. I'll be right back.' He stood up, grimacing at the idea of putting his wet jacket and shoes back on. Not that he had another option. 'Do you have keys? That way I can let myself back in without getting you up.'

Sophie waved in the vicinity of the table before burrowing unhappily back under her blankets.

It took Mike a few seconds to find the keys. Then he moved quickly, tempted to run down to the store, though he kept the urge in check. He wouldn't be much use to Sophie if he slipped on the wet pavement and broke his bloody hip.

Once he was under the florescent lights of the shop, he grabbed a pack of lozenges and a box of tissues. He had to ask for a little help from the assistant to figure out what medicines to get – the packages and names were different from what he was used to at home. Then he paid for them before rushing back to the flat.

He let himself in, grabbing Sophie's glass and refilling it with water. 'You'll need to sit up for a moment to take the pills. Then I promise you can lie back down.' Sophie dutifully eased herself up, but that was all he got for a response. He handed her the glass of water and two pain relief tablets that the assistant had told him would hopefully work for her fever.

She tossed them into her mouth and drank half the glass of water before shoving it at Mike. As soon as it was in his hand, she collapsed back onto the couch, shuddering under her blanket. Mike spent the next few minutes getting her sorted – used tissues in the bin, new box on the table, along with a small plastic bin for the next round of tissues. After washing his hands thoroughly, he checked her cabinets and fridge. He found an empty box of camomile tea, a little honey but no lemon, juice, and a mostly empty fridge.

He frowned at that. Had she been sick like this the whole time, then? He was starting to think she had been. Mike wasn't sure why she hadn't called her son, or even him. Had she been loath to ask for help, or too out of it? He'd find out later. In the meantime, he picked up his phone and started ordering things from a grocery delivery app. The store had some things, but he didn't want to go back there and leave her, and it wouldn't have everything he wanted anyway.

While he waited for the order, he checked her room. If she'd been sweating and feverish for two days, she'd probably spent a lot of that in bed, and likely hadn't had the energy to change the sheets. She'd managed to get into her pyjamas at some point, the clothes from their disastrous – and then glorious – tea date strewn on the floor. He put those in the laundry basket, stripped her bed and put on fresh sheets.

After that, he checked on her again. She still looked sweaty and miserable. He refilled her water and then got a damp flannel, folded it and pressed it to her forehead. Since Sophie was stretched out and cocooned in blankets, there wasn't much room on the small couch , so he sat on the coffee table and held it there.

About thirty minutes later, she'd cooled down a bit and wanted to get back into her bed. He helped her to her room, stepping out when she got in there because she wanted to put on a pair of clean pyjamas. That didn't entirely go to plan, and Mike ended up having to help her get them on. Then he got her back into bed and tucked in, asleep almost as soon as her head hit the pillow.

By then the grocery order had arrived. Mike put away the juice and a few other things he'd got her, including ginger ale and some fresh fruit, but left out the tea, honey and lemons. At that point, he rolled up his sleeves and went back through the cupboards looking for a pot. It was late, but he had no idea what her sleep schedule had been like, or if she'd wake up hungry soon. If he started the soup now, it could simmer and be ready for when she resurfaced. He diced up onions, carrots, garlic and celery, sautéing them while he started prepping the chicken.

After he'd added in the broth, he left it to simmer, once again washing his hands before going in to check on Sophie. She snored softly while he put his hand on her forehead, rechecking her temperature. Cooler, but still warm. At least her fever was responding to the medicine. He opened the packaging to the new thermometer, placing it on the bedside table along with another new box of tissues.

He'd done all he could at that point, so he went back to check the soup. He stirred it, dropping down the temperature to low. Then he went to the couch, grabbed the TV remote and started looking for something to watch to keep him company during what was likely to be a very long night.

Chapter Fourteen

When Sophie woke, she spent a few moments wondering what possible reason there might be, from an evolutionary standpoint, for people to have bad breath. She was positive hers was wretched. Her tongue felt somehow both gummy and thick, like it had been tarred, feathered and topped with a thick duvet cover. Everything ached, she couldn't breathe through her nose, and even though she hadn't opened her eyes yet, she was considering going back to sleep.

She could also hear someone snoring. Not a loud chainsaw of a noise, nor a soft wuffle like her childhood dog used to make, but somewhere in between. For a brief, disorienting moment, she thought it might be Andrew. Who else would be sleeping by her?

Then she remembered the affair, subsequent divorce, and her current near overwhelming desire to staple his bollocks to his front porch. So no, it wouldn't be Andrew.

Sophie cracked open her eyes. Mike lay curled on the bed next to her on top of the covers, fully clothed. He was facing her, his head on the pillow. His hair was tousled, his lashes lying in a dark crescent against his skin. She noted with some amusement that even in his sleep, he seemed concerned, a small divot appearing between his brows, and his stubble had gone far past the five o'clock mark, leaning heavily towards the wee hours of the morning.

He looked tired but handsome and Sophie wondered why on earth he was in her bed.

After a few seconds of her staring at him, Mike seemed to sense her attention and blinked open his eyes. He stared back at her for a moment, his expression muzzy, before his gaze cleared.

'How are you feeling?' The question came out gravelly, sleep-sanded and rough.

And she liked it. She liked hearing him like this and knowing that not everyone got to hear the way he sounded first thing in the morning. Then she remembered he'd asked her a question. 'Like death warmed up, left out, warmed up again, frozen, and then tossed in the bin.'

One corner of his lip curled up. 'A little better then.'

'What makes you say that?'

'Because I got a full sentence that time instead of a mono-syllable.' He reached out and touched her forehead, concern pinching his features. 'Not entirely cool, but you're not as warm as you were. Sit up and I'll take your temperature.' He checked his watch. 'You're due another dose of medicine, too.'

She levered herself up, surprised at how weak and shaky her arms felt. Mike rolled off the bed, bringing her two pills and the thermometer, which he placed in her mouth. When it beeped, he traded it for the pills and water.

He read the digital screen, a slight frown on his face. 'Still a little over a hundred.' He eyed her, assessing. 'Do you feel up to some soup? Or tea? I got you some more camomile. I can put some honey and lemon in it, which will make your throat feel better.'

'You missed your calling,' Sophie said, letting her eyes drift shut for a moment. 'You should have been a nurse.'

'I would make a terrible nurse. People would probably die.'

'I don't believe that for a second. You're too efficient.'

Mike set the thermometer on the bedside table. 'Perhaps, but I also lack patience with most humans, and I find that to be something nurses need a great deal of. What's it to be first – tea or soup?'

'Tea, please.' Sophie watched Mike walk to the door, because even in wrinkled suit trousers, he still had an incredible arse. Quite possibly the world's greatest.

He turned at the threshold and caught her watching him. A slow grin unfurled on his face. 'Lemon and honey acceptable?'

Sophie refused to feel embarrassed about being caught out, so she just nodded and closed her eyes to rest until he came back.

Mike brought her tea, and as soon as she'd drunk some of that down, he brought her a bowl of soup.

She hadn't thought she was hungry, but once she'd started eating the chicken soup he'd brought her, she felt suddenly ravenous. She polished it off quickly, listening as Mike moved around the kitchen with a quiet symphony of cabinet doors and cutlery. When he returned, she was holding the empty bowl in her hands, not quite sure what to do with it.

For some reason, Mike seemed amused by this. 'Would you like more?'

Sophie shook her head. 'Not yet. I was just thinking about the fact that I couldn't remember the last time I'd had breakfast – or I guess dinner? – in bed.'

Mike took her bowl from her. 'To be honest, I've never much cared for it. I always seem to get crumbs in the sheets or spill something, or I get so nervous about doing those things that there's no joy in it.'

'I hate it when I do that – kill my own joy.' Sophie pulled the blankets up higher, though she stayed sitting up. 'Well, it was very good soup, and I don't think I spilled any. Did you get it at the shop?'

Mike shook his head. 'I made it.'

Sophie blinked at him. 'You made it?'

Her question seemed to amuse him, earning her a faint smile. 'Yes,' he said, slowly drawing out the word. He waved a hand at her. 'Why the face? Because that's a very sceptical face.'

'I guess I'm just surprised.'

'That I made soup, or that I made *you* soup?' Mike asked.

Sophie thought about it. 'Both, I suppose. Does it matter?'

'The first could be a little offensive, like you're assuming that I don't know how to cook, but the second . . .' He shook his head again. 'I should keep my mouth shut.'

She'd forgotten that he'd said he could cook – though he'd said he was mediocre, and that soup hadn't tasted mediocre. 'Please don't. It will bother me all day, wondering what you were going to say.'

He sighed. 'The second either indicates that you don't think *I* would be willing to put in the effort to make you a bowl of soup, which is not so much insulting as it is hurtful, or it indicates that you're simply not used to anyone taking care of you at all.' He grimaced. 'I'm afraid that last one makes me a little angry.'

She frowned up at him. 'Why would that make you angry?'

Mike huffed out another breath, strode over and dropped a kiss onto the top of her hair. 'Because you deserve a little effort, Sophie Swann.' And with that, he left the room to deal with the empty bowl, his shoulders tense, his movements clipped.

And Sophie . . . well, she wasn't entirely sure what to make of his behaviour. Despite that uncertainty, however, she felt his words settle into her mind, sinking deep into the fathoms, where they became a little light in the darkness.

When she woke again, she felt a thousand times better. She was also sprawled across Mike, her head on his shirt, which was looking decidedly the worse for wear at this point. The heat of him radiated through the thin material, warming her. His heart beat a steady thump against her ear. She could also hear rain coming down outside the window of her flat, and she lay there for a long time, soaking in the atmosphere and thinking about how cosy she felt. She felt cosseted, warm – taken care of.

It felt wonderful. It felt *essential*.

She couldn't remember the last time she'd felt like this. Edie often did little things for her – picking up her favourite treat from the market or getting flowers for her room. That kind of care had felt essential in a different way. Edie was a bedrock of her life, a friend that she hoped she deserved. Sophie hadn't been ill since she'd moved in with Edie, though her friend had been there for her completely with emotional support, a never-ending supply of tissues and the number for a good lawyer. All of which had been sadly necessary.

But she'd never had the opportunity to take care of Sophie when she was ill. Andrew had, of course, but he'd never done much beyond fetching medicine from the chemist. He'd certainly never cooked for her. So when she tried to cast her mind back over the years to figure out when she'd last been cared for like this, she came up blank.

Which was a depressing thought. What Mike had done shouldn't feel extraordinary. She certainly wouldn't think twice before she cooked for someone who was ill or fetched them things. Except no one had done those things for her. Which was kind of sad, if she was honest. Mike was right. She deserved a little effort.

The one warming thought that came from all of his ruminating was the fact that she'd seen many instances of Tom taking care of Marisa and vice versa. *That's how it should be. If you have a partner, they should be there when you stumble. You should be there when they stumble, too.*

Sophie Swann had considered herself a partner in her marriage, but it suddenly became clear as freshly cleaned glass that she'd never had one herself. She'd had a husband, sure, but not a *partner*.

Oh, she'd figured out long ago that Andrew was an absolute arsehole. But in the messy grief of the dissolution of her marriage, she'd never really come to terms with the fact that she'd been overwhelmingly and disastrously let down by someone who should have been there for her.

Following quickly on the heels of that was this revolutionary and exciting realization that she hadn't done a single thing to deserve any of it.

She had done nothing wrong except try hard with someone who hadn't deserved her effort.

It was a bit of a kick in the gut, if she was honest.

Sophie wasn't sure how long she lay there, dazed with this new thought before she felt the muscles under her shift as Mike moved, his fingers coming up and brushing back her hair.

'I can practically hear you thinking right now.' The sleepy gravel voice was back, much to her delight.

Sophie made a noncommittal noise. His fingers kept sifting through her hair, which made her close her eyes as she enjoyed the simple pleasure of the touch.

'Do you need to talk about it?'

'Maybe. Not yet. Still processing.'

Mike hummed thoughtfully and she could feel the vibration of it. 'Do we still feel like death warmed up?'

'No,' she said. 'We are feeling quite disgusting, though, and hoping our hair isn't greasy at this particular moment.'

Mike laughed. 'Your hair's fine, but I imagine a shower would feel heavenly for you at this point. Feel up to one?'

Was that an offer? She didn't think so – surely he couldn't find her attractive right now. She raised herself up, a dubious expression on her face. Which set him off on another spate of laughter, though this one was mostly silent, his chest shaking under her hand.

'The look on your face. I didn't mean anything salacious by it. You go and get washed. I'll check my email and catch up a little bit.'

She blinked at him. 'Were you supposed to be at work?'

Mike sobered, several emotions imprinting so softly and so quickly across his face that she wasn't sure she caught them, but it gave her the impression that he felt uncomfortable about his answer.

'They don't need me there twenty-four hours a day,' Mike said finally. 'And I'm ahead of schedule, which is a miracle in itself.'

'You don't need to justify your choices to me,' she said, pushing herself to her feet. She wobbled a little and Mike reached out quickly to steady her. 'It was just a question.'

After assessing her steadiness, he stepped back, dropping his hands. 'Go and shower and walk once again among the living. I'll get my laptop.'

The shower felt like magic. Sophie washed her hair and revelled in the remnants of fever sweat and sickness sliding away from her and circling down the drain. By the time she stepped out, she didn't feel one hundred per cent again, but she at least felt mostly human. She dried off, then pulled on fresh pyjamas, leaving the dirty ones on the floor. It felt weird to do that – she was a tidy person – but also wonderful to acknowledge the fact that it was her choice to do so, and no one could complain about it.

It was with renewed spirits that she stepped into her current living room, brushing out her damp hair. Mike was frowning at his laptop, focused and far away in his abstraction. Sophie stole this moment to stare at him openly, taking in the breath-stealing delicious state that was Michael Tremblay, dishevelled. He'd been snatching sleep while he took care of her and she could see it in the faint bruising under his eyes. His hair stuck up at the back, the front ruffled by his fingers, which were now rubbing absently at his stubble.

This moment here, seeing him like this, was enough to make her want him, even half sick and exhausted. She was beginning to think that even on her deathbed, she'd want him enough to use her dying breath to ask him to take off his shirt.

If it had only been about physical attraction, she could have resisted him easily. Or at least taken what she wanted without compunction. But it wasn't only that. Sophie may have had her trust blown to smithereens, and she might not have any faith whatsoever in her own judgement right now, but despite that, she was growing more certain by the day that Mike was a decent man. A good man. She just wasn't sure if he was *her* man, or if she even wanted that right now.

She made an irritated noise – she was so tired of being a mess.

The sound caused Mike to look up, smiling automatically at the sight of her. Like he couldn't help it.

'Do you feel like a brand-new woman?'

Sophie stopped rubbing at her head with her towel. 'Pardon?'

Mike grimaced. 'Something my grandma used to say after we had a shower. She'd ask if we felt like a brand-new person.' He shook his head. 'Ignore my ramblings.'

'I don't think I will.' Sophie went back to drying her hair. 'Because I do. I feel like a brand-new woman.' And it wasn't just because she'd had a truly good shower. It was, well, everything. But before she could say another word, there was a knock at her door.

She frowned, but Mike was already standing, waving her away.

'I'll get it,' he said, snapping his laptop closed. 'You finish what you're doing.' He strode to the door before she could argue, not that she wanted to, and she took another opportunity to watch the world's greatest backside moving away from her.

Chapter Fifteen

Mike had checked the peephole before he opened the door, so he wasn't surprised to see Sophie's son Tom standing in the hallway. It was abundantly clear by the baffled expression on Tom's face that he hadn't been expecting to see *Mike*.

'You,' Tom said, 'are not my mother.' He held his phone out like he'd been about to hand it to someone. One single brow slowly went up. 'Where *is* my mother?' His gaze dropped down and seemed to take in Mike's rumpled and probably unsavoury appearance and got entirely the wrong impression. 'And why are you here?'

Mike couldn't bring himself to be affronted by this, because if he was being honest, he wished he *had* been opening the door after an evening of torridly sweaty sex. He wanted an evening that could only be described as *carnal*. He wanted Sophie with such a blinding intensity that he was certain that if she'd been well, they'd have done things in her flat that would break *laws*.

This sudden frustration coupled with an instinctive need to protect her well-being – she was only now feeling better and she shouldn't have to deal with anything – made his voice sharp. 'Yes, me.' He wanted to growl that it was none of Tom's bloody fucking business why he was there, except Sophie had been ill, her son obviously cared for her, and so it was, in fact, kind of his business.

He sighed, letting his misplaced irritation go. 'Sophie's been ill, so I came to help. She's only just started feeling better, so if this can wait—'

To his credit, Tom was instantly concerned. 'She was ill? Is she okay?'

'Better, yes,' Mike said quietly. 'Her fever has gone and she's had some soup.'

Tom blew out a breath. 'Good. That's good.' He glanced at his phone, his face twisting into a scowl. 'I'm afraid she won't thank me for waiting. Not on this.'

Mike nodded, stepping back to let Tom into the flat.

Sophie was sitting at the table, attempting to plait her wet hair. 'Tom! What a surprise. Well, I guess it's not really a surprise since you're only one floor away, but still.' Her bright expression dimmed. 'Are you okay? Is there something wrong with Marisa?'

Tom pulled up a chair at the table. 'I tried texting you, but you didn't answer.'

'Her phone was dead,' Mike said. 'I put it on the charger, but she's been out of it and I'm afraid I didn't hear it ping at all.'

'I probably had it on silent,' Sophie said.

Mike went and fetched it for her, before heading back into the kitchenette to put the kettle on. From Tom's demeanour, he had a feeling this was a conversation that was going to call for tea.

Sophie, for her part, sounded calm as ever. 'I know that face. What is it, then?'

Tom shook his head, tapped his phone awake and shoved it towards her, his entire body stiff with barely suppressed rage.

Sophie took the phone from him, concern lining every feature, as she peered at the screen.

Then, what little colour she'd managed to regain from soup, fluids and rest, drained from her face. Her hand trembled as she held the phone, her eyes slowly sliding shut.

Mike didn't stop to think twice as he stepped forward and plucked the phone from her loose fingers. He sent a questioning look to Tom, who was holding himself tight and chewing on his lip. Tom managed a terse nod of permission, which was good, because Mike was pretty sure nothing was going to keep him from looking at whatever had bled the joy from Sophie's face.

The phone was open to Tom's Instagram. It was a photo of a man, probably in his late fifties, handsome in a bland, generic kind of way. His arm was around what appeared to be a much younger woman – thirty, perhaps. Her hair was bobbed and sleek, her smile wide as she stared up at the man with open adoration. They were both holding a photo. Mike fished his reading glasses out of his shirt pocket and looked more carefully. Was that an ultrasound photo? He peered down at the text below the photo.

These Swanns are nesting! Can't wait to grow our little family with the greatest man on earth. Thanks for making my dreams come true, Honey Bear.

The endearment 'Honey Bear' was a bit insipid, but nothing to cause the reaction the post was getting from Sophie and Tom. Mike stayed confused until he glanced at the account name, *LiveLaughLori* – or more importantly, the person she'd tagged in the photo, *Andrew Swann*.

Oh.

Oh *no*.

He clicked the phone off, the sound loud in the otherwise silent room.

Sophie had frozen like some sort of ice sculpture while Tom was practically vibrating with anger.

Mike wasn't sure what to do. Did Sophie want comfort? Would she want it from him? He would understand if she never wanted to see another man in her life after that post. The kettle whistled and he escaped for a moment to the kitchen, preparing three mugs of tea before returning to the table. Tom had collapsed in his chair, slumping in defeat, but otherwise the scene was the same.

He set mugs in front of both of them, set his on the table, then took Sophie's hand and lowered himself onto his haunches so he could see up into her face. He wasn't sure what to say. 'Are you okay?' would be a ridiculous question, because of course she wasn't. He finally settled on, 'What do you need?'

She blinked at him, her eyes dry, probably still in shock. 'I don't know.'

Tom rubbed his eyes with the heels of his hands. 'He didn't even tell us he'd remarried, let alone—' He growled and dropped his hands. 'A phone call. Would it be so bloody hard for him to pick up a phone and *call*? He knows, he *knows* what we've been going through, and I'm not saying people can't be happy about things going well for them, but for fuck's sake. I don't even follow her. It showed up because she tagged him.'

Sophie didn't say anything. Her hand in his was icy, and Mike sandwiched it between both of his and tried to rub some warmth into it.

'Marisa's gutted. If he'd just called . . . But we weren't prepared for it. Completely blindsided.' Tom bit off the last word, his jaw tight. He rubbed a weary hand over his face. 'I'm too old to get a surprise sibling.'

Sophie sniffed, then spoke with a quiet voice. 'Remember when you were little and I asked you if you wanted one?'

Tom's expression softened, a faint smile tugging at his mouth. 'I told you I'd rather get a dog. Gemma Davies had been showing off her new puppy and I was extremely jealous.' He reached out and took the hand that Mike wasn't holding and squeezed it. 'I still think I'd rather get a dog.'

Sophie burst out laughing then, though it sounded a little wet, like there might have been some tears mixed in. She laughed until she started hiccupping. 'I'm just.' *Hiccup.* 'So.' *Hiccup.* 'Angry.'

'Livid,' Tom said, giving her hand another squeeze before dropping it so he could clasp his mug, taking a long sip. 'Marisa was quiet when I left. I'm worried about her. I'd have felt a lot better if she'd been screaming into a pillow or even throwing things.' He sighed, his voice going quiet and sad. 'She's still so angry, which is fine, but she's not letting it out.'

The room grew quiet again, Tom and Sophie struggling with this new, unwelcome information. They were both so crushed and Mike wasn't sure what to do. If Rahul had been there instead of Tom, Mike would have hugged him, or at least squeezed his arm or his hand, something to let him know he wasn't alone. Only Mike wasn't Tom's father – which was good, because Tom's father was a complete prat – and to Tom, Mike was basically a stranger.

Fuck it. Mike reached out and squeezed Tom's shoulder. 'I'm sorry your father is being an absolute bell end.'

Tom barked a laugh, the sound obviously surprising him.

Mike dropped his hand, his attention going to Sophie, who was trying to sip her tea even though she was still hiccupping. The tension in the room had dropped, but Mike could still feel the anger, the hurt, flowing off them in waves. They were still holding themselves so tightly, keeping all those overwhelming emotions in.

This, at least, was something Mike understood. How many times had he sat just like this, a toxic mix of grief and rage bubbling up inside him like acid, eating away at his insides until he was hollowed by it. *Content* to be hollowed by it, even, because that meant those corrosive, terrible emotions wouldn't splash over onto his children. They'd had enough grief of their own.

Except he didn't want that for Sophie, or Tom and Marisa. While Tara had been worth the grief, Andrew Swann absolutely wasn't worth this kind of pain. He knew Andrew wasn't the only subject of grief here, but he thought Tom was right – Marisa needed an outlet.

And Mike . . . had an idea. He wasn't sure they'd go for it, but it wouldn't hurt to put it forward. He cleared his throat. 'I have an idea, if you're up for hearing it.'

Sophie continued to hiccup, but he had her attention now.

'Mum, hold your breath,' Tom said, his voice weary now. 'That always helps me.'

'Amaya – that's my daughter,' he threw in for Tom's benefit, 'told me about this place her friend went to after a bad break-up. I thought it might be fun for Sophie's blog, so I looked it up to see if there was one in New York. There is.'

Tom rested his chin in his hand, frowning. 'What kind of place?'

'They're called rage rooms. You go to these places and they put you in safety gear and give you a crowbar or a cricket bat or whatever and turn you loose in a room. Then you smash things. Supposed to be very cathartic.'

'Smash things?' Sophie asked. 'What kind of things?'

Mike shrugged. 'Dishes, printers, whatever they have.'

Sophie turned to Tom.

Tom tilted his head to the side, considering. Finally, he looked at Mike. 'Couldn't hurt.'

Mike pulled up the website on his phone. 'I'll book us a slot.'

Chapter Sixteen

Sophie adjusted the safety glasses on her head, the clear plastic doing nothing to obscure the room they were all in. The gloves felt loose, so she tightened the straps on her wrists. The baseball bat felt solid in her hands when she picked it up. All in all, she felt better, stronger, more steady than she had in ages, like at any moment roots might shoot out of her feet, snarling into the earth below her.

It was possible that the cold medication was making her a little loopy.

Marisa stood next to her, a crowbar in her hands. She looked determined and not a little bit scary. Tom didn't seem to think anything of the fierce expression on his fiancée's face as he leaned down to press his lips to her temple. That earned him a brief flash of a smile.

Mike stood on Sophie's other side, spinning a cricket bat experimentally in his hands as if testing its weight. 'Do they even have cricket over here?'

'Not that I've seen,' Tom said. 'But I also haven't been looking.'

Mike hummed thoughtfully as he examined his bat, then turned his attention to Sophie. 'How are you feeling?'

'Powerful,' Sophie said. 'And a bit sweaty in this get-up.'

'But you're feeling well?' Mike asked. 'You're not pushing it?'

Sophie shook her head. She'd managed a quick nap and another bowl of soup before leaving her flat. She didn't feel totally well, but she was on the mend and well enough for this.

'It looks like we're about to go collect forensic evidence or clean crime scenes,' Marisa said. 'Or maybe create crime scenes.'

'You *really* need to stop watching all of the true crime shows,' Sophie said. 'If that was your first thought.'

Marisa eyed her. 'Oh really? And what was yours?'

Sophie sighed. 'Like we're about to clean up a crime scene.'

'Pretty sure crime scene techs don't have baseball bats,' Tom said. 'But maybe they should.'

Kim, the woman in charge of their session, came back into the room and clapped her hands. 'Okay, waivers are all signed and you're good to go. Anyone have any questions about the rules, or anything else?'

No one did, so Kim barrelled forward. 'The room's big, but it's not infinite. Be aware of where the members of your party are at all times. It's not fun if someone ends up in the emergency room. You have thirty minutes. If you need anything, hit the intercom, otherwise have fun, kids!'

Kim went through the door with a cheery wave, leaving them alone in a white room which was bare except for a wall-mounted shelf with a few other weapons for their use, as well as a table with some mismatched plates, and a box full of electronics and other items for them to destroy. A single, lonely printer rested on the floor next to the table. The room was very quiet, possibly soundproofed, making the thud of Sophie's bat hitting the ground as she tapped the floor with it echo loudly.

'So,' Tom said. 'Who goes first? I was thinking—'

Marisa let out a guttural yell, raised her crowbar and rushed the printer. She slammed the crowbar down onto the casing as she screamed, the plastic shell quickly shattering underneath the force of the metal. The rest of them remained quiet, unmoving, as Marisa screamed, her teeth bared, the metal bar flashing as she brought it down over and over again. The printer bounced with the force, pieces flying this way and that. Marisa didn't even seem to notice. She kept hitting the printer, venting her rage, until there was nothing left but a pile of mutilated plastic.

Then she straightened, her breath coming in short pants, a smile on her face. 'That was *amazing*.'

Tom grinned. 'I guess Marisa goes first.'

Marisa put one hand on her hip as she caught her breath. 'Okay, Sophie's up. What's your flavour? Office machinery? Dishes? I think I saw an old phone in the box.' Marisa's grin widened. '*Or*, you could go for door number three.'

She sauntered over to the wall where a paper bag rested next to the door. Marisa had brought it with her but had refused to show it to anyone until now. She pulled out a framed picture of Andrew with the words 'Mr Wicker Man' written across the bottom of the picture with a blue marker.

'Did you just have that lying around?' Mike asked.

Marisa shook her head. 'I printed it out, but I *did* have the cheap plastic frame. I checked with Kim before I brought it in. There's no glass, so we're more than welcome to destroy it along with the stuff they've provided.'

Sophie hefted her bat. 'I think I'd like to work up to that. How about we start small with a plate?'

Mike grabbed one of the plates. 'Do you want to throw it against the wall or smash it with the bat?'

Sophie licked her lips. 'Both?'

Mike snatched another plate. 'As my lady wishes.'

He placed the first plate on the floor and stood back.

Sophie brought the bat down hard, the plate shattering with a ceramic shriek. Elation sizzled along her skin. Sophie had broken lots of things in her life, but never on purpose. Never for *fun*. It felt delicious. Freeing. And she wanted more of it. She brought the tip of the bat down against the larger pieces of the plate, smashing each bit with a satisfying *crunch*. When the plate was nothing but shards, she held out her hand. Mike carefully placed the next plate into it and once again stepped back.

Sophie drew back her arm, moving her whole body until its shape revealed its new true purpose – to hurl crockery with force. She took a long, deep breath. Then she snapped her arm forward, the plate whizzing through the air. It exploded when it hit the wall, shattering into fragments and splinters of its former self. Sophie straightened, her breathing a little wobbly. She felt so . . . free. So good. It was like she was drunk on destruction. Who knew that breaking things could feel so wonderful? She felt like she could leap over buildings.

Tom went next, choosing a computer keyboard for his object. Sophie thought it was pretty satisfying, watching the keys fly every which way as he demolished the keyboard. When he was done, it was hardly recognizable. It always amazed her how much effort it took to make something, how difficult it was to create, but how easy it was to destroy. A factory somewhere had made that keyboard, the machines humming under the watchful eye of an employee. It took parts, labour, skill and time to build. But all it took to destroy it was an angry young man and a few seconds with a baseball bat.

Mike took on what she was pretty sure was a fax machine – although to be honest, she didn't think it mattered what it started out as. The important thing was that by the time Mike had finished hitting it, all that was left was rubbish. Sophie wasn't sure what it said about her that she enjoyed watching Mike bring the cricket bat down with such force, his teeth bared, but there was poetry in his motions. The smooth way his arms swung. The way his back arched on the follow-through to the floor. The satisfying grunt he made when the wood connected with the plastic and metal was almost sexual.

Was that weird? It probably was weird, but she couldn't bring herself to give a single fuck about it.

Watching Mike was *fun*. Maybe it was because he was normally such a careful and controlled man. Maybe it was because he usually moved so gently through the world, quietly righting things one hug and homemade meal at a time. She wasn't sure what it was, but watching him let some of that careful control slip was heady to behold.

The next twenty minutes was an orgy of destruction. More smashed plates, crushed technology, and a truly disturbing amount of giggling.

They saved the picture frame till last.

When Mike put it in the centre of the room, they all waited a moment, like this was a wake and Mike was about to deliver a eulogy. Maybe it kind of was, in a way. Her old life, her old relationship, was officially dead. She never had to see Andrew again if she didn't want to. Never had to make his dinner, pick up his socks that somehow ended up under the sofa all the time, or watch tennis with him on the telly.

As Sophie looked at her son's face, she thought it might be the same for him, too. She'd never have asked that from him, though. Children shouldn't have to pick sides, even if those children were adults. She felt a little guilty about the fact that Tom had, for the most part, lost his father.

The guilt was a nebulous thing, however, and not attached to anything she'd actually done. Just her wishing that she'd chosen better, that he'd had what he needed from a father. Everything else was on Andrew, and if she was being honest, it had been on him for a long time. He was the one that had opted out of time with his son. Who'd left the phone calls, texts and communication to her. He was the one who had stepped out of his former life like it was a suit that no longer fitted, leaving it in a heap on the floor.

Well, she could step into a new life, too. Only *she* would take Tom and Marisa with her.

'I think I should have brought more than one,' Marisa said, eyeing the photograph. 'Because I think we all want to hit it.'

'What if you all hit it at the same time?' Mike asked. 'Or is that asking for a head injury?'

Sophie looked around the room, at the warped pieces of plastic, metal and crockery that littered the floor. She looked at the photo. And the truly astounding thing was, she didn't care about it. Oh, she was angry on Tom's behalf and annoyed at herself for putting up with Andrew for so long, but there wasn't enough hate and fury left in her to swing the bat one more time. She'd expended her rage for now, and her lying shit-weasel of an ex-husband wasn't worth any more of her energy.

'I'll leave it to you two, actually,' Sophie said.

Tom eyed her carefully. 'Are you sure?'

Sophie nodded, stepping back. She felt the palm of Mike's hand come to rest on the small of her back, support offered if she needed it. That gesture, though not large or extravagant, warmed her more than he could possibly know.

Marisa nodded, swapping her crowbar for a baseball bat. She stood next to Tom, expression resolute.

Tom leaned down and kissed her cheek. 'You ready?'

She tipped her face up to him, her smile strained. 'Shouldn't I be asking you that?'

He gave her a lopsided grin. 'You can ask me too, if you'd like.'

'I'm ready,' she said. 'Are you?'

'Yes,' he said, smiling broadly this time. 'I love you.'

'I love you too.' She went up on her toes and kissed him this time. 'Now let's beat the shit out of this photo.'

Tom laughed and they both fell into position. Tom took a moment to adjust his grip on the bat. 'Ready? One, two, *three.*'

The bats came down with force, the picture frame splintering instantly. Tom gave it another whack, laughing as he leaned the tip of the bat against the floor.

But Marisa kept going, smashing the pieces until they were almost dust. Her teeth bared in a grimace, her face red.

After a few seconds, Tom darted around to her other side, trying to approach her safely. 'That's enough, my love. That's enough.' His voice was so soft, so gentle, that Sophie's heart broke.

Marisa's must have, too, because suddenly she was sobbing, collapsing in on herself as she slid to the floor. The metal bat hit with a clang before rolling away. Tom was there in a second, pulling Marisa into his lap. He held her, letting her sob against his chest, his hand smoothing back her hair. He crooned mostly comforting nonsense to her and made soothing sounds as Marisa howled her anger and grief.

Out of the corner of her eye, Sophie saw the door open and shut as Mike slipped out of the room. Before she could think more about that, her attention snapped back to Tom and Marisa.

'It's not fair.' Marisa's voice was heart-rendingly raw as she rasped, 'I wanted it. So much. I loved it and it's not *fair.*'

Tom held her tighter. 'I know, my heart, my love, I know.' He was crying too, his tears no less gutting for all that they were quiet. But Sophie was sure she could see relief there, too, relief that Marisa was finally, *finally* letting it out.

Marisa's sobs were gentler now as she wrapped her arms around Tom and held him just as tight.

Sophie felt a tug on her hand, only then realizing that Mike had come back into the room. He pulled her behind him gently until they were out of the door, shutting it quietly behind them.

Tom and Marisa didn't look up once during their exit, and Sophie was glad. They needed each other right now, not anyone else. Her heart was breaking for them, but it was healing for them, too. Their love, their consideration of and support for each other would see them through this, she was sure of that now. When they grew tired, she would be there to help them until they became strong again.

Sophie plucked the safety glasses off her face and sighed. 'Do you think we can talk the employees into leaving them alone for a minute? I know our time's up, but—'

Mike shoved his safety glasses up until they rested on his head. There were twin indentations on each side of his nose, evidence of where they'd been. Why did she think that was cute?

'I took care of it. There was another group scheduled to come in here, but I managed to talk them into taking one of the other rooms.'

'How did you do that?'

'By offering to pay for their session,' Mike said. 'They were all pretty amenable after that.' He put his hands on his hips and blew out a breath. 'Do you think we should wait for them? Or leave them be?'

Sophie spent a long moment staring at his adorably questioning handsome face. This man. What was she going to do with this man? While the long term was definitely hazy in her mind's eye, the immediate future was crystal clear. She clasped his face in her hands and kissed him. He tensed for a second, surprised, before melting into her.

The kiss started out soft and sweet, but quickly deepened into something that would have Sophie blushing later.

When she finally pulled back, Mike was wide-eyed and out of breath.

'What was that for?' he asked. 'And how can I do it again?'

Her answering laugh was quiet, but no less joyful. 'How about you take me home and we can discuss it later?'

She'd never seen a man shed safety gear so fast in her life.

Chapter Seventeen

Sophie Swann was a Valkyrie. A Boudicca. A warrior queen. Mike had known this, at least partially. He thought that a lot of people fell into the trap of labelling her *soft*. She was kind, thoughtful, warm and funny. These were things that society tended to put into the soft category, but they weren't. Not really. They were strengths, at least to Mike. It took a core of steel to go out into the world every day and be these things despite the never-ending grind of reality. The fact that Sophie was still soft despite what her ex had done to her was unfathomable.

That was bravery. That was strength.

So he'd already known she was tough, but seeing her in the rage room . . . that had been something else entirely. She was *beautiful* in her fury. Mike had never considered himself the kind of guy who would be turned on by watching a woman demolish a microwave oven with an aluminium bat, but apparently he was. He really, really *was*, and he needed to pour a metaphorical ice bucket on that right now. She'd been sick this morning *and* had an emotional bomb dropped into her lap. She may have kissed him, she might be interested in more, but none of that was happening tonight.

Which was why Mike hesitated before crossing the threshold into her flat. Maybe he should leave it here? Give her a kiss, tell her to call him in the morning, and they'd go from there. He discarded that idea almost instantly. Sophie needed someone here with her – that was obvious. If she sent him home, fine; but otherwise, he would stay even if he needed to sleep on her tiny sofa. He wasn't sure he could give her much, but he could give her this. He could be here on a terrible day.

Not that he could put his choice entirely on her and his own sense of altruism. No, Mike also needed to be there for her tonight for his own sake. He wouldn't sleep well in his flat, worried that she was upset or that her fever had come back. It would be one thing if Tom and Marisa were able to be there for her, but they had their own things going on. Mike simply didn't. All he had was work. His children were an ocean away and, frankly, doing much better than he was. They didn't really need him, at least not right now.

He was the one who could be here for Sophie at this moment. He was the one who *wanted* to be here. If anyone in the city of New York was going to hold Sophie Swann, it was going to be him, damn it.

He stepped into her flat, turning to lock the door as she flipped on lights.

'I can stay.' He hadn't meant to blurt the words, but now that they were out, he didn't have the heart to take them back. 'I mean, I'd like to stay.'

Sophie turned, her expression quizzical.

Nerves got the better of him and as Mike's mouth opened, all manner of nonsense babbled out. 'I mean, if that's what you'd like. Obviously, I can leave if you don't. It's up to you. I can sleep on the couch. Or not.' He rubbed a hand over his face. 'What I mean is, you've had a shit day and I didn't think you'd want to be alone, but also I wanted to be here, but nothing has to happen, I mean you had a fever last night and—'

'Mike.' Sophie dropped his name gently, cutting off the flow of words.

'Yes?'

'I'd like you to stay,' Sophie said.

'Oh, thank god,' Mike said. 'I meant it about the couch, though. Whatever you need. I—'

She held up a hand, palm out, an amused smile on her face. 'You've already slept in my bed. It would be a bit silly to get weird about it now.' She stepped over to him, slipped her arms around his neck and planted a lingering kiss on his lips.

He chased after it automatically, pulling her close, feeling her soft body against his while he tasted her. He groaned from the simple pleasure of it. Sophie Swann was a joy to hold.

When she pulled back from the kiss, Mike felt dazed, his body practically humming. He brushed her hair away from her face with his fingertips, enjoying the way the strands slid against his skin. 'You could get weird about it if you want to, you know.'

She laughed. 'I know, but honestly, I'm exhausted. Pulling on my pyjamas and curling up with you sounds like about all I can handle right now. Is that okay?'

It sounded like pure, unadulterated bliss, if he was honest with himself. 'Yeah, it's okay.' He brushed her hair back again, just because he could.

She studied him for a long moment. 'Are you going to be okay? The night by the carousel . . .' Her words drifted off, turning them into a question.

The answer should have been simple, but that snarl of feelings was still thrashing around in his chest and he wasn't entirely sure he could handle it. All he did know was that he couldn't walk away right now. Didn't *want* to walk away right now. There seemed to be an inevitability about Sophie Swann that he couldn't entirely fight. 'Tonight is okay,' he finally said.

She accepted this with little in the way of reaction beyond a slight tilt of her head. 'And tomorrow?'

'How about we deal with tomorrow, tomorrow?'

'Fair enough,' she said, before leading him into the bedroom.

Sophie put on clean pyjamas – a worn camisole top and shorts, and while Mike found them intriguing, he could also tell they were comfort pyjamas for her. He made do with his boxer briefs, and in no time at all, his head was on the pillow, the sheets cool against his skin. After Sophie had responded to a text from Tom, she set her phone down and curled up against Mike, easing her body against his. It took a little adjusting, and a bit of giggling – not all on her part because she'd found one of his ticklish spots by accident – but they ended up with Sophie's head on his chest, one of her legs thrown over his, and her hand flat on his belly. It was an intimate position for them considering she hadn't seen him naked yet, but it didn't feel that way. It felt . . . right.

Mike had one hand buried in her hair, the other tracing patterns on her back. Her skin was soft and her hair smelled like peaches and honey, and he thought that if he were a cat, he might be purring right now, he was that content.

Sophie sighed, settling deeper into his hold. 'Did I remember to thank you for tonight? If not, thank you. It was exactly what I needed. I think it was what Tom and Marisa needed, too.'

'You're welcome.' He pressed his lips to the top of her head and smiled. 'Want to talk about it at all?'

'No,' Sophie said quickly. She sighed again. 'And yes, but I don't want to be one of those people that talk non-stop about their divorce.'

'You're not,' Mike said, settling his head back against his pillow. 'But if you were, that would be okay. Divorce is hard.'

'There's just such an indignity to it.' She moved so that her chin rested on his chest so she could see him. 'Do you know how I found out that I was getting a divorce?'

Mike prepared himself. He already knew he wasn't going to like it. 'How bad was it?'

'I went in for a check-up at the GP.'

Mike could already see where this was going, his gut pre-emptively filling with cold dread and hot rage. 'He didn't.'

Sophie grimaced. 'He did. Something wasn't right and my doctor ran some tests, including to check for an STI. I never would have thought of that – why would I? I'd been married for ages, if not happily then at least monogamously, I thought. I was doubly lucky that it was one of the ones that could be treated with antibiotics.'

'I deeply regret not hitting his photo with a bat.' Mike was amazed how calm his voice sounded. Inside, it was an entirely different manner.

'Thank you,' Sophie said, turning so she could watch her finger as she traced it down his chest. 'She was his assistant, you know. Which means everyone at work knew. They knew and not a single one of them told me.'

'What did he say when you confronted him?'

'He said maybe if I'd tried a little harder, paid more attention to him, or spent more time on my appearance, he wouldn't have been driven into another woman's arms. Also, he was in love and they were moving in together. He'd already talked to someone about putting the house on the market.'

Mike whistled, long and low. 'Wow, he doesn't do things in half-measures, does he? That's brutal, that is. He's also full of shit.' He touched her chin, nudging it until she was looking at him. 'You know he's wrong, right? Absolutely, completely, mind-numbingly wrong.'

She gave him a faint smile. 'Thank you.'

He clucked his tongue. 'Oh no, none of that. You sound like you bought some of his rubbish. Let me be very clear about a few things, Sophie Swann. Everything that man said to you was a poorly constructed Jenga tower of lies to give himself an out. To keep himself blame-free. Try harder? What utter nonsense.' He brushed a thumb over her cheekbone. 'I may not have known you long, but I know you enough to know you put every bit of yourself into the things you do. I have no doubt that you were a good partner to that man. I have serious doubts as to whether he was a good partner to *you*.'

He felt the edge of his thumb grow damp, and he swiped at the tear that had crawled its way down her cheek. 'He's not worth even that. As to your appearance . . .' Mike blew out a slow breath. 'Well, I think we both know I'm horribly biased when it comes to your appearance.'

'You are?'

He nodded slowly. 'I am, because I happen to think you're a beautiful woman with a hell of a swing.' He leaned until he could brush his lips against hers. Then he did it again, because life was short, unpredictable, and kissing her made it worth it. 'Which it turns out I'm very into.'

She hummed in response, swooping in to steal a kiss of her own.

'You know,' Mike said, trying to sound casual, but not quite managing due to the breathlessness of his words, 'if you decided to murder him, I'd happily give you an alibi. I'm very good under pressure and I don't mind morally grey areas when it comes to protecting my friends. I would have no problem lying on the stand.'

Sophie huffed a laugh. 'You know, Edie said almost exactly the same thing.'

'Really?'

'Yes, only with more profanity and a list of murder suggestions. She was quite graphic and oddly specific, so I guess less "alibi" and more "accomplice". She'd never really been fond of Andrew and with the divorce . . . well, I believe she said she, "wouldn't piss on him if he was on fire". Which never made sense to me, because if you hate someone, you would think you'd still want to wee on them, even if it meant inadvertently saving their lives.' She shook her head. 'I didn't argue with her too much when she said it, though, because she was practically spitting, she was so angry, and also drunk, and I was mostly concerned she would actually go after him in that state.'

'I think I like Edie,' Mike said.

Sophie screwed up her face. 'I'm starting to wonder if I attract bloodthirsty people. First Edie's threats, then Marisa's threats and her decision to call Andrew the Wicker Man, with all that entails. Now you're willing to cover my murderous tracks.'

'I don't normally consider myself a bloodthirsty person, but I think I'd make an exception for your ex. Death isn't good enough for him. I cannot believe he not only did that to you but tried to place the blame at your feet.'

'I can believe it,' she said, her last word cracking on a yawn. 'Sorry.'

He tucked her head back against his chest. 'Go to sleep. Everything will keep until the morning.' He wasn't even sure she'd heard the last bit before she started snoring.

Chapter Eighteen

When you're far from home, sometimes you find yourself missing the things you don't even like about where you live. Even the tube, where you're jammed up against strangers, trying to ignore the fact that you're touching so many people at once and you're so close to someone that you can hear their audiobook even though they've got earbuds in. The wonderful thing about New York is that the subway can fill that gap for you. You can travel about the city, watching the confusing display of human theatre on the train, everyone wondering if the man spouting poetry was naked when he got on, or if he stripped after, but no one actually acknowledging his presence. You can spot a rat running across the track and smile because it reminds you of the mice on the rails at home.

– Excerpt from Swanning About

When Sophie woke up the next morning, she was alone in her bed. There was no sign of Mike at all, and for a brief moment she thought maybe she'd dreamed the whole thing. Like maybe the Instagram post, the rage room, and Mike holding her while she slept had all been some sort of fever dream, beautiful and terrible all at once.

It made her sad.

The feeling only lasted until she stepped into her kitchenette and found a note propped up against her teacup. Mike had laid out mug, tea bag and spoon, and filled the kettle so all she had to do was turn on the burner. Such a little thing, but it warmed her to her toes. She plucked the note from the counter and read Mike's neat, slanted script.

Had to go to work and didn't want to wake you. If you're feeling up to it, I'd like to make you dinner tonight. 7 p.m.? – Mike

Sophie stared at the note for a long time. Then she set it aside and put the kettle on. Once her tea was brewing, she put the toast in the toaster and checked her texts. There was one from Manny, asking her if she could walk Stanley Poochie this afternoon. She said yes to that one without thinking. The other from Mike, wishing her a good morning with a selfie of him with his coffee in some sort of office. That one she didn't answer straight away.

Once she was able to sit at her table with her tea and toast, she messaged Edie to see if she was up for a video chat. Edie responded by calling her.

When Sophie opened the chat, her friend appeared to be wearing overalls, her eyes framed in plastic protective eyewear. It was so close to what Sophie had been wearing the previous night that it took her a second to say anything.

'Sophie, light of my life,' Edie said, shoving the glasses up onto the top of her head. 'I saw the Instagram post. Are you okay?'

'Yes, of course.' Sophie paused, a thought suddenly occurring to her. Even though she was alone, she leaned close to her screen and whispered. 'Oh god, Edie, tell me you didn't kill him.'

Edie blinked at her for a moment. 'Not yet. He's annoying but not *that* annoying. For now, I think the paint ought to do it.'

Now it was Sophie's turn to be confused. 'Wait, what are you talking about?'

Edie scowled. 'What are *you* talking about?'

'I thought you'd finally gone through with it and killed Andrew,' Sophie hissed.

Edie rolled her eyes. 'I would *not* do time for that man.' She put her hands on her hips and squinted up at the sky. 'Not that anyone would find the body. I'm eighty per cent certain I could pull off a perfect murder.'

'Edie!'

'Okay, more like seventy.'

Sophie briefly considered banging her head against the table, but ultimately discarded the idea. 'If you aren't pulling off the perfect crime, what are you doing?'

Edie shrugged. 'What do you think? I'm annoying the neighbour.'

'Not that again,' Sophie said with a groan.

Edie's eyes narrowed. 'He's my nemesis. Do not downplay the power of that. It's an important relationship. You have to *nurture* it.'

Sophie nibbled her toast as she considered the most diplomatic way to phrase her question, but then blurted it out anyway because after all this was Edie, woman of very little filter. 'Aren't you concerned that doing things to prolong a feud with your neighbour because he annoys you is both immature and, well, giving him power over your decisions?'

'What's so great about being mature?' Edie waved a hand dismissively. 'Mature is boring. Name one fun thing about being *mature*. I mean, I'm an adult. I pay my bills. I work. My house is mostly clean and I eat my vegetables. As far as I'm concerned, that's mature enough. If I want to engage in an on again, off again cold war with the neighbour, or hide dead fish in the wheel rims of Andrew's car, why can't I?'

'Besides possible legal reasons?' Sophie should probably ask about the fish, but plausible deniability was a *thing*.

Edie crossed her arms, her voice strangely ominous. 'Everyone needs a hobby, Sophie. My therapist said so.'

Sophie felt the familiar sensation of losing all control over the conversation with Edie. The thing with Edie's arguments was that you usually knew there was something not quite *right* about them, but it was difficult to figure out exactly what that thing might be. 'I'm almost positive your therapist meant something like knitting or betting on the ponies.'

Edie shook her head. 'Dr Gatwa doesn't approve of the ponies but does approve of me airing my feelings.'

'Not sure she considers revenge and minor property damage the same thing as "airing your feelings" but how should I know, I don't have a degree.'

'There's no wrong way to feel something, Sophie,' Edie said. 'There are all kinds of studies that say repressing your feelings causes stress, which leads to health issues. Do you want my heart to explode or my hair to fall out, Sophie? Do you?'

'No, I don't. Marisa would probably ask how the majority of Londoners haven't dropped on the spot. She finds most of us to be repressed.'

Edie put her hands on her hips again. 'That's a bit of a sweeping judgement.'

'I know. So, what are you doing to the neighbour now?'

'He complained about the paint again. It's peeling a bit on *one side*. You can barely see it, but from the way he's carrying on, you'd think the house was falling down, or that I'd left an entire lorry to rust in the front garden.' She deepened her voice, impersonating the neighbour. 'You may not care about property values, but the rest of us do.'

'Weren't you planning on painting anyway?'

'Yes,' Edie said. 'But I don't enjoy people telling me what to do. I'm using this as a teachable moment. He's going to learn.' Her voice dropped into the ominous octave again. 'Or else.'

Sophie had a feeling she knew where this was going and braced herself. 'What colour, Edie?'

The grin that slowly unfurled on Edie's face was Cheshire cat in nature – if said cat had been raised by Machiavelli and Giulia Tofana. It was a little frightening. She drew in a large breath, then said the next word slowly, like she was savouring every letter. '*Orange*.'

'Like a pumpkin, or . . . ?'

The grin kicked up a notch and Edie steepled her fingers together. 'Practically neon. It's not a colour that appears in nature. He's going to be *outraged*.' She cackled. 'I want to see how high I get him to count this time. Last time it was to thirty.'

'Count?' Sophie asked the question, even though she was worried about the answer.

'To find his patience.'

'I see.' Sophie took another bite of toast. 'The neighbourhood is going to hate you.'

Edie shrugged, completely unconcerned. 'How are you feeling, by the way? With everything?'

Sophie spent a moment catching Edie up, giving her only the broad strokes – her illness, Mike's help, the Instagram post, the rage room, and then finally getting to the reason she'd called – the note.

Edie's brows went up. 'He's cooking you dinner? At his flat?'

'He didn't specify where,' Sophie admitted, 'but probably.'

'Do you think this is just a "I want to make you food and spend time" kind of dinner or "I want to fuck you against the wall in the hallway as soon as the front door shuts" kind of dinner?' Both options were listed matter-of-factly, like Edie considered them to be on the same mysterious level, equal in every way.

Sophie wasn't entirely sure how to answer the question. 'Is that second dinner a real option?'

'In theory? Oh, yes.' Edie's sigh was wistful. 'Those dinners used to be my favourite.'

Rather unfortunately, Sophie's imagination decided to helpfully provide her with an image of what Edie's second dinner concept might look like, and so both her and Edie were silent for a moment, each lost in their own daydream. Well, daydream for Sophie. Probably memory for Edie. Or memories.

Sophie took a long sip of her tea, her throat suddenly dry for some reason. 'If we are using the second option as a sort of catch-all for sex in general, and not being fucked against a wall specifically, then I think both options might be on the table.'

Edie nodded. 'Do you want both options?'

She remembered the feeling of him under her. His kiss. Everything. 'Yes,' Sophie said. 'I think I do.'

Edie shrugged. 'Then what's the problem?'

'He freaked out before. He might not be ready for this.' Sophie stared down into her teacup, like it might give her answers. 'My ego was pretty bruised the last time he called a stop to things. If he did that during sex—'

'Yeah,' Edie said, scrunching up her nose. 'That would be a blow. You could talk to him, you know. Have a plan in place in case he changes his mind again. So you don't get hurt as much.' Edie's eyes narrowed. 'You know that it wasn't about you, right? Any of that?'

'Yes,' Sophie said, but when it was clear that Edie wasn't buying it, she sighed. 'Mostly.'

Edie crossed her arms and scoffed. 'God, I hate Andrew. You, my friend, are hot. Gorgeous. Sculptors would be lining up to carve your likeness, but they're too busy weeping at the beauty of your smile.'

Sophie laughed. 'You're ridiculous.'

'You love it.'

'I do.'

Edie nodded. 'Right, so I don't think you have anything to worry about, but what it comes down to is how you feel. Do you want to go, yes; but also do you want to go enough to risk the possibility that it might not go how you're hoping?'

Sophie took a big breath and let it out, slumping her shoulders. 'Yes, I think I do.'

'Good.' Edie nodded sharply. 'I support you. Did you bring that green wrap dress?'

Sophie picked up her phone and walked to the closet to make sure. 'I did.'

'Wear that. It's a good colour on you.'

'Thanks, Edie.'

'No problem,' she said, giving Sophie a lazy little salute. 'What are friends for?'

Before Sophie could answer, there was some commotion in the background. Then a man's voice. 'What have you done now, you little demon? Is that *orange*? Who paints their house neon orange? It's like a nuclear Wotsit. What is *wrong* with you?'

Edie grinned wickedly, waggling her fingers in a wave. 'I'd better go. Knock 'em dead, Sophie.' She kissed the air, then turned off the screen.

Sophie texted Mike back. *Seven it is. Can I bring anything? Your flat or mine?*

His response came with gratifying speed. *Just yourself. Mine, if that's okay?*

When she replied that it was, he sent her his address. Now she only had to keep herself from fixating on it all day.

She got some of her own work done on the post for the following day, including some last-minute edits. Then, when she'd got tired of staring at her screen, she dressed and popped down a few blocks to a bakery she'd spied on earlier walks. She wanted to check on Tom and Marisa, since the day before had been a lot for them emotionally, and while she couldn't make that better, she could bring an array of pastries, which at least wouldn't make the situation worse.

Pastries in hand, she knocked on Tom and Marisa's door.

After a few seconds Marisa answered, and though she looked worn and tired, she also seemed steadier. She had wrapped a thin blanket around herself like a robe and one of her hands snuck out of it to wave Sophie into the flat.

'I wanted to check on you,' Sophie said. 'But just in case talking was the last thing you wanted to do, I've also brought pastries. I got a few different ones. I thought we could cut them into pieces and share so we could try several.'

Marisa padded over on bare feet, peering into the box. 'You're an angel.' She kissed Sophie's cheek. 'Thank you.'

'Tom at work?'

'Yeah,' Marisa said with a sigh. 'He wanted to stay home, but I told him to go. We can't afford more time off and anyway, I'm feeling okay. Better. Yesterday helped.'

Sophie fetched plates for them, handing one to Marisa. 'I'm so glad.' Then she grabbed a butter knife and started slicing the pastries in half.

'How about you?' Marisa asked as she clutched her plate. 'How are you feeling about everything? He's your crappy ex. Can't be fun to have everything shoved in your face like that.'

Sophie considered this as she filled her plate. 'I feel okay? I mean, I'm still angry. He could have handled everything so much better than he did. I can't tell if he's being malicious, or if his cruelty is simple thoughtlessness. I'm not sure which is worse, or if it even matters.'

'Do you want something to drink?' Marisa asked. 'Tea, water, juice?'

'Water, please.' Sophie took a spot on the couch, putting her plate on one of the side tables for now, freeing her hands to take her glass from Marisa.

Marisa followed her to the couch, somehow managing to carry her water glass and plate without dislodging her blanket robe. 'As for whether or not it matters, I personally don't think it does. Both are cruel. The only difference is motivation.'

Sophie bit into a chocolate croissant, the pastry flaking onto her lap. 'When I woke up this morning, I mostly felt relief. Like, he's her problem now. Or his own problem. I don't know.'

Marisa fiddled with the cinnamon roll on her plate. 'Does it ever go away? The anger. The sadness.' She closed her eyes. 'Sometimes I'm just so *tired*.'

Sophie reached over and squeezed her hand. 'I know, darling. Grief is different for everyone, but I think . . . I think it doesn't fully go away, really. And I don't believe that's a bad thing. Our grief simply becomes part of us – like weaving in new thread on a tapestry. The composition is changed, but change isn't bad. The pattern is simply more complex now.' She stared at her croissant. 'Acknowledging the pain in ourselves makes us stronger, I think. The important thing is to not let it eat you up inside. Which I know sounds very trite.'

A single tear dripped down Marisa's cheek and she sniffed. 'Tom seems to be handling it so much better than I am . . .'

Sophie set aside her food and wrapped an arm around Marisa's shoulder. 'He just handles things differently, that's all. We all have to come at grief in our own way.'

Marisa sniffed again, then put her arms around Sophie's neck and squeezed her tight. 'Thank you. I can't wait to be part of your family. You know that, right?'

Sophie hugged her back. 'As far as I'm concerned, you already are.'

Marisa gave her an extra squeeze and then let go, obviously shaking off her tears with a deep breath and a straightening of her spine. 'Tom said the rage room was Mike's idea. You'll have to thank him for me.'

'I can pass along your thanks at dinner tonight,' Sophie said.

Marisa clapped her hands together once, her face lighting up. 'Dinner?'

Sophie nodded. 'He's cooking.'

'He sure is,' Marisa said, fanning herself.

Sophie laughed. 'Do you need me around tonight, darling? I can always postpone—'

'Don't you dare,' Marisa said. 'I'll have a quiet night with Tom. It will be good for us.'

'You let me know if you change your mind,' Sophie said. 'I can reschedule in an instant. Mike will understand.' And wasn't that a grand thing to know? Sophie realized that she could tell Edie at least one fun thing about being mature – you could rest easy in the knowledge that your date really would understand and not take their feelings of disappointment out on you. It seemed like the lowest of bars, but her ex wouldn't have been able to clear it.

'I appreciate it,' Marisa said. 'But I want you to go have some fun. You deserve it. Here's hoping Mike can give it to you.'

Sophie held out her croissant. 'I'll cheers to that.'

Marisa tapped a piece of cherry turnover against the croissant and smiled.

Chapter Nineteen

Mike prepped for his date like some men planned for the apocalypse. He'd gone into work early and skipped lunch so he could leave with enough time to prepare. He bought the ingredients for dinner, three different kinds of wine, and a few things for a cheese plate. He cleaned his flat, going so far as to get some flowers for the table. Then he showered, shaved and put on cologne. He was standing there in his boxer briefs, his bottom lip between his teeth, when the nerves really hit.

He had no idea what to wear. Go casual with jeans and T-shirt? No, that didn't seem right. He hated polo shirts, so those were out. A suit? A suit was probably too much. He ran his hands over his face and groaned. These were decisions he usually didn't fuss much over. He put the effort in, of course, but Sophie . . . he wanted to be more for Sophie.

He checked the time. Six. Making it eleven in London. Mike grabbed his phone and typed furiously into the group chat, thankful that his family tended to be night owls.

Mike: Help. SOS. Or maybe SOD?

Rahul: What on earth is an SOD?

Amaya: You should know, brother, you are one.

Rahul: Oh, ha ha. You missed your calling, sister. Should've gone into stand-up.

Noah: Play nice, children. Did you miss the part that said, 'Help'?

Mike: Save Our Date. I was trying to be clever.

Rahul: Well, that was your first mistake.

Amaya: Shut up, Rahul – DAD HAS A DATE. Is it Sophie? Please let it be Sophie.

Mike: Who else would it be?

Amaya: I don't know, some local skank. Who knows what he's getting up to over there unattended.

Rahul: And you call yourself a feminist.

Noah: We only support home grown, organic skanks.

Amaya: Feminism is here for the skanks, too. I love skanks. Though I'm not sure I meant to imply that Sophie was one.

Mike: I'm once again regretting summoning the group chat for help.

Amaya: Sorry, Dad! What's going on? How can Barney and I support you in your hour of need?

Rahul: Getting a little concerned about you and that plant.

Noah: Focus.

Rahul: Ficus?

Noah: I want a divorce.

Amaya: Dad, are you pinching the bridge of your nose right now and counting to ten? I bet you are.

Mike was, in fact, doing exactly that and wondering why he'd thought his children would be helpful.

Noah: Sorry, Mike. How can we help?

Mike: I don't know what to wear.

Noah: So you summoned the gays. Smart move. Or it would be if your son could dress himself.

Rahul: I still don't understand why you hated that shirt, but I got rid of it!

Amaya: I want pictures, Noah.

Noah: Done.

Amaya: You remain my favourite brother-in-law. Dad, do you have options?

Mike took photos of the three outfits he had and sent them. Instead of a reply, he got a link to a group video chat, which he regretted clicking on before he'd even touched his thumb to the screen. Rahul and Noah were cuddled together on the couch, Noah with a stemless glass of wine in his hand, Rahul with a beer. Amaya joined a second later from Mike's flat, sitting in his easy chair, her arm around Barney the plant.

After greetings were exchanged, Mike checked his watch. 'I have fifty minutes until she gets here, and I need at least ten of those to finish cooking.'

'Right,' Noah said, straightening up. 'The suit is out. Too formal for a dinner at home. You also want to consider your layers – you don't want too many to take off.'

Rahul turned to his husband, an amused expression on his face. 'I'm trying really hard to not think about my father's sex life and you're not helping.'

Amaya's lips were pursed, her gaze on the ceiling. 'What about that thin grey jumper Noah got you for Christmas?'

Mike shook his head. 'Didn't bring it.'

Noah tapped his fingers along his knee. 'Okay. Turn the camera and show me your wardrobe?'

Mike did as he was bid, thumbing through the options.

'Wait,' Noah said. 'Go back. The dark purple one.'

'Really?' Mike asked, though he was already grabbing the hanger. 'I usually wear it with a suit, which tones the purple down a bit. You don't think it's too flashy?'

Rahul rolled his eyes. 'You want to be a little bit flashy, yeah?'

Noah smiled. 'There's a reason male birds are usually so brightly coloured. You've got to shake your tail feathers. Besides, that colour will bring out your eyes.'

Mike set up his camera on the dresser as he shrugged into the shirt. 'If you say so. What should I pair it with?'

'Jeans,' Amaya said. 'The dark pair. Roll up the sleeves of the shirt, but don't tuck it in. And Dad? No socks.'

He frowned at her. 'Really?'

She nodded slowly. 'Really, Dad. You want to look clean and like you made an effort, but also like you're slightly undone and halfway to the bedroom. Also, no one – and I mean no one – looks sexy while they're hopping around removing their socks.'

Mike's fingers slowed as he did up his shirt. 'I really don't want to know what you're basing this opinion on.'

Amaya rolled her eyes. 'Don't be a prude, Dad.'

Mike put on the jeans, finishing up the outfit with his watch.

'We need a fit check, Dad,' Amaya said. 'Walk back so we can see the outfit and turn and walk towards us. Like you're on a runway.'

Mike, feeling faintly silly, did as she asked. He held out his arms. 'What do we think?'

Noah huffed. 'I wish I was there to help. Run your fingers through your hair a bit. It's lying too flat. A little more. Okay, there. Perfect.'

Rahul leaned over and kissed Noah's temple. 'And that's why I married you.'

Noah grinned, blushing. 'Because I know how to dress a man?'

Rahul snorted. 'I'm sure that helped, but I meant because you give a shit.' His voice softened. 'You're a good man, Noah Tremblay.'

Noah leaned into him. 'Thanks.'

Amaya sighed. 'This is why I'm single. You two have set a high standard.' She lifted Barney onto her lap. 'In the meantime, it's just me and Barney, but we both think you look great, Dad.'

'Okay,' Mike said, running his hands down his shirt. 'Okay.'

'And Dad?' Amaya said.

'Yeah?'

Her smile was tight-lipped, but genuine. 'You've got this.'

'Thanks,' Mike said. 'All of you.'

'You're welcome,' Rahul said. 'Now we're signing off so we can continue to enjoy this short span of time where a child isn't yelling at one of us, but we're here for emergencies.'

'Yes,' Noah said. 'We love you!'

Their screen disappeared, leaving only Amaya and the plant. 'Have a good time, Dad. Don't do anything I wouldn't do.'

'What, exactly, would be on that list? Wait, I'm sorry I asked that.'

'Don't worry, I'm not going to tell you, so I guess you'll just have to wing it.' For some reason, that made Amaya cackle. 'Love you, Dad!' Then her screen also vanished.

Leaving Mike alone with a dinner to finish preparing and palms that were sweaty from nerves.

'Right,' he told himself, wiping his palms on his thighs. 'Better get on with it.'

By the time Sophie knocked on his door at five past seven, Mike was ready to crawl out of his own skin. He pulled the chicken out of the oven to let it rest before discarding his oven gloves and striding towards the hallway, his pulse erratic.

Then he opened the door.

Sophie was . . .

. . . was . . .

. . . a sadist, clearly.

Mike's throat went dry as he looked at her.

The green dress she was wearing hugged her body like it never wanted to let go, which might have been him projecting a bit. He followed the line of it down to where it draped around her legs. When the dress stopped, his gaze kept going, tracing her calves, her ankles, and the gold strappy sandals on her feet. She looked *edible*. His body was somehow hot and cold at the same time, and he could hear his heartbeat in his ears. He was gripping the doorknob so hard, he was pretty sure his hand had fused with the metal.

Mike knew he was staring. Knew he should probably stop, but he couldn't seem to get his body to work. Sophie wasn't moving either. She was cradling a bottle of wine, her eyes wide, her lips parted. She wasn't making eye contact but seemed to be staring at a point just below his chin.

He had no idea how long they would have stood there gaping at each other – hours, months, ice ages – if one of the other people on his floor hadn't walked past while talking loudly on his phone. They blinked at each other, the spell broken.

Sophie held out the bottle of wine. 'For you.'

Mike took it with his free hand, shaking out the other as soon as he'd prised it off the doorknob. He ushered her in, certain his cheeks were flushed.

They paused in the hallway as Mike shut the door, both of them temporarily stuck in the awkwardness of the moment. Then they both lurched forward, Mike going in for a hug, Sophie going in for a kiss on the cheek.

Somehow Sophie ended up kissing Mike's ear and he ended up with his hands on her hips. Mike chuckled softly as he set the bottle of wine down on a side table. 'Let's try that again.' He leaned in and pressed his lips to her cheek. 'You look stunning.'

Her breath hitched. 'Thank you.' She didn't step back.

Neither did Mike. His face hovered next to hers as he breathed her in, their skin so close he could feel the heat of her. She smelled like peaches again, like something that would melt in your mouth.

She laid her palm on his chest, sliding her hand up over his collarbone and onto his shoulder. 'This looks good on you.'

'Thank you.' His voice was raspy to his own ears, hoarsened by an overwhelming tide of lust. One of his thumbs was tracing small circles on her hip while the other hand slid around to the small of her back. The air between them was so thick, he was pretty sure it could no longer be categorized as a gas but a solid.

She licked her lower lip and he tracked the movement like his life depended on it. 'Mike?'

'Hm?'

'You should kiss me now.'

'Oh, thank fuck.' He pulled her to him as she lunged forward, causing them to not so much kiss as crash into each other, not that either of them noticed. Mike was too busy tasting her mouth, enjoying the exquisite feel of her tongue against his. She was clasping his back with one hand, the other in his hair, gripping the strands tight. He groaned into her mouth.

She nipped his lip, kissed along his jaw, pressing wet, biting kisses down his neck. Mike sucked in a breath, cradling her to him, not knowing how much of this he could take, while also hoping she wouldn't stop.

He slid his palm down her hip, her thigh, pulling her knee up to his waist, opening her up for him. He wasn't sure when he'd pinned her to the wall, but he used the surface now for leverage.

Sophie arched against him, pushing herself against the seam of his jeans. He used the hand at her knee to trace down her thigh, fingers dipping down until he could feel the satin of her underwear. He traced around the edge there, his touch a teasing whisper. Now that he had her there, in his arms, panting his name, he wanted to take his time. He wanted her wet and needy. He wanted to spoil her with attention, lavish her with touch, with pleasure. Basically, he wanted her as undone as he was.

He kissed a line down her throat and licked the part of her collarbone that was exposed by the dress. His fingers brushed across her left breast, satisfaction welling inside him when he felt the hard peak of her nipple through the soft fabric. He cupped her gently before drifting further down to the hem of her dress, pulling it up and out of the way until he could see a hint of the fabric hugging her hip, following it along her rounded belly, down to the part pressing against him that was dampening more and more by the second.

Green.

She was wearing the green knickers he'd first spied in her suitcase, and he was pretty sure he whimpered. He brushed a thumb right against the wet cloth and Sophie gasped. Her lips were red from his kisses, her skin flushed, her eyes sparkling – she was so beautiful like this. He wanted to see more of it, more of her. He wanted to be greedy and gorge himself on her.

Sophie started undoing the buttons on his shirt, her fingers trembling, and that hit him hard, too. Knowing that he wasn't the only one bowled over by their sheer bloody chemistry.

He took over for her, undoing the buttons slowly, his gaze never leaving hers. 'Is this what you want?'

'Yes,' she breathed.

'Then it's yours.'

She glided curious fingers over his collar, his chest, his belly button. The soft exploration continued over his ribs, ticklishly, making him squirm.

'What do you want?' she asked.

He plucked at the ties of her dress. 'Can I?'

She nodded and he was undoing the bow, hands pushing back the fabric. Now it was his turn to explore, fingertips brushing over the stretch marks on her hips, the swell of her belly, up to the edges of her bra. 'Beautiful, so beautiful.'

He kissed her again, long and slow, not dissipating the heat between them, but stoking it higher despite his slower pace. When he pulled back, he kissed her cheeks, her eyelids, the tip of her nose, while his fingers traced along the silken edges of her knickers. He put his mouth next to her ear, his breath making her shiver, and he smiled.

'I'm going to take these off,' he said. 'Then I'm going to get on my knees and taste you. Is that okay, Sophie?'

She let out an unsteady breath.

He clucked his tongue. 'That won't do, I'm afraid. I'm going to need a yes or a no here.'

'Yes.' The word came out fervently, if still unsteady.

He kissed her mouth, hands sliding over her backside and tickling the backs of her thighs. 'That's what I needed to hear.'

She gazed up at him, her expression glazed with want. Mike was certain he could get drunk from that look.

'If you want me to stop, if you don't like anything I do, you tell me, and I stop. Understand?'

Sophie nodded, swallowing hard.

Then Mike slowly, reverently, lowered himself to his knees. He might regret it later – there was only a thin rug here over the hardwood – but right now, he didn't care. All of his attention was on his hands as he slid that last remaining scrap of cloth down her hips, past her knees, and to the floor. He touched one foot. 'Up.'

She stepped out of them as he'd asked, smiling as he tossed them over his shoulder.

He peered up at her, naked now except for her bra. Mike wanted to store away the sight of her, keeping her like this in his memory forever. Then he dragged his fingers up her calf, lingering for a moment at the back of her knee, before pulling it over his shoulder. He watched her for a second, making sure the wall was holding her up. Her breath was coming in short bursts as she stared down at him, her eyes wide.

He turned his head and kissed her knee. 'You leave this here if you can, okay?'

She nodded.

He traced his fingers teasingly right around the areas where she really wanted his touch. After a few passes, he dipped in closer, just enough to get his fingers wet, then brushed them up and around her clit, only to start the whole process over again.

Sophie was glaring down at him, her palms pressed flat against the wall. She looked deliciously frustrated. '*Mike!*'

'Hm?'

'Please get on with it!'

He laughed against her skin, making her shiver. 'So impatient.' He leaned in, spread her with his fingers, and licked.

Sophie moaned so loudly that she clamped a hand over her mouth, her eyes wide.

Mike laughed into her skin. 'Is that what you wanted?'

She nodded, her hand still clamped over her mouth.

'Well, far be it from me to deny you.' His voice sounded smug, but there was the faintest quiver to it, hinting at his own struggle. As much as he'd been teasing Sophie, he'd also been teasing himself. Desire was a blade that cut both ways, and he'd sliced himself up good and proper this time. It was a relief to take himself off the leash, to finally, fully, put his mouth on her.

She tasted like salt and musk, the flavour exploding across his tongue, lighting up the pleasure centres of his brain. He felt like one of those old pinball machines when all the lights flashed at once. While he licked, he slid one finger inside her, stroking until he found the spot that made her smack her palms against the wall and gasp.

He added another finger, stroking her, feeling her body arch, her muscles tighten. She was already on edge, but he wasn't ready. Not quite yet.

He stopped moving his fingers, but kept them in that sweet spot while he nipped kisses along her belly, her hips.

She growled in frustration, her hand digging into his hair and pulling.

He pressed his forehead against her stomach and let out a breath. 'Fuck, I love it when you're demanding. You want me to let you come? Is that it?'

She made another frustrated sound. Sophie wasn't much of a talker and though her cheeks were flushed, he couldn't tell if she was too turned on to talk, or if she was shy. There was a bit of irony here, that she was usually so good with words, and he wasn't, their roles reversing in the bedroom. Something to think about later. For now, he'd let her off the hook.

Sort of.

He clucked his tongue. 'Now that won't do at all.' He flexed his hand, and she sucked in a breath. 'Is that what you want, Sophie?'

She nodded, her lips parting as she panted, her body taut.

'Okay,' he said. 'I'll let you, but on one condition. I need you to look at me. Eyes on me, gorgeous.'

Sophie blinked down at him, her eyes so wide, the pupils blown. Her chest was heaving. She looked absolutely wrecked. Mike didn't think he'd ever been so turned on in his life. He began moving his fingers with slow, even pumps.

Her eyes started to drift closed, and he stopped.

Sophie growled again and he laughed.

'Cruel of me, I know, but I will give you what you want. You just look at me, Sophie, and I'll give you everything.'

Sophie stared down at him, her fingers curling against the wall.

Mike leaned in, not breaking eye contact, not even to blink. He started moving his fingers again. Then, while Sophie watched, wide-eyed, he traced his tongue up along the seam, before sucking her clit into his mouth.

She shattered, her mouth open on a silent scream, her body arched. Mike stared up at her in wonder. Sophie aroused was a hell of a sight. Sophie having a bone-melting orgasm was a vision.

He wanted it seared into his brain forever. Heat licked up his own spine and he had to shove his hand into his jeans and squeeze, trying to stave off his own orgasm. He hadn't messed his jeans since he was a teenager, and he wouldn't have felt shame over it now, not after watching that, but he wanted to wait. He wanted to focus on her right now, see how long he could draw the orgasm out.

Mike eased her through the aftershocks, waiting until her body relaxed before he reluctantly withdrew his hand. Her eyes were closed, her breathing slowing, as she rested limply against the wall. Mike drew her leg down so that her feet were both flat on the floor again. Then he wrapped his arms around her waist, resting his cheek against her belly. He closed his eyes and breathed in the salt of her, the scent mixing with the smell of peaches and sweetness he now associated with her.

He was going to be hopelessly turned on by peach Soleros for the rest of his life.

Sophie put a hand on his head, gently stroking his hair. After a few moments, she let out an unsteady breath. 'Well. I guess it was one of *those* kinds of dinners.'

Mike burst out laughing, his sides shaking as he held her. He was laughing so hard he was wheezing, and he wasn't entirely sure why.

Then he looked up at her. 'You were really beautiful in that dress.'

'You were handsome in that shirt.' She waved at the shirt, which he'd thrown behind him at some point and was now hanging off a decorative plant.

'You're fucking stunning now,' he said, planting a kiss on her stomach.

'Are you stalling because you're not sure you can get up off your knees?'

'Yes,' Mike said. 'You might have to help me up. The floor is suddenly killing me.'

Sophie reached down and grabbed his hands, pulling him up to a standing position. As soon as he was upright, she kissed him long and slow.

When he pulled back, he glanced at the kitchen. 'I really did make you dinner, you know. There's a whole chicken in there. Roast potatoes. A salad.'

Sophie hummed. 'Can we reheat it later?'

'Of course. Maybe. Possibly.' He kissed her again. 'There's a good chance it will be entirely ruined.'

Sophie tilted her head to the side. 'Do you care?'

'Not even a little bit. That chicken is on its own now. I can always get a takeaway.'

She sighed happily and tightened her arms around his neck. 'Then I think I'd rather you take me to bed.'

He grinned. 'Dessert first. I like it.' He nuzzled along her jaw.

'Mike?'

'Yes?'

'I meant now.'

'Thank fucking hell, I'm dying here.' Then he lifted her off her toes, spun her around and herded her in the direction of the bedroom.

Chapter Twenty

Mike's bedroom was utilitarian and anonymous in the way of temporary flats, but it had a queen-sized bed which was crisply made. This was one of the little upsides of being single at her age – the men were less likely to have beds that were just mattresses on a bare floor. They were also more likely to have clean sheets. Or indeed to have sheets in the first place.

He came up behind her, his arms going loosely around her waist, as he tucked his face against her neck and shoulder. Not doing anything. Just holding her for a moment and seeming perfectly content to do so. Sophie thought this might be the most perplexing thing about him – while he seemed wary of entering a relationship, he also clearly craved the physical intimacy, or at the very least enjoyed it.

And that was dangerous to Sophie. Even now, she wanted to tempt him into wanting more. She liked spending time with him. Talking with him. If the hallway was any indication, she was going to enjoy having sex with him. She just *liked* him. He obviously also liked her, but the danger lurked in the next step. Sophie could easily see herself wanting more with Mike, maybe not now, but at some point, and she still wasn't sure he was ready for that.

What she needed were some firm boundaries. Rules in place, a plan for how to deal with the eventual fallout, much like Edie had said.

And she had better bring it up fast, because Mike had brushed her hair aside so he could nibble her neck and his hands were no longer still. His fingers danced along her stomach and hips in a very distracting manner. She cleared her throat. 'Mike?'

His response was a hum.

'We should probably go over some things.'

Mike found a spot that made her weak-kneed and hovered there, raking it with his teeth.

'Mike.' His name came out in a gasp.

'I got a test about eight months back. No one since then. I can pull up the results on my phone if you'd like.' His voice was a low rumble, his hands kneading her hips.

Gratitude filled her at the offer. After what Andrew had done, her trust was fragile when it came to sex. 'Please. Thank you. Why did you request a test?'

'I had a suspicious rash that turned out to be from a new detergent. I'll leave you with that amazingly erotic image in your head while I go find my phone.' He squeezed her and kissed her again, then pulled away, making it only a few feet before he stopped, pulled a throw off the bed and wrapped her in it. 'Be right back.'

Sophie sat on the bed and waited, wondering at the fact that she hadn't thought of the blanket first. She wasn't shy, but she hadn't exactly paraded around naked for the two men she'd slept with after Andrew had left. She'd had a few drinks in her for courage for the first one, and it had been mostly dark, for which she'd been grateful. For the second one, she hadn't even managed to get fully undressed, and that had partly been why she hadn't asked for a repeat performance.

With the exception of Andrew and a few doctors, she hadn't shown a man her naked body in full lighting since she was twenty. Things had changed since then, certainly, her body shifting with time, not to mention the fresh and shiny dents in her confidence that her ex had left. There had been that nagging doubt that he'd left because she was no longer a person worthy of love or desire, even if Edie repeatedly told her that those things weren't true. Had in fact followed Sophie through the house one day with a novelty megaphone, shouting that at her until Sophie had burst into a fit of giggles.

With Mike, she simply hadn't thought anything of it. *He* wasn't even fully undressed yet, but there was something about the way he looked at her, the way he touched her, that told her more than any words how much he desired her. The man made her feel beautiful.

Mike returned holding his phone. 'Sorry, I took a moment to put the food in the fridge. I don't like my dates to end with food poisoning. Or to start with it. Really, food poisoning is unwelcome at all stages.' He handed over his phone to her, the screen showing the part of his medical file that listed his test results, which were when he'd said they were, and were indeed negative.

'I don't know – I've had some dates where I would have welcomed food poisoning,' she said, staring at the screen. Relief seeped into her that he'd been telling her the truth. 'Do you want to see mine? After Andrew…well, I requested them again after the antibiotics just to make sure.'

Mike shook his head, taking the seat next to her on the bed. 'Only if it would make you feel better for me to see them. With your history, I trust this wouldn't be something you'd lie about. I also bought condoms today. They're in the bedside drawer.'

She handed him back his phone. 'Very prepared.'

'Just hopeful.'

'Thank you, for all of this.'

He was watching her now, eyes assessing. 'What else do you need, Sophie?'

She gave a little laugh, the sound coming out tinny and false to her ears. 'Am I that transparent?'

'No,' he said slowly. 'I don't think you are. I just know you.'

She dropped her gaze, suddenly very interested in the floor. 'I think we should set expectations.'

He leaned back on his hands, his expression thoughtful. 'What does that mean to you?'

'You're only in New York for what, two or three more weeks?'

He nodded. 'More or less – possibly a little more.'

'What if we didn't think about after that? Neither of us are very sure what we want long term, and I'd like this to be a pleasant memory when we're done.' She frowned slightly. 'Do you think that's cold?'

He watched her, his expression thoughtful. 'No, I don't think it's cold. Smart, probably, because you're right.' His voice softened. 'I want this to be a good memory, too. I'd like to think we'll be friends in the end, no matter what.'

'So we have fun while you're here. Enjoy our time. When you leave for the airport, we can let it naturally transition into whatever we want. Not a hard and fast rule, but at least we're on the same page.'

'I can live with that.'

They regarded each other quietly, neither of them speaking. Sophie couldn't help but notice that Mike's ardour had, ah, *cooled*. 'I killed the mood, didn't I?

Mike's lopsided smile was wide and genuine. 'Oh, sweetheart, it would take a lot more than a five-minute – and very necessary – conversation to turn me off. I have an almost entirely naked woman in my bed. Wild hounds couldn't keep me away.'

She glanced rather pointedly at the front of his jeans.

He laughed before rolling onto his side, nudging her down onto the mattress. 'We can fix *that*.' He peeled back one side of her blanket cocoon. 'It's not like it's a hardship.' He pulled back the rest of the blanket, his eyes blazing with anticipation. 'Oh no, we have to do foreplay. Such a travesty,' he murmured, drawing a finger down her sternum before tracing along the line of her bra. 'Whatever will we do? However will we cope?' He kissed her chest, eyes sliding closed as he breathed her in. 'Never have two people had to overcome such odds. Now sit up so I can get this bra off.'

She pushed him away with a laugh so she could do as he asked, nodding at his jeans. 'Those off as well.'

Mike rolled off the bed, landing on his feet, and immediately started pulling off his jeans.

'And you might joke, but most men want to get straight to the good part,' Sophie said, reaching around to unhook her bra.

Mike froze with his trousers at his knees so he could look at her, his expression bewildered. 'It's all the good part.'

She frowned at him. 'You really mean that, don't you?'

'Yeah,' he said, stepping out of his jeans. He straightened, his thumbs inside the waistband of his boxer briefs. 'These too?'

She nodded, tossing her bra onto the floor.

'You don't think this is the good part?'

'Oh, I do, it's just that a large proportion of the penis-wielding population would disagree with you.'

He shoved his boxers down. 'They're welcome to their incorrect opinion.'

Sophie forgot whatever she'd been about to say as he stood up again, fully naked before her for the first time. Her mind completely whited out, the mental equivalent of elevator music taking over as she drank him in. He wasn't chiselled, but he had the definition of an active man, with broad shoulders and good proportions. She was already fond of his chest, her hands itching to run through the hair there again. He turned for her perusal, hands out, blushing almost boyishly when he faced her again. He cracked his knuckles, an anxious gesture that somehow made him more attractive to her than any amount of grandstanding would have done.

'Do I pass muster?' He looked down at himself, moving restlessly, like he might bolt from the room if she gave him a negative answer.

She could only do what he had done for her and show her honest appreciation of him. 'You are quite possibly the most attractive man I've ever met.'

His head snapped up at that, his flush spreading to the tips of his ears. 'I'm what?'

She shook her head. 'Michael Tremblay, you are entirely worth looking at, and this is the best dinner date I've ever had in my life.'

He cracked a laugh. 'I haven't even fed you yet.'

'Am I wrong?'

'No,' he said, climbing towards her onto the bed until she was flat on her back with him above her, his weight on his elbows. 'You're not wrong. Best dinner ever.' His grin turned wicked. 'But then, I've already eaten.'

She rolled her eyes, but she was smiling.

Mike watched her for a moment, his expression turning into something warm and tender, before he lowered his mouth to hers. The kiss started out slow, lazy, and Sophie was starting to understand that when Mike kissed, he did it with his entire body. It wasn't just an action of lips, tongue and teeth. It was hands in her hair, coasting down her sides, tickling the backs of her knees. She could feel the rumble of his response through his chest, which was pressed to hers. Their legs tangled and shifted. He was a tactile man, hellbent on touching every nook, every hidden secret place on her body, mastering every bit of her topography.

While Sophie hadn't had that many partners, she'd had a lot of sex over the years, and would have considered herself to be somewhat knowledgeable about the subject. Now, with Mike, she was starting to wonder if she'd been doing it right all this time – or, more accurately, if her partners had been. It wasn't like he was doing new things, but more like he was going about them in an entirely different way. She'd been getting a scoop of vanilla ice cream, not realizing that there were places that would give you three scoops and unlimited toppings.

Mike took his time. If something he did made her moan, caused her breath to hitch, or got any reaction, he *lingered*. It was like he was starving for touch, the way he went after her. And to be honest, she was no less hungry for him.

He brought her to orgasm again using his fingers before he even reached for the condoms, his hands shaking with barely repressed need as he slid one on. He hitched up her leg slowly, his eyes never leaving her body, as he let out a breath. 'Beautiful. Absolutely beautiful.'

He lowered himself into the cradle of her thighs, his hands cupping her face. 'We still good?'

In answer, she wrapped her arms around his shoulders, pulling him in for a kiss.

He eased into her, his movements measured, rocking deep with each thrust. She shuddered from the pleasure of it, her eyes drifting shut against her will. Everything felt so *good*.

Mike nipped her lip. 'What did I say about eyes on me?'

'Bossy,' she murmured. 'I would never have thought you'd be so bossy in bed.' She must have liked it, however, because she was soon gazing up at him, watching his eyes darken like the fading light through the curtained windows.

'You don't like it?'

She smiled. 'Didn't say that, did I?'

He gave a low, breathy laugh as he lowered his head to her nipple and sucked.

Sophie cried out, arching, heat building rapidly inside her. Mike spread her wider, deepening his thrusts, but keeping the same maddening pace. Sophie writhed beneath him, gasping his name, trying to get what she wanted – she was so *close*.

'What do you need?'

'Faster.' She practically sobbed the word. 'And touch me. I need – I need you to touch me.' She knew she was being vague, but her thoughts were jumbled, and she wasn't used to asking for what she wanted. Worse, she wasn't used to anyone giving a damn.

Mike seemed to understand, shifting so he was on his knees, placing his thumb over her clit and rubbing in circles as he thrust into her.

Sophie fractured into a thousand glittering pieces as pleasure shot through her, only to dissipate slowly, leaving her a puddle of sated human. Mike followed soon after, his body caging hers, and her name upon his lips. He collapsed on her when he was done, chest heaving like a bellows, his body deliciously heavy on hers. She had little energy left but found enough to stroke his back as she held him.

Then, surprisingly, his chest started to shake.

Oh no. Oh god. Was he *crying*? She really hoped he wasn't, not because she had an issue with men crying, but her ego couldn't take it at this particular moment and – no, wait. He was wheezing.

'Are you *laughing*?'

He nodded, his face buried in her shoulder.

'Why?' Was laughing worse than crying? She supposed it depended on what he was laughing about.

'I was thinking' – he wheezed another laugh – 'about when we met.'

Sophie couldn't figure out the connection. 'Okay . . .'

'Even monkeys in the trees do it.' That sent him into another paroxysm of laughter.

'*That's* why you're laughing?' She smacked him playfully on the back. 'It wasn't even funny when I said it!'

'Yes, it was.' He leaned back to look at her. 'It's even funnier now.'

'Why, exactly?'

'I don't know.' He started shaking again with a fresh wave of laughter. 'It just is.'

'You're ridiculous.'

'I know,' he said, tucking his face into the space where her neck and shoulder met. 'But I hope you like it.'

'Yeah,' she said. 'I guess I do.' Then she couldn't help it. She started laughing right along with him.

Chapter Twenty-One

They slept for an hour or so after the laughing fit, then they woke up to make love again. After that, they were rightfully starving and Mike pulled on a pair of joggers to raid the kitchen. He brought back the fruit and cheese plate, along with sandwiches he'd made out of the cold chicken, and one of the bottles of wine. Neither of them could be bothered to reheat the actual meal.

They ate it in bed with their fingers, Sophie wearing one of his shirts, her hair sticking up at wild angles. He was afraid to look in a mirror. He probably didn't look any better. For once, though, he wasn't concerned about getting anything on the sheets while he ate.

Sophie took a big bite of her sandwich, a napkin spread over her lap, which Mike thought was pretty funny since she wasn't actually wearing any clothes. 'This chicken is really good.'

Mike lounged on the bed, slicing the Brie one-handed. 'I did have an actual dinner planned. A whole date, even.'

'So, what did I miss?'

Mike used the knife to slide the hunk of Brie onto a slice of apple. 'Well, first, I was going to invite you in and hope you didn't notice that I was so nervous I was basically covered in sweat. I'd planned on distracting you away from this very obvious fact by showing you my post-dinner cheese plate.'

'Good plan,' Sophie said, setting down her sandwich on the napkin so she could sip her wine. 'That would have worked. I'm often hypnotized by cheese.'

'Who isn't?' Mike asked, tossing a grape towards his mouth, only for it to hit the side of his face and land unceremoniously on the duvet.

Sophie picked up the grape and held it out to him.

'That's probably the least hygienic grape ever. Do you know where this bedspread has been? Because I do.' He leaned forward and snatched the grape with his teeth.

'Then why did you eat it?'

'I'm a filthy man.' He grabbed another bit of cheese.

'Okay then, filthy man. What else?'

'While the chicken was resting, a little dancing. I made a playlist. A little salsa in the kitchen. Then dinner, where I would regale you with charming anecdotes about my life.'

'Like what?'

'I don't know, I don't have any. I'd planned on either making some up or deflecting and asking you questions about *your* life.'

'Hm, yes, good plan.' She finished off her sandwich.

'Then, if things were going really well, I was going to ask if you wanted to watch a movie and work my courage up to holding your hand. My first bold move to seduction.'

She almost choked on her sandwich. 'First bold move, huh? What would you call that thing we did on the couch in my flat?'

'Hot, that's what I'd call it.' He finally abandoned the cheese in favour of his sandwich.

They ate quietly for several moments, enjoying each other's company, before a question occurred to Sophie. 'Were you really nervous?'

'Terrified,' Mike said. 'I wanted this to go well.' He canted his head, gazing up at her. 'Did it?'

'Spectacularly well,' Sophie said. 'A couple of times.'

He laughed before remembering something she'd said earlier. 'Hey, what did you mean when you said, "It was one of *those* kinds of dinners"?'

'Something my friend Edie said when I mentioned your invite. She asked if it was a proper dinner or the kind where we'd have sex against the hallway wall.'

Mike blinked, his half-eaten sandwich only part way to his mouth. 'Is Edie psychic?'

'No,' Sophie said. 'A little terrifying at times, and you don't want to cross her, but not psychic.'

'Because that wasn't my plan at all.' He took a sip of wine, setting the glass back on the bedside table when he was finished. 'It was that dress's fault. As well as your underthings. And the sight of you in them.' He fell back onto the bed, slinging his arm over his eyes with a groan. 'I was basically all over you as soon as you walked in the door, pawing you like an animal.'

Sophie bit into one of the apple slices, the flavour pleasantly tart and sweet. 'Did you hear me complaining? Your plans were lovely, but this way I still had a nice dinner *and* I got to paw you in your hallway.' She smiled at him as she took another bite. 'I blame the shirt you were wearing, as well as the jeans low on your hips. And the sight of you in them. Top date marks all around.'

He leaned across their makeshift picnic and kissed her. 'How lucky I am that you've dropped the bar so very low.'

She kissed him this time, and he tasted apples and wine on her lips.

He pulled back just far enough that he could talk. 'Are you still hungry?'

'No,' Sophie said. 'Why?'

'Because I think it's time for dessert.'

'What else did you get for dessert? I've already seen your cheese plate.'

Mike grinned. 'You.'

'Oh,' Sophie said, not moving from where she sat poised a fraction of an inch away from him. 'Then we'd better put all of this stuff away, hadn't we?'

Mike had to go into work early the next morning, since he was still trying to catch up from missing work when Sophie had been ill. He hated leaving her all warm and sleepy in his bed, but he also didn't want to wake her. She'd had precious little sleep as it was. Then again, so had he, which might explain why he whistled all day at work.

Sometime around midday, his phone buzzed. He dug it out of his pocket quickly, hoping it was Sophie, but it was a message from Amaya. She'd taken a photo of her stretched out on the patio on a towel, soaking up the sun, a pair of sunglasses on her face. Next to her sat Barney the plant, wearing a matching pair. Underneath the photo was the message: *#twinning*.

Mike: Cute.

He set the phone down, getting back to some of the notes the clients had sent him on the design suggestions he'd emailed them earlier in the week. It wasn't long until his phone buzzed a second time. His hopes rose again, but this time, it was a photo of Rahul, Noah, Stella and the baby, lying on their living-room floor. They were all wearing sunglasses, though they didn't match, except for the baby. Someone had tried to create glasses for the baby out of construction paper, but baby Archie seemed to be more interested in chewing on them. The message under their photo said: *#twinningsquared*.

Mike gave in and responded. *Very cute as well, though I don't think Archie's glasses are going to work out. Did he eat them?*

Noah: Yes, but we're choosing to look at it as 'bonus fibre'.

Rahul: He doesn't need bonus fibre, btw. We need him to be less regular. Do you know how many nappies I've changed today?

Noah: Yes, my love, mostly because you keep telling me.

Rahul: How else am I going to earn my 'World's Okayest Dad' trophy?

Noah: Just be glad I kept Stella from drawing on the baby with a marker, which was how she was going to problem-solve the glasses issue.

Rahul: I'm going to have to share that trophy with you, aren't I?

Amaya: The important part of all of this is that Barney and I looked amazing. Also, that we successfully tricked Dad into joining the chat. Now we pounce!

Amaya: And by that I mean, how did the date go?!?

Mike: Don't you all have jobs? School? Lives? You're very invested and appear to have too much time on your hands.

Rahul: Dad, we're home with a baby. Amaya's brain is being turned into pudding by her workload. So no, we don't have lives. You're our entertainment. Now tell me how the chicken turned out? Did you do my chicken justice?!?

Amaya: Who cares about your silly chicken? I want the juicy details.

Rahul: Don't knock my chicken. That's my marrying chicken. That chicken won me Noah.

Noah: Yes, it had nothing to do with your handsome face, your inner beauty, or love. It was entirely because of the chicken.

Rahul: The chicken and my thicc thighs.

Amaya: Annnnd we have a new combination of words to be stricken from the chat. I do not want to hear about your thighs. Ever.

Rahul: Jealous.

Mike: You're not really my children. I found both of you under a rock.

Rahul: Father, that is hurtful.

Amaya: I accept that I'm a rock-dwelling goblin. Let's move along. SPILL, DAD.

There was really no escaping it. He had to give them something. *Date went well.* He left it at that. He didn't add unhelpful details like, 'I know what she sounds like moaning my name' or 'she's a blanket thief' or even the fairly mild 'the chicken tastes good even stone cold', which would only invite questions.

Amaya: That's it? Date went well? UGH.

Rahul: This show is boring. Zero stars.

Noah: Did she like the shirt? Will there be more dates?

Rahul: When do we get to meet her?

Amaya: Barney needs a grandma. I'm worried about the lack of a good older female role model in his life. They grow up so quick, Dad, and without good role models, he could turn to a life of crime. My Barney won't make it in the nick! He's too sensitive.

Rahul: How much coffee have you had today?

Amaya: The perfect amount.

Mike set his head onto his desk. Where had he gone wrong? His phone started to buzz continuously, a call coming through. Amaya had probably got tired of waiting for him to respond and called. He answered without looking at it. 'Barney does not need a grandma, and no one is going to prison, you invasive little goblin. I regret educating you – you only use it against me.'

'I take it your children are badgering you again?'

Mike sat bolt upright in his chair. 'Sophie!' Great. Just great. He'd probably not only sounded unwell, but like someone who was a complete bell end to his children. 'Sorry – it's a joke. I don't actually think those things and my children know I'm kidding.'

Sophie laughed. 'I never thought otherwise, though I'd love some context for some of that later. I was calling to see what you're doing tonight?'

Mike frowned at his calendar, which was depressingly full. 'Depends on what time you're thinking.'

'My neighbour Manny is helping with a fundraiser tonight and a few of his volunteers are ill. Any chance you want to help support the senior centre? We'd have to be there no later than six.'

He should tell her no. He had a lot of work to do, and work came first. Or at least it had for the past ten or so years. And where had that got him? He looked at his schedule again.

Fuck it.

'Send me the address. I'll make it there as close to six as I can.'

Sophie made a happy noise. 'Ooooh, thank you! I'll text you the details when I get off the phone.' She paused. 'Thank you in advance. For tonight. Also for last night.'

'The pleasure's mine on both counts.' He hung up after they'd said their goodbyes, finding a few missed messages from his children, mostly more good-natured bickering.

Mike: She said I looked handsome in the shirt and just called to see what I was doing tonight.

Rahul: Yes, chicken for the win!

Noah: Pretty sure shirt for the win.

Amaya: Yes, that's how you win a lady's heart – chicken and shirts. You've unlocked the secret. We are simple creatures, but alas, not that simple.

Mike: She's right. It was probably the cheese plate.

Mike thought it might also be the orgasms, but once again opted out of sharing that particular detail.

Amaya: You made a cheese plate? Excellent choice. No wonder she wants another date. Where are you going? Are you doing something fun?

Mike: She's helping out her neighbour who's running some sort of fundraiser at a local senior centre. So nothing too exciting. Probably a silent auction or something.

Maybe it sounded on the duller side to his children, but Mike didn't think it mattered what he and Sophie did – he always had fun with her. She'd make the evening entertaining no matter what.

With that mindset, Mike was woefully unprepared for what greeted him in the cafeteria of the senior centre. He had not expected the music, the disco ball or the frankly irresponsible number of vodka jelly shots lined up in little plastic containers creating their own poor-decisions rainbow. He probably could have anticipated the tables and chairs, but not the penis-shaped confetti covering the nearest one. He had also not expected to find Manny, Sophie's intimidating neighbour, dressed like a ringmaster, his face in full makeup, which included a great deal of blue glitter.

'Oh good, you're here,' Manny said, rushing towards him. 'How are you with crowd control?'

'What,' Mike said slowly, as he tried to take it all in, 'is happening?'

Manny herded him towards the back of the room, talking as he went. 'Didn't Sophie tell you? It's Drag Queen Bingo.'

Mike peered down at Manny. 'I will admit that I don't know much about being a drag queen, but I thought they usually dressed as women.'

Manny's blue-glitter eyebrows bunched together. 'What? Oh, it's not me. I'd make a terrible drag queen. I'm more of an assistant. I help Dazzle with the sound and whatever else she needs. Look, I really appreciate the help. Bingo is a huge draw and a big money-maker for the senior centre – it pays for a lot of the programmes they offer. My *abuela* goes here, so it means a lot.'

'Your *abuela*?'

'Yeah,' Manny said. 'That's her over there by the Jell-O shots.'

'I didn't know people drank at bingo. Or had disco balls.' Mike came to a stop, pushing the heels of his hands against his eyes. 'Manny, I didn't get a lot of sleep, and right now there's a lot going on here all at once.'

'I feel for ya, buddy, but I don't have time to acclimate you. Doors open in twenty minutes and bingo players are fucking feral. Let me hand you off to Sophie. She's been brought up to speed already.'

Sophie was in the kitchen, helping Tom and Marisa as they finished setting up the kitchen.

'Nachos,' Tom said when he caught Mike's questioning expression. 'Everyone gets a boat of nachos with their entrance fee. Helps create a base for the drinks.'

Marisa filled a plastic container with sour cream. 'There's something about buying Jell-O shots from seniors. People go overboard. It would be a really bad idea not to offer at least *some* food.'

To Mike, the kitchen seemed like a microcosm of the barely controlled chaos in the larger room he'd just left, only a fraction more manageable. There was simply too much to absorb. He turned to Sophie. 'Just tell me what to do, and I'll do it. Should I stay back here and help?'

Marisa jumped in, not giving Sophie a chance to answer. 'Oh no, you're not going to be wasted back here. We're going to use the power of your accent.'

Mike blinked. 'Pardon?'

Tom smirked at him as he tied on his apron. 'She means she wants you to work the room. People buy a pack of bingo sheets when they come in, but they can buy smaller, quick-round games during the evening, too. Marisa wants you to go out there and charm people into spending money.'

'Yes,' Marisa said. 'Trust me. It'll work. TV has trained us to think anyone with a British accent is either a super-villain or intelligent and charming, like Benedict Cumberbatch.' She shooed him with her hands. 'So go out there and *charm*. Channel your inner David Tennant.'

'He's Scottish.'

Marisa scrunched up her face in confusion. 'Isn't that part of Great Britain?'

'Yes,' Mike said.

'So doesn't that make them British?'

Mike waggled his hand back and forth.

'They probably think of themselves as Scottish first,' Tom said helpfully. 'There's a lot of complicated history there.'

'Fine,' Marisa said. 'Channel your inner James McAvoy.'

Mike shook his head. 'Also Scottish.'

Marisa huffed. 'Cillian Murphy?'

'Irish,' Mike said, a bit apologetically.

'Is there anyone *in* England?' She frowned. 'Hugh Jackman?'

Tom snorted. 'He's Australian.'

Marisa threw her hands in the air. 'Daniel Craig? But not James Bond Daniel Craig, more Benoit Blanc – but without the Southern accent. Go be folksy and handsome.'

Mike looked helplessly at Tom, who raised his hands in surrender. 'Don't look at me.'

When that didn't work, Mike turned to Marisa. 'You do know your fiancé is also British?'

'I am aware, yes,' Marisa said. 'But he's on nacho duty. I made a promise after last time.'

Mike wheeled round to face Tom. 'What does *that* mean?'

Tom threw him a pitying look as he transferred grated cheese into a plastic container. 'It means watch out for table five. I've never been hit on so much in my life. Especially watch out for Dolores. She's been known to get handsy. If she does, tell Manny and he'll handle it. She's been warned.'

'Handsy?' Mike clasped the back of his neck with his hand. 'I don't want to be groped by strange older women.'

'Only older women you know well?' Sophie asked. She placed a hand on Mike's shoulder. 'I'm kidding. No one expects anyone to be groped. I'll try to handle table five, but if anyone makes you uncomfortable, tell Manny.'

'I'm more confused now than I was when I came in here,' Mike admitted. 'Who knew bingo could be so fraught with danger?'

'Oh, you poor man,' Tom said, shaking his head. 'You sweet summer child. You have no idea.'

Mike was starting to severely question his choices for the evening.

'I've got you,' Sophie said, taking his arm. 'Just have fun and try to sell as many sheets as you can. Every penny goes towards the senior centre.'

Chapter Twenty-Two

Sophie was starting to understand why Drag Queen Bingo was such a draw. Dazzle Camouflage could work the room, keeping up an engaging patter between the numbers. Manny the Man-tamer, as he was being called, handled the bingo programme on the laptop, the projector that showed the number on the screen, and the sound. Everyone was in high spirits as they competed to win donated prize packages and cash pots. There was a wide range of people there, their only common denominator seeming to be people who liked having a good time.

After two games, Dazzle sang 'Luck Be a Lady' while Sophie and Mike sold the special game sheets. Sophie had a pocket apron around her waist full of cash, which she took back to the person handling the money as soon as the song was over. Mike met her back there to do the same thing, handing her a small plastic container when he was finished. The jelly inside was a vibrant, unnatural blue colour.

'Nothing good has ever come from jelly shots,' Sophie said, having to raise her voice and lean close to him to be heard. This close, she could smell his skin, which smelled as good as always.

'Good and fun aren't always the same thing,' Mike said. 'Besides, I bought them from Manny's grandmother, who's also selling fudge. It's going to a good cause.' His mouth was so close, she could feel his breath. 'Are you going to let the seniors down, Sophie?'

'Well,' she said, 'when you put it that way . . .' She popped the lid, squeezing the sides until she could get the jelly into her mouth. She shuddered. 'It tastes like blue and vodka.'

He laughed. 'I'm told it's easier if you use your finger to loosen the sides first.'

'I've been handling money. No thank you.'

He was still grinning when he downed his, which was green. 'Mmm, chemical lime and cheap vodka.' He threw away the container. 'I'm going to go get us another round.' He strode back to the tray of shots, falling quickly into discussion with Manny's grandmother. She couldn't hear him, but Mike was gesturing to the different colours and she was responding, her hands flitting all over the place.

Sophie tried to picture this same scene when she'd been married and couldn't imagine it. Despite all his bluster about being a pillar of the community and all of that, there was no way Andrew would have come to something like this. He'd talked a lot about the importance of being there for your neighbour, but that rhetoric had all seemed to circle back to supporting local small businesses, mostly his.

Though a little overwhelmed at first, Mike had thrown himself in, which couldn't have been easy. She knew full well how little sleep he'd managed. She'd taken a nap earlier, but he'd worked all day. You wouldn't know it from watching him. All she'd had to do was tell him that someone needed help, and here he was. Not complaining. Not grudging. But like there was nowhere else he'd rather be. He never made anyone feel like they were a burden. Even sleep-deprived and changing her sheets, he'd acted this way.

And this, she thought, was what was so dangerous about Michael Tremblay. Not that he was a stunner, not that he was good in bed, though she liked both of those things, but his kindness and decency. His sense of humour about life.

Because it was those things that would make it very easy for Sophie to fall in love with him, and that was the last thing either of them wanted.

As if feeling her attention on him, Mike looked up at her and winked. Even that was somehow sexy, though she usually thought men winking at her was creepy. She gave him a little wave and a smile, then turned her attention back to the players and put everything else out of her mind.

Five hours later found her and Mike half naked on her couch. The remnants of their dinner was still on the table, curries they'd grabbed from a takeaway place. Mike was rubbing her feet, pausing occasionally to guzzle some water while mumbling about 'smooth-talking seniors and their tricky jelly shot ways'. She was enjoying the foot-rub – there had been a lot of running around during bingo – and was attempting to rub one of his feet while also looking at the photos and short videos on her phone.

Mike groaned.

'You okay over there?'

'A little drunk,' Mike admitted. 'I wasn't expecting to get any drunk. Manny's *abuela* is not to be trusted.'

'I did tell you that Manny said she was ruthless. There you were, an innocent with cash in your hand. Her job was to part you from it, and she was very good at it.'

Mike closed one eye and squinted at her. 'How come you're fine?'

'I gave mine away after the second one,' she admitted.

Mike's eyes widened as he gasped, pausing the foot-rub to point at her. 'Foul betrayer.'

'I told you I didn't want any more,' she said, flipping to a new image on her phone. This one was of Mike holding up a winner's hand in victory. From the way they were both carrying on, you would have thought he'd won the serving tray set. 'Not my fault if you didn't listen.'

Mike sighed. 'It was too loud in there. I didn't hear you properly. I thought you'd asked for more.' He slumped back against the couch. 'I wouldn't have bought you more if I'd heard you say no.'

'Keep drinking water. That will help.'

He dutifully finished off the glass and set it on the table before returning to her feet. 'Did you get any good ones for your blog?'

'Ooooh, yes,' she said. 'Including the one where you were dancing with Dazzle Camouflage.'

Mike let his eyes drift closed, though he was still using his thumbs to dig into the arch of her foot. 'For someone so tall, she was very light on her feet.'

'Dazzle gave me permission to post the video on the blog as long as I link to her website and the senior centre. I'd like to see if we can raise some extra funds for them. They do so many classes and community gatherings – it's a wonderful resource.'

Mike hummed a response, though he was no longer rubbing so much as petting her ankle.

She smiled at him. He seemed so content where he was, the corners of his mouth curling up even now when he was half asleep. She raised her phone and took a picture. Not for her blog, but just for her – something to remind her of a night that was pretty much perfect.

Mike gave a sleepy chuckle.

'What is it?' she asked, setting down her phone.

'Tom dropping that container of salsa.' He cracked his eyes open. 'He'd been so smug in his kitchen refuge, hiding from Dolores. No one was pinching his bum but his fiancée. Then – *crash.*'

It had been a large container, too. Tom had still been mopping when they'd left.

'Did Dolores pinch your bum?'

'Once,' he murmured sleepily, his eyes drifting shut again.

'Why didn't you say anything?'

'Her friend made her apologize and asked me not to tell – she's on her third strike and they were afraid she'd be banned again.'

Sophie frowned. 'If her behaviour is problematic, someone needs to address it.'

'I talked to her,' Mike said, patting Sophie's ankle, his eyes still shut. 'She misses her husband. Married twenty years. Told her I knew what that was like. We bonded.' His words were tapering off now. She'd need to move him to the bed before he passed out, otherwise he'd have to spend an unpleasant night bunched up on the sofa. 'Called me her ride or die. You can't throw out your ride or die, even if she does pinch your bum.'

Sophie covered her mouth to stifle her laugh. 'Oooh, she got you good. Wrapped you right around her little finger, didn't she?'

Mike didn't answer. Sophie sighed and nudged his legs off the couch. 'Okay, let's go. Bedtime for you.'

He muttered something and buried his head deeper into the couch.

'And we'd better give you something for that headache that will probably be coming along really soon.' It took a little effort, but she finally got him up and to the bedroom, tucking him under the covers. He was snoring softly a few seconds later.

Ridiculous man.

But she was happy that he was her ridiculous man, at least for now. Only for now. Her stomach sank, and as she watched him, Sophie thought she might be a little too late. She was more than half in love with him already, and she was going to have to work very hard to not fall the rest of the way.

Thursday evening, which was four days after bingo, Sophie was on the couch with Marisa as Tom made them both dinner. It was a celebration of sorts. Sophie's last post, which had featured the senior centre's bingo night, a few short videos of Dazzle Camouflage being amazing, and a few pictures of Mike charming the players, had garnered three times the usual traffic. The fundraising meter for the centre kept going up, too, with every repost of the article.

'How much is it at now?' Marisa asked.

Sophie handed her the phone.

Marisa whistled. 'That's great. I think that video of Mike and Dazzle waltzing was the clincher. She looked amazing and your boyfriend's pretty handsome. Hate to say it, but sex really does sell.'

'He's not my boyfriend,' Sophie said.

'Sure he's not.' Marisa handed back her phone. 'You just talk constantly, sleep at each other's apartments, and . . .' She stretched to see if Tom was listening from the kitchen, but he seemed to be scowling at the recipe he'd pulled up on his iPad. 'You've been humping like rabbits with twenty-four hours to live and nothing to eat but aphrodisiacs.'

Sophie's brows went up. 'That's . . . graphic.'

Marisa waved it away. 'I'm just saying, you two might not be labelling it, but I am. Friends with benefits don't go on dates. They don't hold hands.' She pointed at Sophie's phone. 'And they don't send you cute morning coffee selfies every day just because.'

'I'm not ready to call it anything else. Maybe when we're both back in England . . .' She let the thought trail off. She'd been trying not to think about that too much. She missed her home, but she loved being close to Tom and Marisa, and she was afraid to bring up the idea of trying to maintain the relationship once they got back to London. Mike seemed okay right now, but she was concerned that pushing him too hard too quickly would make him panic and shut down.

Marisa sent her a commiserating look. 'How much longer is he here again?'

'Two weeks, I think. He said it depended on the job.'

'And we've got you a little over a month,' Marisa said. 'That's not a big gap of time. Just enough for him to miss you.'

'Maybe.' What they had right now was wonderful, but it also felt new and fragile. The last thing she wanted to do was shatter it with too many questions.

'Twenty more minutes,' Tom said from the kitchen. 'Is Mike going to make it?'

'I'll see.' Sophie checked her phone and saw she'd just missed a message from him. 'He'll be here shortly.' Out of habit, she opened up her email app, wanting to see if there was anything dire she needed to handle.

She had two unexpected emails, both of which had subject lines that made her heart rate pick up, though for very different reasons. One was from Andrew. She didn't want to read it, so she forwarded it to Edie as per an agreement they'd made months earlier. If there was anything actually important in it, Edie would let her know. Otherwise, she could delete it.

The other, however, was from someone she didn't know. *KMartin@Halftimebooks.com*
Subject: Swanning About Blog

As Sophie skimmed, her heart rate sped up. She reached over without thinking and took one of Marisa's hands.

'What?' Marisa asked. 'What is it? If it's the Wicker Man, delete that trash.'

'It's not the Wicker Man,' Sophie said absently as she reread the email, convinced she'd read it incorrectly before.

'It's from an editor. She'd like to meet about my blog. I think
. . . I think she wants to see if I'd want to write a book.'

Marisa froze, her mouth open in surprise.

Tom flew out of the kitchen, wooden spoon in hand. 'What
was that? What did you say?'

Sophie blinked at them both. 'It's from an editor. She
knows I'm in New York and she wants to talk to me about
the possibility of making a book for *Swanning About.*'

Tom blinked, stunned.

Marisa threw up her arms and screamed. 'Victory!' She
started punching the air over her head, each punch punc-
tuating a new 'victory'. She threw her arms around Sophie.
'I'm so excited for you!'

Tom came over and joined the hug, being careful to keep
the spoon from hitting them. 'That's amazing, Mum.'

'Nothing may come of it, you know,' Sophie said. 'It's only
a preliminary meeting.'

'It doesn't matter,' Tom said. 'You never thought it would
even get this far. Either way, you've done something you
should be proud of.'

'Take the win,' Marisa said. 'Life doesn't give us a lot of
them.'

'You're right,' Sophie said, hugging them both, and feeling
like she was quite possibly the luckiest person alive in that
moment. 'I'm taking the win.'

Marisa gave one more small punch, her voice quiet this
time. '*Victory.*'

Chapter Twenty-Three

Mike had spent this week in bliss. There had been setbacks at work, which would usually have irritated him, but now only managed to thrill him. Setbacks meant he would be here longer, which meant more time with Sophie, which meant he could probably take her to see a few of the other places he'd found that might be good for her blog. Maybe even convince her to finally go and see a few of New York's tourist highlights, like she wanted. And to see how she felt about testing the kitchen table to find out if it held her weight. Or his kitchen table. He didn't care which. It was the testing part that was important.

Since their dinner date at Mike's flat, they hadn't spent much time apart except for when they were working, both of them aware that their time together was finite. He wanted to squeeze the days for every moment with Sophie he could get. Which was why, despite being worn out from work, he'd made his way over to her flat, stopping to get flowers en route. It hadn't taken him long to see how much Sophie delighted in these small gestures – though he didn't like to dwell on the fact that she probably delighted in them because they seemed like large gestures to her. With the possible exception of her friend, Edie, no one had doted on Sophie in a long time, which was perplexing to Mike. She was so fun to dote on – why hadn't more people figured that out?

He headed towards Tom's flat, as per Sophie's instructions, pausing when he heard someone yelling through the door. He couldn't quite make out the actual words, but the tone seemed . . . happy, maybe? He waited a moment to see if he could hear more, but when nothing else happened, he knocked.

The door swung open, revealing Tom, who was holding a wooden spoon and wearing an apron, and from the expression on his face was either very happy to see Mike or was about to murder him and cook him for dinner.

'Oh good,' Tom said. 'You're here.' He gestured with the spoon in a way that made Mike think rather uncomfortably of a cattle prod.

'Maybe take it easy with that spoon,' Mike said. 'Some of us want to live long lives with both of our eyes.'

'Sorry,' Tom said. 'I'm excited.'

Marisa snatched the spoon out of his hand. 'Come on. I'm starving.'

Mike pulled off his shoes, automatically seeking out Sophie. He found her setting out four champagne glasses, excitement lighting her up so much she glowed. He kissed her on the cheek. 'Dinner that exciting, huh? Those must be some amazing chicken enchiladas.'

Tom opened his mouth, only to have Marisa lunge up and cover the lower part of his face with her hand. 'It's your mom's news. Let her tell it.'

'I got an email from an editor,' Sophie said. 'She loves the blog. Wants to meet up to discuss possibilities.' She started pouring the champagne into the glasses. 'Nothing may come of it, but we decided to celebrate anyway.'

The way jubilation punched through his system, Mike would have thought it was news for him and not Sophie. He was just so *happy* for her. 'Really?' He grinned, striding over to lift her off the floor in a big hug. 'That's fantastic.' He kissed her cheek, setting her back onto her feet.

Sophie flushed. 'Like I said, nothing may come of it—'

Marisa smacked her hand flat on the counter. 'You will not downplay good news and accomplishments in this house. No, you will pick up your champagne glass and let us toast your good fortune, remember?'

'Right,' Sophie said, handing out glasses. Once they all had one, she lifted hers. 'To celebrating possibilities!'

Mike clinked his glass with everyone, all of them smiling as they sipped, the tart, bubbly taste of the champagne sliding over his tongue. He put his arm around Sophie and gave her another squeeze. She smiled up at him and he wondered at the fact that not very long ago, he hadn't known a single person in this room. He'd never heard of Sophie Swann and thought he'd be working non-stop in New York, the days seamlessly blending together in a montage of sameness until he keeled over one day onto his desk.

It seemed such an unsatisfactory way to live compared to this.

'Wait!' Tom said, taking out his phone. 'I want to get a picture. Someday, Mum, you'll get to post about this on your blog – even if it's just to discuss what might have been – and you'll want a photo to mark the moment.'

Marisa moved next to Sophie, and Tom stood on Marisa's other side, the two men bookending the group as Tom got the phone ready. He snapped several pictures and Mike didn't need to see them to know that he'd look happy in every single one.

Because he was.

And way back in the dusty crevices of his mind, a tiny voice reminded him that he'd been happy like this before once, and that was exactly the moment that life loved to kick your teeth in.

Mike ignored that voice all through dinner, several champagne toasts, and taking Sophie back to her flat to love her, gently and thoroughly, until they were both drowsy and sated.

None of that kept the voice from talking, though.

And no matter how hard he tried, Mike couldn't stop listening to the familiar sounds of his own doom.

Monday afternoon found Sophie sitting across from Kenzie Martin, one of the editors at Halftime Books, in a cute little Italian place that smelled like garlic in the best possible way. Kenzie looked younger than Sophie had been expecting, her brown hair back in a ponytail, her outfit casually stylish. She didn't seem to be wearing any make-up beyond her winged eyeliner, which looked good on her. They'd already had lunch as they'd talked, chatting about general things before Kenzie had launched into her proposal.

Sophie was glad she'd stuck to club soda to drink, because she was already feeling overwhelmed by all of it and wanted to keep her head in any way she could.

'So that's my thought. We do the book in two parts – New York and London. Not really a travel guide, but more like a collection of humorous essays. We could make it an interactive book by putting in QR codes to link to your video clips. There are a lot of women out there – *people* out there – that have had to start over like you did. Your stories will make them laugh, but I'm hoping they'll connect a community, too, like your blog has done. What do you think?'

'It's a lot to mull over,' Sophie said. 'I've never even written a book.'

'Everyone's got to start somewhere,' Kenzie said, leaning forward. 'Why not give it a go? I'd need a proposal and sample chapters to take to acquisitions. I've been pitching the idea, but I'll need to show them something. I can send you some example outlines if that would help.'

Sophie chewed on her lip. It was very tempting. She loved the instant connection of writing online, but to hold a book in her hand with her name on it? That would be something special, too. 'When would you need all of that?'

'Soon as you can get it to me. I know you'll need to work on it around your usual posts. The advance might not be much – lots of factors determine that. And those take a while to get to you anyway. Will you be able to extend your stay here, do you think?'

Sophie blinked at her. 'Extend my stay? I've got another three weeks . . . Oh.' That's when it finally landed in her mind that if she was going to get enough material to write a book, she was going to have to explore more of the city. Three weeks probably wasn't going to cut it. Could she stay longer? Her flat might be an issue. She'd have to see if the owner had anyone lined up after her. Edie would be both elated about the offer, and sad she wasn't coming home right away.

Mike . . . she couldn't think of him right now. She'd spent too many years putting Andrew first, putting her own dreams on hold. She wasn't going to do that again. Either Mike understood, or he wasn't the man for her.

'I can see,' Sophie said finally.

Kenzie smiled at her, an understanding expression on her face. 'I've given you a lot to think about, I know. Sleep on it. Run it past your family and that boyfriend of yours if that will help.'

'He's not my boyfriend,' Sophie said. 'But yes, I'd like to discuss it with my family.' Tom and Marisa might see things she was missing.

'He's not? Sorry for the assumption,' Kenzie said. 'But that dancing video . . .' She looked at the ceiling and fanned herself with both hands.

Sophie laughed. 'The one with me, or with Dazzle Camouflage?'

'Touché,' Kenzie said. 'But I meant what I said. Think on it. Talk to the important people in your life. Just don't take too long – I'd like to move forward on this if we can. No matter what, it was great to meet you, Sophie.' She held out her hand.

Sophie took it. 'It was good to meet you too, Kenzie, and I appreciate the opportunity you're trying to give me.'

'Don't get me wrong,' Kenzie said. 'I'm not giving you anything except a chance you've earned, but I've been around long enough to know that just because something is an opportunity, it doesn't mean you'll want to take it. There are lots of different dreams out there. Maybe this one isn't yours.'

'Wise,' Sophie replied, and they said their goodbyes, Sophie promising to get in touch soon. She thought Kenzie might be on to something when she said that there were a lot of different dreams out there, but as she made her way back to her flat, she was pretty sure that this opportunity, this dream, was one she wanted very much. She just wasn't sure what it was going to cost her in the end.

And whether or not that cost would be worth it.

Chapter Twenty-Four

Mike didn't get a good chance to really hear about Sophie's meeting with the editor until two days later, because work had been busy. He must have been feeling nostalgic, because he'd asked her to meet him at the carousel. They were walking hand in hand along the water, the sun shining, the sky blue, everything looking like one of those no-filter Instagram posts.

Which was a shame, really, because Mike's good mood was evaporating by the minute. No, that wasn't entirely accurate. It wasn't that he was unhappy; he wanted this for Sophie. Mike wanted her to have this success, to hold that book in her hand and to shove it down her crappy ex-husband's neck. Even though the last part would probably never occur to Sophie, Mike wanted her to have the perfect revenge of living well. She deserved that.

Even if he got left behind in the process.

'So you'd be here indefinitely?' Mike asked, keeping his voice level. He didn't want to give any hint of his turmoil, didn't want to do anything that would bring down her joy and sense of accomplishment.

'I guess that's one way to put it. I've started putting together an outline for the proposal for Kenzie. It's going to take weeks to get enough content to fill out the kind of book she's talking about. Obviously, I'll come back to London at some point, but in the meantime, I'll be happy getting more time with Tom and Marisa.'

He hadn't missed that *I'll*. Mentally, for her it was a done deal – at least her part of it. He forced himself to smile. 'That sounds great. How are they doing?'

Sophie considered her answer for a minute as they walked, her head turned towards the river. 'Better, I think. The kind of things they've been dealing with . . . it lingers. Grief takes as long as it takes, and I'm happy that they're not pushing each other to try and get better, faster – whatever that means. I'm not as worried about either of them as I was, so that's a relief.'

Mike nodded, his chest feeling tight. 'You're going to have your plate very full. Is it . . . that is, do you still want to see me? You know, while I'm still here? I don't want to get in the way of your work.'

She tipped her face up to him, bemused. 'Of course I do.' She grinned. 'I need someone to go with me to all of the stuff that Tom and Marisa won't go to.'

'I see how it is,' Mike murmured. 'But I will be forever avoiding table five, at least metaphorically.'

'Speaking of which, what are you doing tomorrow?'

Tomorrow he'd be duct-taping his own mouth shut to keep himself from trying to talk her into coming back to London with him, that's what. 'Work, of course. After that, no plans.'

'How do you feel about roller skating?'

'Like I'm going to break a hip, why?'

'There's a place Manny was telling me about that's part roller rink, part bowling alley. On Wednesdays one of Dazzle's friends does tarot readings at a table in the roller rink. I'd like to get my fortune read. I want to see if there's a dark-haired stranger in my future.' She batted her eyelashes at him.

Me, he thought. *I'm your dark-haired stranger*. He was also hoping she'd take a long trip to faraway lands, or whatever the usual tarot reading clichés were. He didn't care who told her to come back with him, to stay with him, so long as she did it. These thoughts circled in his head, quiet but constant, and he dismissed them all, because ultimately he'd rather punch himself in his own face than step between her and her chance. She deserved that at the very least. He wouldn't say or do a single thing to make her feel otherwise. 'I'm definitely up for bowling. Fair warning, prepare to thrash me. I'm basically shit at bowling.'

'Understood.'

'And I can't tell you whether or not I'm going to be able to roller skate at all. It's been ages since I've tried, but I'm up for whatever it is you'd like to do, as always.'

Sophie beamed up at him, her smile wide. She pressed her lips to his chin, his cheeks, his mouth. 'Thank you, Mike.'

'For what?'

She bumped him with her hip. 'For supporting me. I know you're busy. You can't be getting much sleep, and yet you come along with me on my adventures anyway.'

'I happen to like your adventures,' Mike said. 'I'm happy to be part of them.'

For at least the little time they had left.

The roller rink had been loud, blasting songs Mike hadn't heard in at least ten years, every roller rink and bowling alley operating in the same liminal space of timelessness the world over, where the past and future careened past each other. Mike wasn't sure how they did it, but every bowling alley he'd ever been to had somehow managed to give the feeling of being built sometime around 1982, no matter what time it had actually come to be.

Because of this, his ears were still ringing slightly as he walked into the office for work, and the Spice Girls song 'Wannabe' was etched into his brain, never to leave.

Not that they hadn't managed to have a good time. Sophie had beat him twice on the bowling lanes, and was a slightly better skater than he was, which wasn't saying a lot. He hadn't tried to skate since Amaya was thirteen.

And afterwards . . . well, they'd kind of both won there.

Due to the fact that his mind was far away and his hearing not at its normal levels, it took Mike a few seconds to figure out that someone was speaking to him.

'Mike – got a second?'

He looked up to see Larry Whetherman, the architect on record and his boss, striding towards him. Mike liked Larry – he was mellow, efficient and listened well, something that very few people seemed to actually do. Larry was one of the reasons Mike had taken this position in the first place, and while he was pleased to see him, he hadn't been expecting to. 'Hey, Larry.' He got up and shook the man's hand. 'What are you doing here? I thought you'd had to go to Chicago this week?'

Larry waved this away. 'Change of plans. Speaking of which, that was the reason I tracked you down.'

Mike gestured to a chair next to the drafting table he was using. 'What's up?'

Larry pulled up the chair, taking a seat. 'I'm sure you were frustrated by the delays this week—'

Mike shook his head. 'I think we've both been at this long enough to know that these things happen. It's fine.' More than fine, but he wasn't about to get into that with Larry. They weren't that close, and it wasn't any of his business.

'I know, but you've always worked so hard to get things in early, and I know when you got here that you wanted to get back to London as soon as you could. I looked over everything and talked to the key players, and we all agreed that there was no reason you needed to delay your trip back.'

Mike's brain stuttered to a stop, positive that he'd heard him wrong. 'Pardon?'

'You get to go home! Wrap up whatever you need to today and book your flight. Anything else we can do remotely, I'm sure, but worst case scenario we could always fly you out for a quick trip.' Larry's face held the wide grin of a man imparting great news. News that he was sure would be met with equal levels of excitement. Larry had no idea that it was the last thing Mike wanted to hear.

His grin started to falter at Mike's apparent lack of excitement. Shit. Mike couldn't have that. Larry had probably busted his arse to get this for him and it was his general rule to try and keep his various work contacts happy so that they offered him more work in the future – and work was his priority, wasn't it? Work had been the thing that had kept him together all these years. He couldn't cock that up.

'Sorry,' Mike said, faking the most sheepish expression he could manage. He was surprised he didn't baaa at the man. 'Tired, you know. Took a minute to sink in. That's wonderful news.' Mike smiled and it hurt.

Larry didn't seem to notice. 'I knew you'd be happy.' He extended his hand. 'Good work as always, Mike.'

'Thanks, Larry. Pleasure working with you.' He meant it, too. Even if the inside of his chest felt punched in. 'I'll just wrap things up here and get out of your hair.'

Chapter Twenty-Five

I can't seem to get enough of the views of the skyline in this city. Last night we watched the sunset from the waterfront Time Out Market in Brooklyn's DUMBO neighbourhood. DUMBO stands for Down Under the Manhattan Bridge Overpass, though a few people have told me that it's Down Under the Manhattan and Brooklyn Overpasses. Whatever you want to call it, the views from the market are spectacular. You can take your pick from two floors full of different restaurants, then eat your fill while admiring the visual feast that is the East River, Brooklyn Bridge and Manhattan skyline. My only regret was not being able to sample every restaurant. I've linked to the ones we tried, but I'm curious to know if any of my Swannies out there have been? If so, tell me what you got!

– Excerpt from Swanning About

Sophie plunked her head down onto the table, resting her forehead against the cool surface, even if it meant that she could no longer see Edie on the screen. 'I'm now convinced that I no longer know how words work, and I don't know how people write books ever.'

Sophie had spent all of yesterday and most of today working on her proposal. Because she'd had no interruptions, she'd really been able to concentrate, which was both wonderful and terrible. She was glad Marisa and Tom had gone out on a date. They deserved a night out. Unfortunately, Mike had cancelled their own plans – he'd had to stay late at work – which she didn't love but was understandable.

The problem with no interruptions meant you had no excuse *not* to look at your laptop, and Sophie was beginning to hate the small, blinking cursor. Just sitting there, alone on a blank page. It was mocking her, she was sure of it.

When she looked up, Edie blinked back at her from her tablet screen. She was out on her patio, enjoying the evening with a glass of wine. For the first time in weeks, Sophie wished she were there, too. They could split the bottle and Edie would listen, hug her and tell her she was being ridiculous.

'Okay, you're being ridiculous.'

Of course, she could manage most of that without Sophie being next to her.

'Of course I support your ridiculousness,' Edie said, topping off her wine glass. 'It's one of my favourite things about you. If you were one of those people born with a metal rod shoved up your butt, completely unable to bend, who took themselves *so seriously* . . .' She glared off to the side, and Sophie was sure it was in the direction of her neighbour's house. 'Then I'm not sure we could be friends. And since you're one of my favourite people on this entire planet, that would make me bereft.' She set down her glass with a click.

'I appreciate that,' Sophie said. 'And I love you too.'

Zeus, Edie's gigantic ginger cat, leapt up onto the table. Edie scooped him up and deposited him into her lap. 'I have complete faith in your abilities. You're a good writer, Edie, or your blog wouldn't have so many readers. You're getting overwhelmed is all. What's that thing you say – "a little step will do"?'

'I can manage little steps, it's the big steps here that are killing me.'

Edie pursed her lips as she scratched Zeus under the chin. 'Small steps make up big steps. Figure out how to break it down.'

Sophie rubbed her eyes and made a frustrated sound. 'It's not the breakdown that's the problem. It's the assembling.' She slumped in her chair. 'The blog is basically episodic by nature. There's nothing stringing the posts together. I know some of the pieces I'd like to have in the New York bit, but I'm not sure how to connect it all for the pitch. It's like I'm trying to make a book out of Post-it notes.'

Edie continued to pet Zeus as she considered this, only to stop suddenly, a confused look on her face. 'What on earth . . .' She dug Zeus's collar out of his fur, frowning. 'That *arsehole*.'

'What did Zeus do now? Tear up your potted plants again?'

Edie huffed in irritation. 'Not Zeus. My awful neighbour. He put a tag on Zeus's collar!'

'How do you know it was him?'

Edie gave her a flat look. 'Who else would it be?' Her scowl turned thoughtful. 'Though this move is surprisingly creative coming from him. I'm almost impressed.'

'What's the collar say?'

'"For a good time, call . . ." and then it lists my phone number.'

Sophie guffawed and then quickly stifled it. 'Sorry – I mean, the bastard. We ride at dawn.'

Edie set Zeus onto the ground. 'No, no, your first response was correct. It was a good move.' She tapped her fingers on the table, gazing up at the sky. 'I know you won't be home for months, but what do you think about dogs? A big, filthy, smelly dog that barks a lot? Because I'm suddenly thinking of fostering one for a while.' She turned wide eyes on Sophie. 'Maybe a few of them at once. My garden has a fence, and shelters are overrun, you know. I'm only doing my bit.'

Sophie shook her head. 'Do you even want to deal with a dog that barks all the time?'

'Sometimes,' Edie said airily, 'we must make sacrifices for the important things in life.' She sighed, refocusing on the screen. 'Getting back to the topic at hand – I think you're missing a rather obvious through-line. *You*. Readers connected because your words, your situation, all those things resonated with them.'

Sophie straightened. 'Huh.'

Edie waved a hand like she was shooing her away. 'I know, I know, I'm brilliant. Now go and create something amazing. I've got a nemesis to annoy. Love you!'

The screen went dark.

Sophie shook her head. *Edie, what would I do without you?*

She got up, stretched and got a glass of water. Her friend was right – *she* was the structure. She'd just need to move the pieces she had around, figuring out how she wanted to present the story, and—

Someone was knocking at her door. Sophie peeked through the peephole, assuming she'd see her son or Manny, but was surprised to see Mike. She unlocked the door and opened it, a smile on her face.

Which quickly died. Mike looked . . . well, handsome. He was always attractive. But now he also seemed unhappy. She opened the door wider, ushering him in. 'What happened? What's going on?'

Mike stood in her hallway, hands on his hips, the muscle in his jaw so strained that it was ticking as he stared at the ceiling.

Sophie didn't rush him, letting him think while she shut and locked the door. 'Should I put the kettle on? I feel like I've been swimming in tea, but I'm happy to make you one if—'

'I'm going home.'

Sophie froze. 'You're what?'

Mike slid a hand through his hair, stopping at his neck. 'Home. Back to London. My job is finished. I fly out tomorrow.' Each sentence was clipped, giving her the impression of someone ripping off a plaster to try to lessen the pain.

Everything inside Sophie suddenly dropped down like she was in a broken lift, a nerve-rattling swoop and then a freeze while you waited to see if it would go back up or keep going down. 'I thought you still had two weeks?'

'Larry, who is a nice man and does not deserve to be thrown to the piranhas, no matter what my imagination says, worked miracles so I could get back to London.' Mike rubbed his hands over his face, his eyes hollow.

'Oh.' What else could she say to that? They'd both known this was coming, she just thought she'd have more time to prepare. 'Is this the part where you say, "Maybe this is for the best, a clean break" or some nonsense like that? Because fair warning, if you do, I might stab you with a fork.'

He looked at her, crushed. 'No. *No*, Sophie.' He moved towards her then, pulling her into his arms. 'There's no direction I can take to approach this situation where I come back with anything approaching the phrase "for the best". This is, in fact, shit.' He squeezed her tight, rocking her in his arms. 'Absolute shit. Fucking *Larry*.'

She laughed and they both ignored that it sounded slightly damp. She stepped away from him then, turning so she could wipe her eyes. When she turned back around, Mike was examining the table that held her laptop, notes and half-drunk cup of tea.

'How's it going?'

'Mildly terrible,' she said. 'But Edie had some good suggestions.' She sniffed. 'Mike, what if—'

Mike cut her off. 'The only thing I want you to say next is, "What if I look you up when I get back to London?"' He tipped his chin at the table. 'Because as far as I'm concerned, you're where you need to be. You've worked really hard, Sophie. You deserve this. Don't toss it in the bin just for me.'

'Quite an ego on you,' she said, trying to lighten the mood, because he was right: for a brief, frenzied moment, that had been what she'd been about to suggest. 'I was going to say, "What if I make that cup of tea now?"'

He laughed and it didn't sound any better than her laugh had a moment before. 'I don't want a cup of tea.'

Sophie tugged at his hands, leading him back to the bedroom. 'That's okay. I've got a better idea.' She felt hollow inside, already feeling like Mike was slipping away from her. But what could she do, ask him to stay? He had a job. Family. A home. No, she couldn't ask it of him. But this . . . she could do this.

Mike followed her into the bedroom, standing docilely as she stripped away every stitch of his clothing. She couldn't find the words she needed, not this time, so she did her best to tell him through touch.

Stay. Just . . . stay.

A long time later, Sophie lay naked in his arms, head against his chest, as he dozed. The evening light filtered in through the window, and she thought about how much her heart was breaking and what that meant. It wasn't a thought she wanted to dwell on, especially after the way Mike had made love to her, each kiss, each touch, slow and thorough, like he'd been saying goodbye to every inch of her skin. She thought that maybe he, too, had been at a loss for words and was doing the best he could to say what he needed to say.

Like he thought he'd never see her again.

Mike stroked her hair, and she closed her eyes tight, not wanting to cry. 'I can hear the wheels turning in your head again.'

She felt too sad to laugh. 'Is this why you cancelled on me yesterday?'

'Kind of. I was trying to wrap everything up for Larry and it took longer than I wanted or expected. I didn't get out of there until after eight.'

And he hadn't come straight to her. Probably hadn't wanted to drag the goodbyes out. Well, that quite clearly told her where she stood, didn't it?

'What time's your flight tomorrow?'

'Six in the morning.'

He likely wouldn't be staying at hers tonight, then. Still, she found herself asking anyway. 'Lot to do back at the flat?'

'No, I got most of it done before I came over. I just need to go and get my bag and then head to the airport. Until then . . .' He traced her jaw, lifting her face up to his. 'Can I stay here? With you?'

She should say no. It *hurt* and there really was something about drawing these things out. But she didn't want to say no, so she didn't. In fact, she didn't say anything. She kissed him instead, telling him again without words how much she wished he'd stay. That for the first time in a long time, someone would choose her.

But if he heard her, it didn't stop him from walking out of the door.

Chapter Twenty-Six

Mike left Sophie's flat at an hour too late to be called night and too early to be called morning. When he got back to his rented flat, he showered, but didn't bother shaving, telling himself that there wasn't enough time, but really, he just didn't want to look at his own face. He was a little afraid of what he'd see there. He went into autopilot mode, getting dressed, locking his flat and handing in the keys.

Rideshare to the airport, ticketing, boarding, then a long flight with a child kicking the back of his seat that Mike didn't say anything about, convinced he deserved it.

London was . . . London. He didn't notice much of it. Just went back to his flat, wheeled in his suitcase, watered Barney, who had a label sticking out of his pot bearing a speech bubble that said, 'Welcome home, Gramps!' The plastic brontosaurus now had a friend – what looked like a small plastic capybara.

He spent a moment wondering at what point capybaras had evolved to roam the earth, because he was certain that it hadn't been at the same time as brontosauruses, but then what did he know?

Then he collapsed onto his couch, fully clothed, exhausted and aching. Maybe he was getting ill. He kind of wished he was. Ill he could handle. This . . . this just sucked.

Exhaustion eventually got the better of him, dragging him into a heavy, blissfully dreamless sleep. He got up at some point. Messaged his kids back, even though a second later he couldn't remember what he'd said. Thought about showering or doing anything and just . . . couldn't.

He considered the coming days. Going to work. Coming home. No dance classes or bingo halls full of old ladies pinching his bum or dates where he ended up sick in the toilet. No adventure. His future was grey around the edges. Not forever – Sophie would come back to London eventually. Six months from now. Unless it was longer. Unless she fell in love with New York or met someone there who could give her the things she needed.

What would he do if she didn't come home? Would he fade from her memory until she couldn't remember why she'd liked him in the first place? Would she realize she could do better?

Mike didn't have any answers, or at least not any answers that he liked, so he collapsed back onto the couch and slept.

When he woke up again, Amaya was hovering over him, poking his side with her finger. 'Oh, good. You're not dead.'

'Of course I'm not dead,' he croaked. 'Why would you think that?'

Amaya straightened and put her hands on her hips. 'You didn't hear us knock or let ourselves in. Rahul has been making a god-awful racket in the kitchen as he makes breakfast—'

'Hey! Be nice! I'm feeding you!'

Amaya tipped back her head. 'I love you!' Then she refocused on Mike. 'You haven't so much as twitched. Stella climbed on you and Archie was crying because he's a baby and you haven't moved. You're usually a light sleeper.'

'Jet lag,' Mike mumbled, sitting up and putting his feet on the floor. 'Really nasty jet lag.' And the fact that he felt like his soul had been removed with a rusty spoon. 'What are you all doing here?'

'We're here to greet our dad after he's been away for weeks, that's what, you ungrateful old man.' Rahul popped into the room, setting a mug of coffee with milk in front of him on the table. 'Here.'

'What he means,' Noah said, coming into the room cradling a cooing Archie in one arm while Stella dangled off the other, 'is that we missed you, wanted to see you, and wanted to check on you because we were concerned.'

'If I'd wanted to say that,' Rahul said dryly, 'I would have.'

'Your last couple of texts didn't sound very good,' Amaya said, ignoring her brother.

'I'm fine,' Mike lied. He held out his arms. 'I just needed a hug from my favourite girl.'

Stella squealed and hurled her small body into his arms, almost giving him a black eye with her flailing hands.

Amaya shook her head. 'Ouch, Dad.'

He squeezed Amaya's hand. 'You know you're my other favourite.'

She snorted. 'Good save.' The humour fled her face as she stared at him. 'You look like hell, Dad, and *don't* tell me it's jet lag. I've seen you jet lagged. This isn't it.'

Mike set Stella down and grabbed his coffee. 'I don't know what you're talking about.'

Amaya crossed her arms and sighed, turning her face towards her brother. 'A little help?'

Rahul pulled one of the kitchen chairs into the living room, setting it across from Mike. Then he got his own mug of coffee and sat. 'Dad. We love you.'

Mike sipped his coffee. 'Waiting for the punchline there.'

'No punchline,' Rahul said.

Mike's eyes narrowed over the rim of his cup. 'Is this an intervention?'

'Yes,' Amaya said.

'Kind of,' Rahul added. 'When Mum . . .' He paused, clearing his throat. 'When we lost Mum, I was a mess. We both were. You held us together. I can't imagine what that must have been like for you – how hard it was. We're so grateful—'

'But you don't need to do it any more,' Amaya finished. 'We're grown up, Dad. Rahul is married to a man who is waaaay out of his league and has two of the cutest kids in the universe.'

Rahul shot her a look. 'And this brat is well on her way towards her degree. We're thriving. So cut it the fuck out, Da.'

Mike choked on his coffee, setting it down quickly before he spilled it. 'Excuse me?'

'Language,' Noah murmured.

'Sorry,' Rahul mouthed.

Noah handed Archie to Amaya, then took the seat next to Mike. 'What your two children are trying to say is that they love you, they know something is wrong, and you don't need to pretend it's not in order to protect them.'

Mike stared at all of them in turn, his hands shaking for some reason.

Noah placed a hand gently on Mike's arm. 'I think we've made it very clear, Mike that we're very invested in your drama, and unless you want to be cancelled in season two, you're going to need to start opening up and dropping the juicy bits.'

'I didn't understand half of that,' Mike said.

Amaya cuddled Archie, keeping her tone sweet for the baby even if her words were not. 'What he means, Dad, is stop with the stiff upper lip bull—" She cut herself off, glancing at Stella. "Uh, stuff, and *tell us what the ffff…fudge is going on.*' She threw Rahul a sympathetic glance. 'Sorry. It's surprisingly difficult to watch my own mouth, apparently.'

Mike tried to tell them he was fine. He really did. He opened his mouth, but couldn't quite make himself say the words. Then finally, *finally*, something deep down inside him snapped, and everything came bubbling up, the barrier shattering so completely that he didn't think he'd ever be able to put it back up again.

'I fucked up,' he said simply. 'I think I really fucked up and I'm not sure how to fix it.' He glanced guiltily at his granddaughter. 'Sorry, Stella.'

She patted his leg. 'Papa says bad words are okay when you're hurt.' She leaned in close, peering at him with a worried expression. 'Are you hurt?'

'Yes,' he said. 'Very much.'

'Okay,' she said. 'Then no time out. Daddy says it's a loophole.' She turned to Noah. 'Papa, what's a loophole?'

Rahul made a choking sound and turned his head, hiding his expression.

Noah managed to keep a serious expression on his face. 'I'll explain later, love. Right now, we're talking to Grandpa Mike.'

As everyone in the room watched him expectantly, Mike took a deep breath and told a highly edited and sanitized version of what had been happening.

By the time he'd finished, they'd moved into the kitchen and everyone else was eating what appeared to be a very nice breakfast while Mike held his head in his hands and thought seriously about climbing under his kitchen table and never coming out.

'You know,' Amaya said, spearing the end of a sausage with her fork, 'you said a whole lot of words there, but I didn't hear the important ones. I bet she didn't, either.'

Mike looked up at her, confusion on his face.

Noah rolled his eyes. 'Men.'

Rahul looked at him. 'You *are* men.'

'I know,' Noah said glumly.

Amaya made an exasperated sound, set down her fork, grabbed one of her father's hands and pushed it down to the table. 'Dad. Do. You. Love. Her?' She enunciated each word slowly and crisply.

'Oh god, so much.' His hand was still shaking slightly as he wiped his mouth. 'But that seems – doesn't that seem fast to you?'

Rahul shrugged as he grabbed a cloth and wiped Archie's face. 'Time has always seemed pretty meaningless in these things. I knew I wanted to marry Noah five minutes after I met him.'

Mike frowned at him. 'You did? You never told me this.'

Now it was Rahul's turn to frown. 'I've told you how we met.'

Mike shook his head. 'But not the part where it was practically love at first sight.'

Stella perked up. 'Story time?' When Rahul didn't immediately start speaking, she added a drawn out, 'pleeeeassssse?'

Noah threw them all an apologetic look. 'Sorry, this is one of Stella's favourites.'

'Sounds like I might need to hear it again as well,' Mike said.

Rahul sighed. 'Okay, so I was cooking at this fancy event, and I nipped outside for a cigarette break—'

'Which is bad for you, and you should never do,' Noah told Stella.

'Right,' Rahul said, 'and I heard this one guy going on and on about something. When I looked up, I saw the most beautiful man I'd ever seen in my entire life. I think my heart literally stopped for a second.'

'For the record,' Noah said, 'I was not the one going on and on. That was Gerald, an awful man trying to tell me that B-movie horror films were the worst thing to happen to cinema and if I liked them, I not only couldn't call myself a film lover but had horrible taste and a brain made of cottage cheese.'

'And Noah just looked him dead in the eye and told him that men who are snobs about art forms and make sweeping judgements about something as subjective as taste in films have tiny dicks, and then he turned and walked away.' Rahul was laughing now, his eyes shining.

Noah sighed. 'He was my ride, too.'

'That right there was when I knew,' Rahul said. 'There was no way I was going to let him walk away, so I ran after him, introduced myself and asked him out.'

Amaya sighed wistfully. 'And he said yes, and you fell in love?'

'No,' Rahul said, pausing to cover Stella's ears with his hands. 'He told me to eat shit. My timing wasn't great, admittedly.'

'Your timing was atrocious,' Noah said. 'I was fuming.'

'Right,' Amaya said. 'Forgot that bit.'

Stella pushed away Rahul's hand from her head and he smiled at her. 'I told him if he ever changed his mind, he should call me, even if it was just for a drink or whatever and gave him my number.'

Noah reached over and picked up Stella's cup before she knocked it off the table. 'I found the piece of paper he gave me a few days later when I was checking my pockets before I put my clothes in the wash. I was in a better mood then and I liked that he hadn't pushed when I said no. So I texted him.'

'He took some convincing,' Rahul admitted. 'We hung out as friends for the first month or so.' His mouth curved into a small smile. 'Then I played my ace.'

Stella looked up at Noah. 'Then what did he do?'

'He sweet-talked his friend who manages a small indie cinema into giving him the keys. We had the cinema entirely to ourselves and when I walked in, he'd set up a small table for dinner for two. We're talking cloth napkins and candlelight. He'd cooked for me. We had dinner and watched the original *Creature from the Black Lagoon* and *Anaconda*.'

'Basically,' Rahul said, 'I killed it.' He turned to his dad, his face suddenly serious. 'You did not.'

'I know,' Mike said, swallowing hard. 'I should have said something. Told her . . . I don't know.'

'Dad,' Rahul said, sounding exasperated. 'You should have *stayed*. You should have stayed and given it a shot. Told her how you felt. If it was important to both of you, you'd have worked it out.'

Mike felt so *tired* all of a sudden. 'We'd made a plan. Once she was back in London, we'd talk. Decide what we wanted to do. It was what she wanted.' His voice, when he spoke again, sounded small and miserable. 'What if she's not inter-ested in working it out?'

Rahul leaned back in his chair, making an exasperated noise. 'Well, you're never going to fucking know if you don't try, are you?'

'Loophole, Daddy?' Stella asked as she lined up her straw-berries before popping them into her mouth one by one.

'Yes,' Rahul said without missing a beat. 'Loophole.' He sent Noah an apologetic look.

'We are going to get so many notes home from school,' Noah said with a sigh. Rahul just winked at him.

'Oh, god,' Mike moaned. 'What am I going to do? She probably hates me.'

'She's probably angry,' Amaya said. 'Or hurt. But that's fixable, Dad. I'm just surprised at you. Running away isn't your usual way of doing things. You don't buckle when things get hard.'

'I got scared and I panicked,' Mike said. 'I'm just not sure what to do next.'

'That's easy,' Amaya said. 'You're going to eat the nice breakfast your son has made or he's going to think he's a shit cook and complain about it for weeks.'

'Hey now,' Rahul said.

Noah smiled crookedly at him. 'Accurate.'

'Loooophole,' Stella murmured, grabbing another strawberry.

'Then,' Amaya continued, 'you're going to shower and shave, because you look awful and smell worse and none of that is going to help your case. Then we're going to help you figure this out.'

Stella peered up at her aunt.

'Yes, darling, loophole,' Amaya said, smoothing her hair. 'I have a gigantic ouchie and it's called Grandpa Mike.'

Stella nodded and went back to her strawberries.

'I can't just take off to New York,' Mike said. 'I have a job, you know.'

Amaya pinched her eyes shut and sighed. 'For such a smart man . . . Dad. You have like eighty billion annual leave days saved up. You never take them. So take them. Tell your work it's a family emergency or something. It's not even really a lie. We're your family and we're declaring an emergency.'

Mike dropped his head. 'That didn't even occur to me.'

Noah sighed. '*Men.*'

Amaya reached across the table and grabbed Mike's hand. 'Look, I don't know Sophie, but I've read her blog and I've listened to you talk about her a lot. Still, I can only guess at what she's feeling, but my guess is that she's pretty sensitive to rejection after her divorce. You already freaked out on her once. She needs someone to make some effort and pick her. Give *her* the chance to choose you.'

Mike nodded absently – not because he wasn't listening, but because Amaya's words made him think of that first dinner with Sophie. He needed to reach across the table, just on a much bigger scale. 'I have no idea how to do any of that. Simply flying back isn't going to cut it.'

Amaya looked at him patiently. 'Doesn't her best friend live in London? Isn't she someone you can ask?'

Mike grimaced. 'Yes, Edie, and right now she probably wants to put my body in an unmarked grave somewhere. Can't say I blame her.'

'Grovel,' Noah said. 'A lot. Eventually to Sophie, but start with Edie.'

Mike dropped his face back into his hands and groaned.

Stella frowned at her grandfather, concerned. 'Is Grandpa okay?'

'He'll get over it,' Rahul said. 'As soon as he gets back to New York.'

Chapter Twenty-Seven

Edie peered up at Mike, and though she was a head short-er than him, this obviously didn't faze her in the slightest. He wasn't sure what to make of Edie. Her house was . . . well, it was bright orange, a colour he mentally referred to as nuclear Irn Bru. There were at least twenty wind chimes hung about the place, causing a good amount of ruckus even though it wasn't very windy today. She seemed a little eccentric, but Sophie thought the world of her, and that was enough for him.

'I'm not sure I like you much right now,' Edie said, her mouth pressed into a thin line.

'I'm not sure I like me much either right now,' Mike said, raising his voice to be heard over the wind chimes as the breeze gusted. 'But I need some help.'

Edie didn't unfold at that; her arms stayed crossed, her chin up. 'And why should I give it?'

'Because I'm hoping that, in the long run, it will be good for Sophie.'

Edie dissected him with her gaze. 'If you're not out-of-your-mind, head over heels in love with my friend, you're not stepping past this threshold. So let's hear it.'

'Whatever I am is for Sophie's ears,' Mike said, and as he moved forward, Edie stepped back, letting him into her home.

It was . . . not what he'd expected. While the outside was jarring to every one of his senses, the inside was beautifully put together. Whatever else Edie was, she had an artist's eye. 'You have a lovely home.'

She smirked. 'Surprised?'

Mike considered denying it out of politeness but decided that Edie wouldn't appreciate that. 'Yes.'

'The outside has been temporarily sacrificed to an ongoing feud with my neighbour,' she said, leading him into the kitchen. She filled a kettle and flicked it on, leaning against the counter. 'Okay then, let's hear your pitch.'

By the time Mike had finished explaining his idea, they were seated at a cosy kitchen table, their mugs empty, and Edie was no longer watching him like she was considering where to bury his corpse.

She frowned thoughtfully down at her empty mug. 'You're going to need my help, obviously.'

'I would love it, yes, but I'd understand if you're hesitant. I'll of course pay for the costs.' Mike did have some savings – and a credit card – if push came to shove.

Edie waved her hand. 'I could use a holiday anyway.' She tapped her fingers on the table quietly as she thought. 'What will you do if she doesn't want to play?'

Mike swallowed hard at that thought, Edie unknowingly voicing his fear. He let out a long, slow breath. 'Then I'll know where I stand. At least then I'll know I didn't walk away – that I tried.'

Edie smiled at him then – it was small, and close-lipped, but it *was* a smile. She held out a hand. 'Okay, Mike. I'm in.'

He took it, laughing, as he gave her small hand a shake. 'Thank you, Edie.'

She shook her head. 'I wouldn't thank me yet. It's up to Sophie now.'

'I know,' Mike said, feeling so much lighter now. 'But I'm thankful nonetheless.'

Sophie nodded, rapping her knuckles on the table. 'I'd better go and pack. Oh, and Mike – do be a dear and go out in the back garden and turn on all of the bubble machines for me? My neighbour is working outside today and if I'm going away, I need to get in some last volleys before we leave.'

Chapter Twenty-Eight

Marisa watched her with concern and Sophie couldn't help but feel the reversal in their roles. She'd gone from caregiver to the one needing care and much like Marisa, she was getting heartily tired of her own bullshit. Tom, in age-old British tradition, was making a pot of tea like it might possibly solve every single problem in their lives.

Marisa unpacked the small bag of groceries she'd fetched for Sophie, putting them away neatly in the kitchenette while Sophie continued to nest on the couch. 'You still haven't heard from him, then?'

'No,' Sophie said. 'It's fine, though. For the best.' She'd had plenty of time to work on her book proposal, for example. Which, ironically now that she was miserable, seemed to be chugging along at a good pace.

Marisa shook her head. 'Sophie, if everything was fine, you wouldn't have been wearing the same pyjamas for three days and you wouldn't be speaking to me from a blanket cocoon.'

The blanket cocoon had been going on for a week, but at least she *had* changed her pyjamas. 'I've been working,' Sophie said defensively.

'Have you?' Tom asked. 'Because from where I'm standing, you've been pushing pieces of paper around, muttering and eating nothing but gummy bears.'

'I mean, I don't know a lot about writers,' Marisa added, 'but from what I've seen, that sounds like writing to me.'

'If that's all it involves, how do their books get finished?' Tom asked.

Marisa just shrugged before folding up the shopping bag and turning her attention back to Sophie. 'We're concerned is all.'

Sophie scowled, which didn't have quite the impact she was hoping for since she was still wrapped up in a blanket like a sausage. 'I'm *fine*.'

Marisa shook her head. 'I say this with absolute love, but you are full of shit right now.'

Sophie wanted to double down on the lie but what was the point? They all knew she wasn't fine. She just wanted to be.

'So the man you're in love with is a bit of a git,' Tom said. 'Welcome to dating.'

'I don't want to be in love with him,' Sophie said. The cold reality she'd been facing was that not only had Mike been able to walk away, but he'd been able to stay away. No messages. No video chats. *Nothing*. If she needed a clearer example that all of the feelings were at her end, this was it.

Tom sighed and put a mug in front of her. 'No one *wants* to fall in love, necessarily. We can't really choose these things. Do we need to go back to the rage room? We can print out two pictures this time?' He looked at his fiancée. 'I suppose you're going to tell me violence doesn't solve anything.'

Marisa smiled at him. 'I'm an American, sweetheart. I literally cannot say that phrase with a straight face.' She gave Sophie a hug, squeezing her tight. 'We're making you dinner tonight. Then you're going to go to bed at a normal hour and get some sleep. Things will look better tomorrow, I promise.'

'That's not a thing you can actually promise,' Sophie grumbled.

'Yes, I can,' Marisa said with an impish grin. 'Don't doubt my magic.'

'I've learned not to argue with her, Mum,' Tom said. 'She's usually right.'

Sophie was glad she'd gone to bed early because otherwise she would have murdered the person knocking on her door. She looked blearily at her clock. *Six A.M?* She might still murder them. She cocooned herself back in her blanket and made her way to the door. She was so angry that she didn't even look through the peephole, merely opened the door wide and saw . . . 'Edie?!?'

Her friend stood in front of her, a paper bag and a tray with two takeaway cups in her hands. Edie frowned at her. 'Good god, it's worse than I thought. Well, let me in and tell me you love me.'

And while Sophie did let her in, what she did instead was burst into tears.

After a bout of crying that ended in hiccups, Sophie was handed a bacon and fried egg sandwich and a cup of tea. Once she'd eaten every bite, Edie bundled her off to the bathroom with strict orders to wash the misery off herself and dress like a functioning human being.

'You're being mean!' Sophie yelled from the bedroom. She was pulling on the outfit Edie had laid out for her, which included comfortable shoes. While she did feel infinitely better being clean, she didn't say that to Edie.

'No, I'm not,' Edie yelled back. 'I'm being firm and no-nonsense. Tough love, my friend. Now hurry up.'

'Are we on some kind of schedule I don't know about?' Sophie asked.

'Yes,' Edie surprised her by replying. 'Luckily, we're not late since I factored in some showering and crying time. What I didn't factor in is arguing, so chop-chop!' She clapped her hands twice with the last two words.

'Rude,' Sophie mumbled, but she continued to get ready.

Edie eyed the side of the Staten Island ferry from their perch at the railing. 'Maybe I should have gone with this colour orange for the house. I quite like it.'

Sophie grinned at her. The ferry lumbered along, white tumbled water in its wake. Sophie loved it. She loved everything about it, from the wide range of people on board, to the sea spray in her face, to the views. For the first time in over a week, she felt *good*. 'You can always repaint the house.'

Edie didn't reply but looked beyond Sophie with a grin. 'Finally.'

Confused, Sophie turned. Her confusion morphed to surprise to see Marisa weaving her way towards them.

Marisa greeted them with a hug. 'Oh good, you're on the best side to see the Statue of Liberty. Well done, Edie.'

'Not that I'm not happy to see you, but what are you doing here?' Sophie asked.

'I'm here to play tourist with you,' Marisa said. 'We thought it best if I tagged along to make sure no one got lost.'

Sophie's surprise turned back into confusion. 'We?'

Marisa nodded. 'We.' She reached into her handbag and pulled out an envelope. 'This is for you. It will explain everything.'

Sophie took the envelope reluctantly as she examined their smiling faces. 'Okay. I guess.' It was a nice envelope, the cream-coloured paper thick. Her name was neatly printed along the front in familiar handwriting and her heart sped up. With shaking fingers, she tore open the seal. Inside was a folded slip of paper with '*Read me first*' printed on it, along with a smaller unsealed envelope. She dutifully opened the folded paper and read.

Dear Sophie,

If you're reading this, it means you at least opened the envelope. I'm grateful for that. I wouldn't have blamed you for chucking it into the sea immediately (or at least into the bin. Littering off the ferry is probably forbidden). I'm sorry for how I left things. I feel like I'm always apologizing to you, or maybe it's just that the times I've had to apologize loom large in my mind. You are the last person in the world I want to hurt, but I've managed to do it anyway. With that in mind, I'd like to tell you this – today is your choice. At any point if you no longer wish to participate, if you decide it's not worth the bother, I will understand. Today is about you, Sophie. No one else.

With that in mind, I've put a smaller envelope inside this one. It contains the first clue on a scavenger hunt through the city. If you want to play, open it. If you don't, hand it back to Marisa.

Mike

Sophie folded the note, her hands less than steady, her vision prismed by tears. 'What is this?'

Edie plucked the letter from her. 'If I may?' When Sophie nodded, Edie skimmed it. 'A scavenger hunt. Seems pretty straightforward to me.' She handed the letter back to Sophie. 'The question is, do you want to play?'

Marisa handed Sophie a tissue. She took it, wiping her nose. 'If I don't?'

Edie shrugged. 'We see the Statue of Liberty and then go about our day.'

Sophie sniffed. 'And if I do?'

Marisa shrugged. 'You open the next envelope, and we go on an adventure.' She touched Sophie's shoulder. 'Why don't you think on it? You have an entire ferry ride to make up your mind.'

Sophie decided this was wise, so that was what they did. They watched the water go by. They enjoyed the new views of the city. When they passed the Statue of Liberty,

Sophie didn't say a word, simply drank her in. She was beautiful.

As they docked on their return trip, she opened the second envelope and took out the note.

Chapter Twenty-Nine

'I can't believe you haven't made it to Chinatown yet,' Edie said. 'Look at this place. I could spend *weeks* here.'

'I'm afraid all you'll have is the amount of time it takes to eat lunch,' Marisa said as she led them to a place where they apparently had a reservation. Even though today had already been full of surprises, Sophie was still astonished to see Manny there holding a table for them.

'Finally,' Manny said. 'I was starting to get looks from people who wanted our table.' He handed an envelope to Sophie as they all took their seats and settled in. Sophie tore it open immediately.

Dear Sophie,

I'm going to write these as if you're opening all of them, as if despite everything, you're choosing to play along. This might be foolishly hopeful, but if so, then that's how I want to be. I'd rather that than be wisely hopeless, at least with regard to you. I think you'll like Chinatown. It's a colourful place, full of hidden corners and a variety of eateries. Welcome to Joe's Shanghai. I picked this one because they're credited with bringing xiao long bao, aka the soup dumpling, to New Yorkers. Enjoy your meal and your time in a place almost as vibrant as you. If you so choose, Manny has another envelope for you.

Mike

Sophie didn't ask for the next envelope. Much as she had on the ferry, she put the decision aside as they ordered their meal. They stuffed themselves on soup dumplings, rice cakes, noodles and Peking duck. It was only as they sipped tea, their bellies full and the bill whisked magically away by Edie, that she thought about what she wanted to do.

She thought about the hurt she'd felt during the past week and, not for the first time, she thought about the hurt she might have caused. Only instead of brushing that aside as she had been, Sophie fully examined that thought. This entire time, she'd been wallowing in the fact that Mike had so easily walked away. That he hadn't talked to her, hadn't tried, hadn't said, 'To hell with the mature, measured response and waiting – I want to know where we stand now.'

It still hurt. Sophie hadn't realized how much she'd wanted him to do that until he'd gone. But the thing was, she hadn't done that either, and she could no longer pretend that Mike had walked away unaffected, or she wouldn't be here. With that in mind, she realized she'd made another assumption. 'Edie, did Tom and Marisa send for you? To visit me, I mean.'

Edie drained her cup. 'Nope. Imagine my surprise when none other than Michael Tremblay arrived on my doorstep, asking – practically begging – for my help.'

'This was all your idea, then?' Sophie asked.

'No,' Edie said with a tiny shake of her head. 'It was Mike's, but he needed help getting hold of everyone, and with some of the finer details.'

Sophie turned to Manny.

'Mike sent Marisa armed with a care package for Stanley Poochie,' he admitted. 'I figured, well, even if you told him to fuck off, at least you'd get a good meal out of it.' He sighed. 'Besides, I kind of owed him for the bingo help.' He tilted his head to the side, questioning. 'You want the envelope?'

'I think I do,' Sophie said, and held out her hand.

The next envelope took them to Central Park South. Manny didn't go with her, but Edie and Marisa were apparently along for the ride. Sophie assumed that they'd be meeting Tom in the park, since the pattern appeared to be a new person joining her at each location, so she was surprised when they got to their destination and he was nowhere in sight. There were, however, several black carriages lined up at the edge of the park, each with a well-groomed horse attached.

A young woman waved at them from a spot next to one of the horses. She was short, with tanned skin and purple streaks in her black hair, and though she seemed to recognize them, Sophie had no idea who she was . . . until she grinned. Sophie might not know the face, but apparently Mike's lopsided grin was etched deeply into her memory.

She waved back, before offering a hand. 'You must be Amaya?'

'In the flesh,' Amaya said, handing her an envelope. 'I hope it's okay that I'm here. I know you don't know me but . . .' She waved at the carriage, with its handsome chestnut-coloured horse and elegantly dressed driver. 'Look at this? Basically, I weaselled my way in.' She nodded at the envelope, now in Sophie's hands. 'Whether or not you decide to keep playing along, I hope you take pity on me and let me ride in the carriage.'

Amaya put her hands together in an adorable caricature of supplication. 'Please. In return, I can tell you things. Embarrassing things. Funny things. Delightful things. I've been given permission to let you into the family vaults and answer any questions you might have.'

'Well,' Sophie said, opening the envelope, 'hard to say no to that.'

Dear Sophie,

You're standing in a bit of New York history. Designed by Frederick Law Olmsted and Calvert Vaux, Central Park opened in 1858. You're about to spend almost an hour riding through this urban oasis. And because I know you: yes, there are photo stops and yes, the tour I booked includes treats for the horses. I'm reasonably certain this horse won't eat your shirt like that Highland steer, but take care regardless. Use the pictures for your blog or keep them for yourself. Like everything else today, this is for you, and how you decide to use it is your choice.

Mike

PS Assuming you don't run off with the carriage driver, Amaya will give you the next envelope at Rockefeller Center.

The ride was a delight. The afternoon air was hot and sticky, but no one cared. They posed for photos at each stop. The driver charmed them with facts and stories about the park and the city and Edie could not get enough of his accent. Sophie wasn't entirely certain, but she thought they might have exchanged numbers at the end of the ride.

They walked to Rockefeller Center, stopping to get water along the way. Sophie thought Tom might meet them there, but no one greeted them. She didn't expect Mike to turn up yet . . . but she hoped a little. Not that she wasn't having fun. Edie and Marisa were two of her favourite people and in almost no time at all, Amaya was acquiring similar status. She didn't *need* Mike to be there, but it turned out she wanted him to be there.

After poking around the gardens and taking a few more photos, Sophie asked Amaya for her next clue.

Sophie found herself holding her breath as they took the lift up to the observation decks of the Empire State Building.

There was just something magical about the place. Tom met them when they got out, handing her another letter with a smile. 'Pretty cool, isn't it?'

Sophie wasn't sure if he was referring to the building itself or the day in its entirety, but the answer was the same either way. 'Yes, it is.' She took the next note from him.

Dear Sophie,

I was right, wasn't I? The Empire State Building is magic. It's grand in an old-fashioned way and it's often referred to as an 'architectural marvel'. It's the kind of building that makes you believe in higher beings, because what mere mortal could conceive of it? It's a creation that makes me fall back in love with my profession every single time I see it. As I write this I realize that you, Sophie, are a bit like the Empire State Building. Classic, unique and with the ability to make me believe in things greater than myself.

Mike

PS All that being said, I also recommend the exhibits. I think you'll especially enjoy King Kong's hands.

Chapter Thirty

Sophie was getting tired by the time they got into the lift to leave the Empire State Building. It had been a long, wonderful, exhausting day.

As they stood in the lobby, Tom handed her the final note. 'If you decide to follow this one, you're on your own.'

Sophie didn't hesitate to take it from him, but she didn't open it, either. She looked at all of them. She knew what she wanted to do, but that didn't stop her from wanting to hear what they had to say. She trusted herself more than she had when she'd arrived in this city, but what was the point of any of it if she didn't ask for help from the people she loved best? 'What do you think?'

It was Amaya who spoke first, her expression thoughtful. 'I'm in the unique position here of knowing Michael Tremblay better than anyone and you barely at all.' She frowned. 'Except, I feel like I know you. My dad doesn't talk about anyone, Sophie. Not really. He's created this safe little bubble for himself, focusing on me and my brother to the exclusion of everyone else.' She huffed out a frustrated breath. 'It's maddening. And adorable. But you? He talks about you. I don't think he even realizes how much. I'll be honest and say that he's not perfect. I mean, who is?' She smirked. 'Even *I'm* not perfect, and I'm pretty great.' Her smirk became a full grin. 'My dad has been very clear that I'm not to try and sway, bully or convince you into any sort of decision.' She rolled her eyes at this. 'Which, okay, accurate, so I'll just say this: I have never, in my entire life, seen him do anything like this. He lights up for you, the way he used to light up for my mum.'

She hugged Sophie then, squeezing her tight. 'It's been great to meet you, Sophie Swann, and if you decide to take a chance, I'd like to be the first one to welcome you into our family.' She stepped back, her grin wicked. 'I'm well aware that's getting a bit ahead of things, but this way when I get home I can tell Rahul I got here first.'

Edie hugged her next. 'I was going to remind you to trust yourself, but honestly, I think I want you to date him just so I can be an honorary aunty to Amaya. I adore her.'

Sophie laughed. 'Thank you for coming all this way. I love you.'

'I know,' Edie said, 'but what else would you expect? I would cross the world for you, my friend, several times over.' And with that she stepped away, looping her arm through Amaya's and escorting her outside to wait.

Marisa hugged her and kissed her cheek. 'Whatever you choose, I support you.'

'Thank you,' Sophie said. 'That means the world.'

Marisa didn't go outside, but made room for Tom, who hugged her tightest of all. 'What are you going to do?'

She looked up at her son and voiced the last lingering sliver of fear that had been hiding in her all this time. 'What if it's a mistake? What if he's like your father and I just didn't realize?'

Tom snorted a laugh, shaking his head. 'Mum, do you really think any one of us would have helped if we thought that was the case? Edie would literally murder for you and Marisa would hide the body.' He held her shoulders and squeezed. 'And I love you. So much. I know you feel guilty about Dad, but I also know you did your best. You never once made me feel like I wasn't loved. Like my fiancée said, we support you whatever choice you make.' He gave her another little squeeze and dropped his voice. 'And for what it's worth, cock-ups aside, this man has fallen all over himself for you.'

Sophie sniffed, hugging him again. 'I love you too, you know.'

'I know,' he said. 'You got on a plane for me.'

'I think,' Sophie said, 'that it's time I did something for myself.' And with that, she took the final envelope and wished her loved ones on their way.

Inside the envelope was an address with the note, '*Message me when you get here*'. When she typed it into her phone, she saw it was only about a fifteen-minute walk from where she was. Though she was tired, she decided she needed that time to settle herself.

The address led her to a giant glass building and following Mike's instructions, she texted him as soon as she arrived. In response she was messaged a virtual ticket for the Summit Experience, whatever that might be. Her heart in her throat, she found an attendant and was directed to Air: Transcendence One.

Sophie stepped out into a world of air and reflection. Every side of the room was clear glass, revealing New York in all its glory. Above and below her were mirrors, reflecting the sky, the buildings and herself. She moved carefully, her shoes covered by the little disposable booties they'd given her on arrival.

In the centre of all of this, looking handsome and anxious, stood Mike. She stopped in front of him, not saying a word.

He stared back, wrecked in a way she had never seen before, his pupils so wide she could only see the thinnest line of colour around them. Mike cleared his throat. 'There are over 30,375 feet of mirrors in this space, which is about nine and a quarter kilometres. I'm still not sure why Americans don't use the metric system. The imperial system is nonsense.'

Her mouth twitched. 'Did you bring me all the way here to talk to me about the metric system?'

Mike seemed to collapse in on himself. 'No, Sophie, god, no. I—' He closed his eyes, letting out a breath. 'That wasn't what I wanted to talk about at all. 'The day they told me I could go back to London, I should have gone straight from work to your flat, got down on my fucking knees and told you that I loved you. Told you that I didn't care how long you needed to stay here – I didn't want to wait and see. I wanted you to know that no matter where you go, whatever adventures you have, you'll either take me with you or come back to me when they're over.'

Sophie sucked in a breath, but didn't get a chance to respond.

Mike took one of her hands in his. 'I love you, Sophie Swann.' He blew out a long, unsteady breath. 'I think I've loved you since the moment you started talking to me at the airport, and I'm sorry it's taken me this long to figure it out.' He tugged at her hand, pulling her towards one of the windows. 'But I thought maybe, if I brought you here, you could understand.'

He took a deep breath and then let it out. 'The Summit building is the tallest building in Midtown Manhattan, and while the Empire State Building feels like the past, like a bedrock, Summit blends art, technology and architecture into something uniquely wonderful.' He looked around the room, and there was an expression of wonder on his face. 'You stand in here, and you see the future. You feel small and gigantic all at once. It's like staring into infinity.'

He looked down at her. 'That's how I feel when I'm with you.'

Sophie's eyes filled with tears as she threw her arms around him. She didn't have words, not yet. But she would. She knew she would.

He rested his cheek on the top of her head. 'I am so, so sorry that I didn't talk to you when I should have. That I ran. Please give me a chance to make that up to you. I don't deserve it, but I want it anyway.'

'Okay,' Sophie said, staring up at him. 'But I need you to do one more thing for me first.'

'When you said "anything", I'll admit this option never occurred to me.' Mike stared down at the dishes Sophie had put in front of him at Xi'an Famous Foods. 'This seems like a trap. Why would my path to forgiveness be paved with good food?'

'Because,' Sophie said, 'I wanted noodles. Lunch was hours ago. You also promised you'd come back here after you shamed your family name.' She sighed happily. 'I've been dreaming about these dumplings.'

Mike sighed too, but it was slightly less happy. 'This is far better than I deserve. Bring it on.'

Thirty minutes later, Sophie was carrying several take-away boxes and Mike was sweating through his shirt.

'I think it was especially cruel to film it,' Mike said. 'And to send it to my children.'

'Why?' Sophie asked. 'You didn't throw up this time. Aren't you proud?'

He fished another ice cube out of a plastic cup and put it into his mouth. 'I'm feeling a lot of things right now, but pride isn't one of them.'

Sophie laughed as she slid an arm around his waist.

'Are you sure you want to do that?' Mike asked, even though he was already putting his free arm around her. 'I'm pretty disgusting right now.'

'Maybe,' Sophie said. 'But you're *my* disgusting.'

Mike pressed a kiss to her forehead. 'I cannot feel my lips right now, which is a shame.'

She laughed.

'Thank you,' Mike said softly.

'For what?'

'For giving me another shot,' Mike said. 'For taking a chance on me.'

Sophie squeezed him, and he was momentarily grateful he had clothes back at Tom's flat. He really was sweaty.

'That's what you do for the ones you love,' Sophie said.

'And do you love me, Sophie Swann?' His tone was light, but he meant the question all the same. 'I almost blacked out from anxiety earlier, but I'm pretty sure I'd remember a declaration of love.'

His tone was playful, but Sophie knew it had been eating away at him, waiting for her response. She was grateful, though, because she felt like she had finally figured out the words she wanted to say. They walked quietly for a moment before she pulled him away from the foot traffic until they were under a large tree jutting out of the pavement. 'How about this – I love you, Mike Tremblay. I love the way you're there for me, even if it takes you a second. I love how thoughtful you are and how you talk about your kids. I can think of nothing I want more than to have you by my side for the rest of my life. I'm not sure what that's going to look like or how that's going to work, but I'm willing to figure it out.'

Mike took her in his arms and kissed her. What else are you supposed to do when the person you love says something like that?

When he finally pulled back, Sophie was smiling at him. 'Liked that, did you?'

'Yes,' he said, wrapping his arm around her shoulders and pulling her back into the middle of the pavement, manoeuvring her until she was on the inside part away from the road. 'Not as poetic as mine, but it will do.'

She jabbed him in the side with a finger and laughed.

Mike sighed. 'I'll have to go back to London in two weeks, but I can come back soon. One of my children helpfully pointed out that I have a lot of annual leave saved up, and it's about time I took it.'

Sophie shook her head. 'Don't you want to save some of that for an actual holiday?'

He pulled her close and gave her another kiss. 'Sophie Swann, you *are* my holiday. One I'm hoping I can keep around for the rest of my life.'

'I think,' she said, 'that I'd like that very much.'

'Me too,' he said. 'Because I love you, I need you, and I'm not letting you go.' Then he leaned over and gave her another kiss, just because he could, and because he wanted to, and because he thought that no matter how much time they had, he'd never be able to kiss her enough.

But he was certainly going to *try*.

Epilogue

Sophie Swann stared up at the seatbelt sign with dismay. 'I hate this so much.'

'I know,' Mike said. 'Flying is unnatural. I've read your book. But you're going to do it anyway because you're a good mum and you love your family.'

'I know.' Even though her palms were sweating, Mike was still holding her hand. She loved him for that alone.

'We could do the boat again,' Mike offered with an evil grin. 'There's still time to leave the plane. They haven't shut the cockpit door.'

'No, *god*, no.' Sophie had taken a ship when she'd first moved back home to London. It turned out that, while she wasn't afraid of ships, she hated cruises.

Mike cupped her face in his hands. 'Don't think about the plane. Just keep doing your grounding exercises and know that I'm going to be sitting right here the entire time.'

'Okay,' she said with a nod.

'If it helps, focus on what happens after we land.'

'We go to Tom and Marisa's?'

'Well, I was thinking of the hotel where we're going to take nice, hot showers, and then I was going to see if we could get hotel security called on us in this hotel, too.'

Sophie blushed. 'Never again. I couldn't look that security guard in the face.'

Mike stared at her innocently. 'They just wanted to see if you were okay. There'd been all this *moaning* and for so long, too.'

She slapped his chest with her palm. 'I'm serious. We can never go back there.'

'I don't know,' Mike said. 'I thought they were nice. The guard even brought me that ice bucket with the Gatorade in it as an apology for the interruption.'

Sophie groaned, thumping her head against his chest.

'And I did need the electrolytes.'

'I really hate you right now.'

'Maybe,' Mike said. 'But you weren't thinking about the plane, were you?'

She blinked in surprise. 'No, I guess I wasn't.'

He grinned at her. 'Don't worry. I plan on distracting you the entire flight.'

'What else could you possibly distract me with?'

He leaned back against his seat, taking her hand and absently playing with her fingers. 'I was going to remind you of the fun things you have to look forward to – lunch with Kenzie. It will be nice to see your editor again, right? And talk about the new project?'

'Right,' Sophie said, closing her eyes. Her book, *Swan Dive*, hadn't been a runaway bestseller, but it *had* sold, and enough that her publisher wanted another book. Sophie was happy with that, and it would be nice to see Kenzie in person. 'What else?'

'Dinner tonight with your family, Manny and Stanley Poochie.'

'I can't wait.'

'Wednesday, I'm taking you salsa dancing and to the carousel.'

She smiled at him. 'Are you recreating our first date?'

'Yes. I'm trying to redeem myself.'

'Pretty sure you did that last time we went.' The third time Mike had taken her to the carousel, he'd proposed. Sophie hadn't thought she'd marry again, but with Mike . . . it felt right with Mike. 'You didn't panic and shove me into a car that time.'

'No, but I did sit in someone's dropped ice cream cone.'

'I forgot about that.' She hadn't. The ice cream had been chocolate. The placement on his trousers had been . . . unfortunate.

'Oh no you didn't. You took a photo. It's favourited on your phone. I've *seen* it.' He raised her hand to his lips and kissed it. 'But I appreciate the lie.'

'I wanted to document our engagement. Is that so wrong?' She batted her eyes at him and he smiled.

'Brat.'

'You love me,' she said, before bringing them back on-topic. 'Okay, so Wednesday we go to the carousel, and you try to leave with your dignity intact.'

'What's left of it.' Mike sighed. He leaned back into the seat and closed his eyes. 'I swear, any time I go out with you, something like that happens. I'm a little shocked you married me.'

She nudged him with her shoulder. 'I like adventure *and* comic relief.'

He grinned.

Sophie waited for a few seconds before she lost patience and poked him.

He laughed. 'Do you want me to tell you about Thursday?'

'Yes.'

'On *Thursday*, after I feed you and keep you in bed as long as I can . . .'

She glared at him, which only earned her another laugh. 'Get to the best part.'

'I happen to think that last part was pretty good.'

She continued (mock) glaring.

'Fine. On Thursday, we go over to Tom and Marisa's flat where you're going to bask in the joy of holding our granddaughter for a little while, and then we're going to help them pack up their flat.'

'That's good, but it's not the best part.'

The plane started to move then, all of the machinery making noise that made her shoulders want to hitch around her ears.

Mike leaned in close to her so she could hear him over the noise. 'The *best* part is that on Monday, we ship off their stuff and they come back to the hotel with us and then on *Tuesday* we get back on this plane and take your family home. What do you think of that, Sophie Tremblay?'

'Our family,' she corrected automatically.

He smiled his crooked smile. 'Our family.'

It was weird having a new name after all these years. She hadn't wanted to keep Swann, though she still had it as her pen name. For a bit, she'd considered taking her maiden name again. Mike had told her he didn't care *what* name she used as long as she came home to him at night.

In the end, she'd gone with Tremblay. Much like marrying Mike, it had felt like the right move for her.

'That's not the best part,' Sophie said.

Mike pulled back, confused. 'It's not?'

She shook her head. 'No, the best part is that on Friday, Edie has invited us all to dinner, and your family will be there, and my family will be there, and then all of my absolutely favourite people will be in one place. *That's* the best part.'

'You're right,' Mike said. 'My mistake.' He kissed her then, soft and sweet. 'You know what the best part is right now?'

'No.'

'It's that we're in the air and you didn't notice,' Mike said. 'It's that we get to spend the rest of this flight talking about all the good things in our lives right now, and even though it's a long flight, we'll still have things left over when we step off this plane. Our happiness will be so apparent and disgusting that people will want to throw things at us.'

Sophie tilted her head to the side. 'How long do you think it would take us to list all the good things?'

Mike frowned, thinking. 'Forever, probably.'

'That's a long time.'

'The thing is,' Mike said, 'is that we'll keep making new ones as we go, so the list is sort of regenerative.'

'We'll probably have a lot of bad things as well,' Sophie said. 'Just because that's how life works.'

'We don't need to list those, though.'

'We don't?'

'Why would we want to waste our time on the bad things? They'll happen, we'll deal with them and move on.' Mike shook his head. 'We only have this one life, and I don't intend to waste it. I've already spent too many years closed off.'

Sophie thought about that as she watched him. She didn't think she'd ever get tired of his face – the blue-green of his eyes, the curve of his lip. 'Do you count those years as wasted, then?'

'No,' Mike said. 'Not any more. Because now I know I was waiting for you.'

She snuggled into him and Mike put an arm around her, tugging her close as they tried their best to get comfortable on the plane.

'You know,' Sophie said after a minute, 'I think I'm going to have to slightly revise my position on planes.'

Mike peered down at her. 'Are you feeling well? Have you been replaced by some sort of pod person?' He held up two fingers. 'How many fingers am I holding up?'

She poked one of his ticklish spots. 'I was *saying* that if I hadn't got on that first, horrible flight to New York, none of this would ever have happened. I never would have met you. I wouldn't have my book deal. My kids might not be moving home. None of it would have happened without that first plane trip.'

'I don't think that's entirely true,' Mike said.

'You don't?'

'I think the popularity of your blog would have brought you to someone's attention at some point, and with Marisa not having much family besides us, the odds were high that they would end up moving closer to you at some point.'

Sophie scrunched up her face. 'But what about us?'

Mike didn't hesitate. 'We would have found each other.'

Sophie was surprised at how confidently he said that. 'You think so?'

'I don't believe much in fate,' Mike said, 'but I do believe that some things are inevitable, and for me, you, Sophie Tremblay, are *inevitable*.'

She laughed. 'I thought I was a choice?'

He looked at her, his expression perplexed. 'It's not really a choice when it's always the same answer. The answer is always you.' He shrugged. 'In light of that, what choice is there?'

Sophie wasn't sure how to respond to that except to give him another kiss, tell him she loved him, and to spend the rest of the flight discussing their inevitable future.

Together. Always together.

Acknowledgements

I think if anyone knew how much work went into a book making it onto the shelf, they'd all be a little surprised that any of them ever actually made it there. I'd like to thank all of the people who made this one happen.

To the team at Hodder & Stoughton, especially Phoebe Morgan and Jake Carr, for their unwavering support and kindness during this project.

To my agent, Cheyenne Faircloth - this book wouldn't exist without you and Handspun Literary. I appreciate your hard work so much and all of the supportive gifs and adorable animal photos you send on the rough days.

To author Nell Campbell, who answered all of my questions about what architects do all day to help me get it right for the book. I probably didn't, but that's not her fault. As always, all mistakes are mine and mine alone.

To all my writer friends that helped answer questions and talked me down when I would panic and message them, "But what if it's just vibes and banter?!?" Thank you for reminding me that people *like* vibes and banter and that I have, in fact, written a book before and could do it again. So thank you Gwenda Bond, Christina Lauren, Marissa Meyer, Molly Harper, Kristen Simmons, Jeanette Battista, Chelsea Mueller, Jaye Wells, Olivia Waite, Kendare Blake, Allison Kimble, Ryfie Schafer, Arnée Flores, and Martha Brockenbrough.

To my non-writer friends who answer random (and frequently upsetting) research questions with little to no context, make me go outside sometimes, and occasionally feed me. Especially Sarah Keliher, Haiden Lisenby, Anje Monte-Calvo, Megon Shore, Mel Barnes, Devon "Porkchop" Fiene, and Team Crane.

To everyone on the internet who told me their favourite New York stories and answered my questions about what it's like to live there - I wish I could thank you all by name, but you were too many and I have the memory of a confused goldfish. Still, I appreciate your help so much.

Big thanks to my family who still love me even though I imagine living with a writer is not unlike living with a sentient feral raccoon - you have my love and my gratitude, and I promise to occasionally come out of my den and tell you as much in person.

And finally to the readers, booksellers, reviewers and librarians that read, talk about and share my books - I literally couldn't do it without you.

- Lish McBride